SMOKE ON THE WATER

WHEN THE GOING GETS TOUGH, THE TOUGH GET CREATIVE.

First Published in Great Britain 2025 by Mirador Publishing

First edition: 2025

A copy of this work is available through the British Library.

ISBN: 978-1-917411-47-9

SMOKE ON THE WATER

WHEN THE GOING GETS TOUGH, THE TOUGH GET CREATIVE.

A NOVEL BY

DOUGLAS BUCKLAND

Good Friends Are Hard To Come By
Vigilantes, Payback and Poetic Justice
Creative Retribution
The Jackrabbit Boogie
The Counterfeit Express
Catfish Alley
Dust Devils

In urban slang, the saying "there is going to be smoke on the water" means that something is about to go down or that someone is about to behave in an inappropriate, improper, or unexpected manner.

CHAPTER 1

THE CARIBBEAN QUEEN, AN OLD Sea Ray 500 50' motor yacht, slipped her mooring in the Inner Basin, which fronted Independence Square along the Constitution River in Bridgetown, Barbados, at 2:17 in the afternoon. After passing under the Chamberlain Bridge, the vessel passed through the Outer Basin, and along with her five passengers, headed west past the breakwater for the fishing harbor and continued due west setting a course for the Blue Lagoon Anchorage at the southern tip of St. Vincent. The passengers, three Bajan males, one Bajan female and one mixed race, Bajan with Thai, female. Bajan is a common term used to refer to people of Barbados.

The departure of the vessel had been observed with interest by two Bajan men who had been stationed on the Chamberlain Bridge specifically for this purpose. Once the Caribbean Queen was clear of the breakwater protecting the fishing harbor, one of the men took out his cellphone and made a call.

The voyagers aboard the Caribbean Queen were supposed to meet up with some associates at the Flowt Beach Bar, just to the west of the Blue Lagoon Hotel and Marina at 9:00 that evening, but they would fail to make the meeting. Ten miles to the east of St. Vincent Island, the Caribbean Queen exploded violently, totally destroying the vessel and killing most, but not all, of its passengers.

The mixed-race woman had been standing on the swim platform at the stern of the boat watching the phosphorescence in their wake when the explosion had ripped through the hull and she had been blown off the swim platform and clear of the flaming wreckage. She never lost consciousness, but to say that she was not hitting on all cylinders when she stopped skipping across the water like a rag doll, would be an understatement. She was disoriented by the blast and her back and the back of her legs had been singed by the heat of the explosion, but other than this no real damage had been done. Swimming back towards the flaming wreckage, she came across a large, orange, 40-quart hard sided Cuddy floating cooler that she later discovered held several bottles of water, a six-pack of beer, a few packaged sandwiches, and some ice. She grabbed onto the cooler to use as a floatation device and watched the various bits and pieces of the Caribbean Queen that remained afloat eventually burn out and all that was left was a drifting layer of smoke lying on the water. She never saw any evidence that her associates had survived the blast.

With no other option, the woman simply climbed onto the buoyant cooler and straddled it like a horse as the current took her south and west between the islands of Bequia and Mustique in the Grenadines, hoping that a ship or a plane would spot her once the Caribbean Queen was reported missing and the sun came up.

Being so low in the water and without any light or other means of signaling boats or planes which might pass by, the chances of rescue were slim to none during the night. She could see the lights on Bequia to the west, and then Battowia, Baliceaux, Mustique and Little Mustique to the east as she rode the cooler south by southwest through the night. If she could hold out long enough, she should wash up on Canouan, Mayreau or Union Island further to the south. Worst case, she'd run aground on Grenada if she managed to last that long. If she somehow managed to survive the next full day under the broiling tropical sun, she would be in bad shape by the time the sun went down.

She passed by what she knew to be Little Mustique about 4:00 in the morning after the explosion, so she calculated that the current was running about two miles an hour through the unnamed strait between Bequia and Mustique. If she could just hold out for the next four or five hours, she should beach somewhere on Canouan Island. She still had one bottle of water and one sandwich left, so if the current held as it was, her chances of surviving the explosion and being lost at sea overnight were looking much better.

What she failed to take into account was the island of Little Canouan, which is located almost exactly midway between Little Mustique and Canouan, at the bottom end of the Windward Islands. Little Canouan is a small island of only 7.4 square miles that at one time comprised the Petit Canouan Wildlife Reserve. It no longer did.

CHAPTER 2

TAENG SKEETE WASHED ASHORE ON Little Canouan at around 6:30 in the morning the day after being blown off the Caribbean Queen. Little Canouan Island is a little pimple of an island that pokes out of the ocean roughly five and a half miles west by southwest of Little Mustique and about three and a half miles north by northwest of Canouan. The northern coastline of Little Canouan runs roughly east to west and the western coastline runs roughly north-northeast to south-southwest. The rest of the island's shoreline is a roughly semi-circular arc connecting the eastern end of the north coast with the southern end of the west coast. The island really did resemble a pimple as it rose from the sea like a blister. There was little significant vegetation. The island was covered in guinea and signal grass, interspersed with agave, wild jasmine, corac and Spanish needle. At the top of the hill, where the only structure that could be seen from offshore was located, dwarf coconut trees and manac could be seen.

Originally, most of the entire coastline had been rocky cliffs, but some enterprising souls had blasted out a small harbor in the middle of the northern shoreline and built a stone L-shaped breakwater out of the blasted rock. The breakwater shielded the little harbor from the fury of the open ocean when she got angry. The short leg of the breakwater extended out from the original shoreline about 50 yards before it made a 90 degree turn towards the west, creating a protected half mile stretch of calm water protected from the vagaries of the sea. It was onto the corner of this breakwater that Taeng Skeete, the half Thai, half Bajan survivor of the Caribbean Queen finally made landfall.

It was just starting to get light by the time Taeng heaved her cooler onto the top of the breakwater's corner and climbed up after it. Looking inland she spied the small harbor, which could not be seen from out at sea. She estimated that it was about eight to ten acres in extent with a windowless concrete structure where the short leg of the breakwater intersected the shoreline, and a building on the opposite side of the harbor that had been built against the base of the sheer cliff that decreased in height as it sloped down to the shoreline.

The concrete structure to the west looked vaguely familiar, like a much smaller version of pictures she had seen of the Nazi U-boat pens built in Saint-Nazaire, France during World War Two. This structure was topped by what appeared to be a windowless single-storied warehouse or garage, also made of concrete, which ran the entire length of the top of the submarine pen looking structure. Due to the inclination of the topography, the side walls of the harbor rose from the shoreline to a height of about 60', with the entire back wall of the harbor being a sheer 60' cliff. Essentially the harbor had been quarried like a big, rectangular slot cut into the island, with the longer axis running from east to west while the shorter axis ran from the breakwater inland. It was an unnatural feature and out of place on the small Windward Island. There were no piers or docking facilities in the harbor, nor was there any sign of human habitation or industry. The only buildings which she could see were what she now referred to as the submarine pen, the concrete building opposite and the single pastel blue building which sat at the highest elevation at the center of the island.

She was feeling pretty good about surviving her recent brush with death when she heard someone with an attitude yelling at her. A guy had come out of the steel door in the concrete structure to her left, the one at the end of the short leg of the breakwater and was approaching her along the poured concrete path on top of the breakwater.

"Lady, just what in the heck do you think you're doing? You're trespassing, you can't just show up unannounced on somebody's island! Would you mind telling me who you are and what you are you doing here?" shouted the man as he walked towards her.

Taeng watched him approach, and as he got closer, she couldn't help but notice that he wasn't too hard on the eyes, for a white guy. She guessed that he'd be in his early to mid- 30's, about 5'10" tall with a ropy, muscular build with very little fat on him. His long blond hair was tied in a ponytail that reached halfway down his back and from what she could see of him, which was most of him, he was tanned a deep bronze color. He was dressed in a pair of tie-dyed motif board shorts, an old pair of canvas Converse sneakers and nothing else. Taeng was intrigued.

While Taeng was busy being intrigued, the man finally came up to her and once he had taken a good look at his trespasser, he was pleasantly surprised and intrigued with her as well. Taeng had gotten the best out of both of her bloodlines, her Thai and Bajan mix. She stood about 5'7" tall and weighed in at around 120 pounds packed into a 34-24-32 figure, probably a B-cup edging towards a C, if he had to guess. She had flawless, honey colored skin, and had a perfectly proportioned, yet tastefully rounded backside which was again a gift from her mixed DNA. Her Thai blood had allowed her to retain the silky, jet-black Asian hair, but her Bajan blood ensured that it was much curlier than the pure Asian version. She wore it shoulder length with a side part, when she wasn't getting blown off boats and riding coolers all night. Her facial features were stunning. The almond eyes from her Thai side were very exotic and were highlighted by her high cheekbones and lips that were slightly fuller than the pure Asian variety, again due to the Bajan influence. The only thing out of place was her slightly Roman nose, there must have been an Italian in the woodpile at some point in her family's past. In an odd sort of way, the slightly prominent bridge of her slender yet refined nose actually complemented the rest of her facial features. Her figure, athletic as it was, had also benefited from her Barbadian blood in that the entire package had slightly softer edges than a woman of purely Asian ancestry would have possessed. If he had to guess, he'd say that she was in her mid-20's.

Needless to say, she wasn't looking her best at the moment after a night in the water, but the man would have bet good money that she cleaned up pretty good. At the moment she was dressed in a soaking wet pair of cut-off jeans and a crimson bikini top under a very wet Banks beer t-shirt which didn't do much to hide the pert profile of the items concealed by the bikini top underneath.

"Look, asshole, I've just spent the entire night riding this damn cooler from just off St. Vincent to this weird little island of yours. I am not in the mood for your attitude. Let's try that again, shall we?" This response was delivered in melodious Caribbean accented English tempered with what Cody thought to be a Southeast Asian tonal inflection.

Cody was cynical by nature when it came to women. They rarely took the time to really get to know him once they figured out that he had some money and his own island. That said, he'd never had one go to the effort of spending the night at sea before washing up on his island to make his acquaintance.

Taking another good look at his visitor, the man tried again. "Sorry, I don't get many visitors, and my social skills have never been that great to start with. My name is Cody Morgan. I own and operate this island, and I am very pleased to meet you, Miss…"

"Much better, Mr. Morgan. My name is Taeng Skeete. I was on my way from Barbados to St. Vincent yesterday morning when the boat that I and my friends were on blew the hell up and I've been floating down the straits between Bequia and Mustique on this cooler all night long. I could use a shower, a change of clothes and a breakfast. If you could provide them, it would be much appreciated. I'll also need to make some phone calls."

"I heard on the maritime radio about the boat that blew up off Kingstown last night. I'm sorry about your friends. You can leave that cooler here if you like and if you follow me, I'll get you that shower and breakfast. The clothes might be a bit of a problem, but I'll see what I can do in that department."

"Mr. Morgan, that cooler saved my life. There is no way I am going to leave it on this breakwater."

Cody reached down and grabbed the cooler. "Understood. Follow me and we'll get you sorted out."

Taeng followed Cody back along the short leg of the breakwater to the steel door set into the blockhouse. He held it open as Taeng walked into a cavernous room with a polished concrete floor with what appeared to be two large industrial machines of unknown purpose bolted to the floor and humming along in the center of the building.

"What are those for?" asked Taeng.

"The curse of many Caribbean islands is that they are dry. There are no springs or aquifers on this island, and the elevation changes do not cause enough rainfall for a significant amount of potable water to collect. What you see are two industrial sized reverse osmosis desalination plants which provide me with enough potable water to live comfortably on my island," replied Cody.

"How many people live on your island?"

"You've just doubled the population."

This revelation did not give Taeng a warm fuzzy feeling. Maybe she had landed on the island of Doctor Moreau. Perhaps Cody was a reincarnation of the mad scientist in that novel.

"Didn't this island used to be called Little Canouan Island?" asked Taeng.

"Yeah, it was. I bought it several years ago and renamed it Pala Island after the fictitious island in Aldous Huxley's novel 'Island'. An island of science and technology."

Taeng was getting the vibe that her rescuer might not be playing with a full deck, but she needed his help, so she'd play along.

They crossed through the desalination plant to a door on the opposite side of the building to the one they had entered. Leaving Taeng's cooler inside, Cody held the door for Taeng. Waiting outside was a year-old Kawasaki 450X dirt bike. Cody climbed on and told Taeng to hop on behind him. There were no passenger pegs for Taeng to rest her feet on so she had to hold on tight to Cody's waist with her legs spread out like outriggers as they rode up the meandering path paved with crushed oyster shells, to the house at the very top of the island.

During the ride up to the house, Taeng had to maintain a firm grip on Cody since, with no foot pegs, she had nowhere to put her feet and couldn't grip with her thighs as the bike bounced up the path to the house. Her hands had crept from his waist to his stomach while she was holding on to him during the trip and she subconsciously became fascinated by Cody's abs and eventually her libido led her subconscious down the path of thoughts inappropriate to her present situation.

Even though this Cody guy seemed to be a little odd at first blush, he wasn't hard on the eyes. Taeng's mind began wandering into the arena as to what opportunities might present themselves on the island and what she would do if these opportunities presented themselves, as one does after having a near death experience the previous evening. She contemplated the possibility that if Cody didn't turn out to be some sort of psychopathic serial killer, that there might possibly be the seeds of a romantic interlude sprouting on this odd little island. She'd probably find out shortly what Cody's plans were for her, at which point she could figure out her plans for him.

The house had been painted a pastel blue, and was irregularly shaped, something along the lines of a truncated right triangle. The shorter base leg of the triangle faced the harbor, and this was fronted by a spacious patio. The short leg and patio were actually the front of the house. The left-hand side of the house, when viewed from the patio, was the longer leg of the truncated right triangle while the right-hand side would have been the hypotenuse. The rear of the house was where the triangle had been truncated.

They walked up a set of three steps to the charcoal-colored flagstone patio, which was furnished with two lounge chairs with cushions made from some weather and sun resistant material, a large patio umbrella shaded the seating arrangement while a small table was arranged between the lounge chairs.

Behind the lounge chairs two full-length, single pane French doors opened into a spacious living room with an eight-place formal teak dining table in the center. A large L-shaped couch and coffee table were along the wall to the left and a four-stool island was centered between the formal dining table and the fully equipped kitchen counter built along the right-hand wall with a Sub-Zero refrigerator and a Wolf range and oven combo.

Continuing on, if you walked past the formal dining table and then through another set of sliding French doors, you found yourself in a small courtyard with a water feature and tropical plants as a centerpiece. The walkways around the edge of the courtyard were covered, while the middle of the courtyard was open to the sky. Some hanging vines dropped down through the opening in the ceiling to complete the tropical motif.

At the far side of the courtyard, opposite the set of sliding French doors, was a pair of mahogany doors which led to the large master bedroom with its ensuite bathroom. To the right, as you faced the water feature was another set of mahogany doors leading to the guest room, also with its ensuite bathroom.

The two doors opposite on the other side of the water feature from the guest room led to a half-bath with storage cabinets built into the small hallway to the bath while the other opened into the laundry room.

The complicated roofline was tiled with red clay tiles and every open area of the oddly shaped house held tropical plants and flowers. The house would never be featured in Better Homes & Gardens due to its odd shape, but it was open, airy and comfortable.

Taeng didn't know what to make of the only house she'd seen on the island. It was an oddly beautiful house with views of the ocean in all directions, but it seemed a little unusual for a guy like Cody, who appeared to be something of a recluse or hermit.

"Cody, this is a lovely house, but isn't it a bit much for one guy living on an island by himself?"

"Who says that I am always here alone? Maybe I fly in the Swedish women's beach volleyball team on occasion and have myself a party," said Cody as they made their way back into the kitchen area.

"Do you?" asked Taeng as she took a seat at the kitchen island.

Cody had been at the Sub-Zero getting out the makings for some Spanish omelets and had just placed them on the kitchen counter. Without turning to face his guest, he placed both hands palm down on the kitchen counter and sort of leaned into them.

"No, I don't. You are the only social visitor I've had in years, and I am really glad that you washed up on my shores."

Turning around, Cody crossed his arms across his bare chest and looked at Taeng.

"Ms. Skeete, I realize that you are somewhat apprehensive about me and my situation here, and rightly so. There is no need to be. I am what some people refer to as a savant, in my case an engineering savant. I am not autistic in the least; I just enjoy solving problems. That said, my social skills are somewhat rusty due to lack of use, but other than that I'm a pretty regular guy."

"A pretty regular guy that just happens to live on his own island," clarified Taeng.

"There is that. Hold that thought while I make us some breakfast."

Cody whipped up a breakfast of two big three egg Spanish omelets with toast which they washed down with coffee. After a night on the water, Taeng discovered that she was famished and wolfed down her omelet and three pieces of toast before Cody could get half of his breakfast down his neck.

Cody cleaned up the kitchen and washed the dishes, he'd never bothered to install a dishwasher as it was usually only him in residence, before he poured them both another cup of coffee and they retired to the couch on the other side of the living room.

Taeng needed some context for the unnatural situation she found herself in, so she just bluntly asked Cody what the heck he was doing out in the middle of nowhere on his own little island.

"I can understand your anxiety, so let me give you the CliffsNotes version."

Taking a sip of coffee, he began, "I was born in Landers, Wyoming back in 1995. My parents ran a lumber and building supply outfit there and I grew up doing all the things that young guys grow up doing out west: hunting and fishing, football, chasing girls, and so on.

"When I was in middle school, it became apparent that I had an unnatural aptitude for math, science, and things mechanical. My parents and the school nurtured this aptitude all through high school and I decided that I wanted to be an engineer. I applied to Rensselaer Polytechnic Institute in New York and was accepted on a full ride scholarship. I earned dual undergraduate degrees in Mechanical and Materials Engineering then stayed on to get my doctorates in both.

"After obtaining my doctorates, I was scouted and then hired by Lockheed Martin to work in their Skunk Works program designing the next generation manned and unmanned aerial vehicles with an emphasis on developing hypersonic vehicles. At this point in time, no successful propulsion system had been developed for these aircraft. Anyhow, after a few years I got fed up with the engineering bureaucracy at Lockheed and set up a consulting firm, which consisted of me, to work with commercial aviation on airframe and aircraft engine design.

"I never gave up on the idea of a workable hypersonic propulsion system, and one evening, while sitting alone in my apartment in Denver, I had a 'eureka moment' concerning the turbine-based combined cycle system, commonly called TBCC, and after a year I had perfected a propulsion system, on paper anyhow, that utilized a turbine engine at low speeds and a scramjet engine at high speeds. The turbine and scramjet engines would share a common inlet and nozzle, but with separate airflow paths.

"Needless to say, this caught the eye of DARPA, the Defense Advanced Research Projects Agency, who wanted this propulsion system for themselves, but I had already filed a patent on it. This propulsion system would power aerial vehicles to Mach 5 and above. The problem was, aerodynamic heating at these speeds created temperatures hot enough to melt conventional metallic airframes, so utilizing my materials engineering knowledge, I developed a composite material consisting of high-performance carbon, ceramics, and metal alloys for use in the engines and in the airframes. I filed for a patent on this as well.

"DARPA caused my patent applications to disappear before they could be published and swore me to secrecy under pain of imprisonment, death, or worse. That said, although they were assholes about it, they paid me an unbelievable amount of money to use my inventions and they also pay me an astronomical retainer's fee to ensure that I did not share my knowledge or work with any foreign power and consult solely with them. They also sweetened the deal by somehow getting the government of Canouan to delist this rock as a wildlife reserve, there is no wildlife on this rockpile anyhow, and sell it to a holding company in the Bahamas. I am the sole employee of said company.

"During the Cold War the British still technically owned this rock and it was they, not I, who carved out the harbor and built the other infrastructure around it, which you may have already noticed, contains a rather large submarine pen. You may have also noticed the communications' tower behind the house festooned with various dishes, antennas and so forth. This is for my communications and internet connections, but since the CIA and the NSA come out on occasion, I am sure there is some spy stuff on that tower as well, but that's not my problem.

"Anyhow, that's me, what about you? There must be a back story about you getting blown up and set adrift. Care to share?" asked Cody expectantly.

Taeng thought about how she should respond. Cody seemed like a good guy in his own weird way, but she'd only known him for a few hours at this point.

"Don't take this the wrong way, but my getting blown overboard like I was may not have been an accident. There may be some people back on Barbados who might be looking for me that neither you nor I want to meet. If I can borrow a phone, I'll call some friends in Bridgetown to come and get me, and you won't be in any danger by association."

"Were you involved in anything criminal?"

"Not at all! In fact, we were trying to stop a criminal enterprise," exclaimed Taeng.

"Well, I'm not going to tell you what do, especially since I don't have enough information to propose a strategy, but I would suggest that you consider staying dead for a while longer, at least until you can figure out what is going on back in Barbados. You can stay here as long as you like and playing dead will keep you from becoming a person of interest for either law enforcement or the criminal enterprise you spoke of earlier."

Taeng had to admit that hiding out for the moment sounded like a pretty good idea. "Okay, I'll take you up on your offer, but I'll still need to contact some people in Barbados soon. Can I reach Bridgetown from here?"

"Darlin', you could reach Mars from here, but first things first. If you go to your room and pass me out your wet laundry, I'll get it washed and dried for you while you shower up. You'll find some of my old gym shorts and t-shirts in the middle dresser drawer. The shorts are definitely too big in the waist, but nothing a safety pin can't cure," offered Cody. "The door locks from the inside, you'll be safe," he added.

Taeng really didn't feel comfortable getting naked in Cody's house, but she couldn't keep her saltwater-soaked clothes on much longer before the salt crystalized and started rubbing her raw.

"Okay, that would be great," replied Taeng as she stood up and headed for the guest room after Cody had pointed it out to her.

A few minutes later she came out dressed in a pair of old Rensselaer gym shorts and a Bob Marley and the Wailers t-shirt; she was trying to keep the shorts from falling down around her knees while at the same time holding out her previous attire for laundering.

Cody had already gotten a safety pin out of a kitchen drawer and came to her rescue. Trading her the pin for the clothes, he headed towards the laundry room while she modified the waistband of the shorts.

"Hey! Something is missing here," yelled Cody from the laundry room.

When Taeng got there, she asked what he was talking about.

"Well, there is a t-shirt, a pair of cut-offs, a bikini top, but no bikini bottom. Now either you are a free-spirited type who goes commando, that is sans underwear, or you do not feel comfortable enough to let me handle your bottoms, no pun intended. If you keep the bottom half of your bikini on underneath those shorts, you are going to get chafed raw as they dry out."

Taeng looked him in the eye for a second, scanning for any sign of an ulterior motive, then scowled and walked back to her room to take off her bikini bottoms and then going commando in Cody's gym shorts.

Going back out to the laundry room, she approached Cody and handed over the lower component of her bikini to a smirking Cody. He took a long look at the crimson briefs before commenting that there wasn't enough material in them to make a decent handkerchief, let alone cover Taeng's tight little package, but he did concede that the material was somewhat elastic so if it were to be tugged up snug enough, it could probably get the job done.

"It does the job, I usually tug it up until it creates what is sometimes referred to as a 'dromedary's digit' and call it good. You will likely never see this, so I'll just leave that to your imagination," smirked Taeng.

"I believe the term is actually a 'camel toe'. This being said, the term 'likely' was the operative term in that sentence, Ms. Skeete, leaving the possibility open that I will see those crimson butt-huggers in action at some point in the future. I play the long game," informed Cody with a smile.

To be honest, Taeng thought he might actually see that bikini bottom in action in the future as well if he played his cards right. Regardless, she'd need to get some new clothes and toiletries if she was going to play dead on the island of Pala.

"I can't keep running around in your old clothes and the one set of mine. I can't see Amazon delivering here, so how do we go shopping?" asked Taeng.

"I'll show you tomorrow. You aren't afraid of flying, are you?"

"Are you a pilot as well?" Taeng was beginning to think that this Cody was a jack-of-all-trades.

"Technically no, but I can fly."

"What does 'technically no' mean?"

"Well, my pilot's license is a forgery, but I've got 537 real flying hours in my logbook."

Taeng just rolled her eyes and went to her room to take a shower, with the door locked. She wasn't to the point where she trusted Cody yet, and she wasn't sure that she trusted herself in the event that he turned out to be untrustworthy. Time would tell.

CHAPTER 3

THE FOLLOWING MORNING TAENG CAME out of her room dressed in her original outfit of cut-offs, the red bikini top and Cody could only assume the matching hipster bikini bottoms, although this could not be confirmed. She had also decided to ditch her original Banks beer t-shirt and had opted to retain the Bob Marley and the Wailers model. She found Cody already up and in the kitchen making pancakes. He took a long appraising look at her from his position in front of the stove and said, "You clean up pretty well for a castaway and a good night's sleep seems to have agreed with you as well. Do you want blueberries and walnuts in your pancakes?"

"Stupid question. Only morons would opt out of blueberries and walnuts in their pancakes. Yes, I feel much better after a night in bed as opposed to riding a cooler on the high seas and having my own clothes on again is also a plus. Your shorts fit me like a pair of ghetto rags."

"Just curious, but are you going commando this morning or are you sporting that sexy little red hipster bikini bottom?"

"I don't think I know you well enough yet, Mr. Morgan, to discuss my choice of undergarments, or lack thereof, with you, so I guess you'll just have to remain curious," replied Taeng as she took a seat at the island.

"They say curiosity killed the cat. Do you want me to have a curiosity induced heart attack before these pancakes are ready?"

"I thought you were the nerdy type, but you seem well versed in ladies' swimwear and the various styles, not many guys know the difference between a tie-side bottom, a hipster bottom or a Tonga bottom. You also seem familiar with the crude and vulgar terminology for what those bottoms can do to the female anatomy when worn too snug. Why are you so inquisitive about my choice of underthings, or lack thereof?"

"First, I am not a nerdy type, I am an engineering savant. There is a subtle, yet distinct difference. Secondly, I am a fairly young, red-blooded American male and you are one of the few women, and the only really attractive one, to ever visit my island. I am simply trying to find out more concerning the habits of the rare and elusive attractive female of the species."

"Did you just try to flatter me, Mr. Morgan?"

"Sort of, how did it go down?"

"Well, I appreciate the compliment, but if you are trying to flirt with me, you'll need to tighten up your game if you plan to get anywhere with it."

"Lucky for me that you are playing dead for a while here on the island. Think it'll give me enough time to get my game sorted out?"

"Depends on how long I have to be dead, that could take a while," Taeng said. The fact was, she was kind of enjoying the flirting even though it was somewhat clumsy and needed some fine tuning. Depending on how everything eventually turned out, and how long she had to play dead, Taeng got the feeling that her time on Pala Island with Mr. Morgan might be rather stimulating.

After their blueberry and walnut pancake breakfast, Cody told Taeng to take care of her morning ablutions and then meet him back in the living room in 15 minutes. Back in the living room Taeng watched as Cody emerged from the master bedroom. He'd ditched yesterday's tie-dyed motif board shorts and had dressed slightly more appropriately in knee length gray and black camo motif cargo shorts, high top Converse sneakers and a Jimmy Cliff t-shirt. He had a pair of classic Ray-Ban Wayfarer sunglasses perched on top of his head and an old, sun bleached, green and black camouflaged Oakley knapsack in his left hand. His long, blond ponytail had been brushed out and secured in two different places by yellow scrunchies, and he'd shaved.

"You ready for a little adventure, Ms. Skeete?"

"Does it entail me getting undressed?"

"Not today."

"Then I'm as ready as I'll ever be, Mr. Morgan."

After closing up, but not bothering to lock up the house, they climbed back onto the Kawasaki dirt bike and headed back down the crushed oyster paved path towards the small harbor. During the ride down to the western side of the harbor where Taeng thought she'd seen the U-boat pens topped by a warehouse, Cody almost dropped the bike a few times. Keep in mind that there were no passenger pegs on the Kawasaki and Taeng had to ride with her legs spread like outriggers which didn't add to the stability of the bike. This riding position also forced her pubic arch, better known as her crotch, to be pressed tightly against the top of Cody's backside, better known as his butt. Cody's 'lizard brain' began to override the other parts of his brain. This, combined with his earlier inspection of a certain, crimson, bikini bottom caused his 'lizard brain' to start painting mental pictures of the anatomical features presently rammed up against his backside as he struggled to maintain his balance on the bike. This led to an occasional loss of concentration, which further threatened the stability of the bike.

"What the heck are you doing?" demanded Taeng after the third or fourth wobble.

"It's not me, it's you!" yelled Cody as he wiggled his butt to make his point.

It took Taeng a moment to figure out what was going on. "You need to put some pillion pegs on this thing," suggested a blushing Taeng as she unsuccessfully tried to get some separation between her crotch and Cody's butt without the benefit of the leverage normally provided by the foot pegs.

"Perhaps, but I'm kinda enjoying the sensation," joked Cody.

"I'm sure that you do, but perhaps you should put your libido in check. I'd like to get down this hill in one piece." Taeng wasn't really joking at this point.

They finally reached the U-boat pens and the crushed oyster trail that they had been riding on led them to a steel door built into the southern wall of the warehouse or shop building on top of the pens. After they got off the bike, each making a concentrated effort not to look at the other as they adjusted their shorts after the butt versus pelvic arch incident, Cody got the bike on the kickstand and led the way over to the steel door. Since Cody was usually the only occupant of the island it wasn't locked, so he held it open and ushered Taeng in. This was not a gentlemanly act so much as Cody just wanting to take a good look at Taeng's backside and the root cause of the near fatal trip down the hill from his house. He decided that the root cause was extremely attractive even if it was well concealed beneath snug-fitting cut-offs.

The warehouse or shop building on top of the submarine pens was 150' long by 75' deep with a 20'ceiling. The original concrete walls, floor and ceiling had been smoothed over with troweled cement and painted storm gray. Although there were no windows in what Cody called his shop, it was well lit. To Taeng's untrained eye, the shop seemed to contain every metalworking, tool and die or machine shop tool known to man. There were a few jigs holding what she thought were pieces of airplanes and boats, but this wasn't her area of expertise. Everything was spotless.

Walking across the shop to the far wall, they entered a concrete stairwell. This led to an observation deck about 30' above the surface of the water that looked out into the covered submarine pens from the north wall. Below them was a 400' long by 150' wide pool open to the harbor surrounded by a 30' wide concrete deck. Running across the width of the concrete ceiling, were two industrial gantry cranes. As Taeng leaned against the handrail of the observation deck and looked out over the cavern, Cody explained what she was looking at.

"Back in the Cold War, Britain built this submarine pen to hold two Oberon-class submarines. Eventually these subs were retired from service, and the newer subs were longer and eventually nuclear powered. This pen, and the shop above it, could no longer conceal or service them. When I got the island, the US Navy helped me get everything back up and running so that

I could continue my work on propulsion systems and they got a secret facility in the event that they ever needed one."

"Is that a seaplane over against the far edge of the pen?" asked a curious Taeng pointing to a single-engine aircraft resting on two large pontoons across the pen.

"I tinker with old World War Two equipment when I can find it. Technically that is an Aichi E13A, better known as a Jake. It started life as a Japanese long-range reconnaissance seaplane used from 1941 to 1945. I found this one rotting in a warehouse on the U-Tapao Royal Thai Navy Airfield. Apparently the Thais operated a few before the First Indochina War. I have totally restored it with a full suite of modern avionics and replaced the original Mitsubishi Mk8 14-cylinder air cooled 1060 horsepower engine with a later, more powerful version of the same engine giving me about 1,500 horsepower now. Originally it had a crew of 3: pilot, observer slash navigator, and rear gunner, but I removed the rear gunner's seat, and it now serves as a baggage compartment. It cruises at about 150 miles an hour and has a range of a little over 1,000 miles. It's a perfect light aircraft for the Caribbean."

"Okay, what are those two things parked below us? One looks like a military boat of some sort, and the other one appears to be a barge of some sort."

"Good eye. Let's take it from left to right. The military boat, as you call it, is just that. It is one of the later versions of the Tjeld class Norwegian patrol torpedo boats, which came without the torpedoes. When used in Vietnam, it was called a Nasty boat. It was built in 1967, it is 80'4" long, it displaces 80 tons fully loaded when it was built although I've stripped off the gun and depth charge mounts and added state of the art radar and navigation. The twin supercharged Napier-Deltic diesel engines provide 3,100 shaft horsepower each to two screws which give it a top speed of 45 knots. If you tone it down a bit to 20 knots, it has a maximum range of just over 900 nautical miles. Again, a perfect boat for the Caribbean.

"The barge is full of diesel fuel. That humming sound you hear is the pair of industrial sized diesel-powered Cummins gen sets in a dedicated room beneath us. The barge holds about 80,000 gallons of diesel. I share the cost with the US Government since I have to power their spy stuff up the hill as well, and we switch it out with its twin as required. The twin is berthed in Kingstown at the moment. Are you ready to go shopping?"

"About that... I don't have any money, my wallet, purse, cash and credit cards were blown up with the Caribbean Queen."

"Don't give it another thought. I have a line of credit on Grenada that should survive a shopping spree from a homeless waif such as yourself. If not, we may need to talk about alternative forms of repayment," informed Cody with a sly grin.

"As long as the alternative forms of repayment does not involve removing any or all of my clothes, then I agree to your terms."

"I can't believe you'd even think that I would consider asking you to undress as a form of repayment! That said, modelling what you purchase should definitely be on the table."

"Modelling I have done before and may do again. Whether your wanton black heart could survive my modelling is an entirely different story," replied Taeng with a grin of her own.

"Does your modelling routine involve a pole by any chance?"

"You never give up, do you? Let's go get on that plane and get out of here. It'll give your vivid imagination a rest and give you something else to concentrate on."

CHAPTER 4

THE AICHI SEAPLANE WAS MOORED nose in to the cement wall of the dock with the front of the two pontoons up against a large inflatable tubular fender which was chained horizontally to the wall and floated on the surface. Since the prop was well back from the front of the pontoons there was no risk of damaging the prop. Mooring ropes were attached to a cleat on the top of each pontoon then angled up and out to two bollards on the top of the dock. The bollards were equipped with automatic tensioning devices that kept the aircraft snug and secure against the fender while taking into account the rise and fall of the tide within the basin, and therefore the submarine pen.

The problem was that even at high tide you were required to climb down a rusty ladder bolted to the wall of the dock before stepping onto the port side pontoon. You then had to grab the trusty piece of 2"x 6" plank which rested on top of the fender and place it from one pontoon to the other. You had to do this so that you could cross to the other pontoon and untie the mooring rope from the cleat on that pontoon, then cross back to the port pontoon to repeat the process and free the aircraft from its moorings.

The next part of the departure process was to grab the paddle that also rested on top of the fender and paddle the aircraft out into the pen so that the aircraft was pointing out of the pen towards the harbor. This was usually not a complicated process, but Cody had never had to do it with another person standing on the port pontoon. This being the case, Cody got down on the port pontoon first, then made a detailed inspection of Taeng's derrière as she descended the rusty ladder onto the pontoon. In the short time that Taeng had been on the island, he found himself doing this as often as opportunity allowed.

At this point, he informed her that Japanese aircraft of the era were very lightly constructed, and she needed to be careful not to damage the aircraft. He showed her the step built into the front of the strut supporting the pontoon and how to climb it. He instructed her that once she was up on the wing, she was to remain as close to the fuselage as possible and wait for him to get up and show her how to get in the middle seat of the elongated cockpit.

Taeng got her right foot on the step, but it was a bit awkward for her so Cody, out of the kindness of his own heart, and possibly his desire get some hands on appreciation of her fabulous derrière, placed both hands on her butt and gave her a shove up onto the wing.

"You did that on purpose!" she scolded.

"Yep, I did. That is one phenomenal tush you've got. Now stand there by the cockpit and hold onto something. I'll be up in a minute."

Cody grabbed the 2" x 6" plank, made his way over to the starboard pontoon and untied that line before crossing back, replacing the plank and grabbing the paddle. He then untied the port mooring rope and began paddling the plane out into the pen.

"I might be missing something here," remarked Taeng cheekily, "but I thought that we were actually going to fly this thing to Grenada. It'll take us a while if we have to paddle it all the way there."

"Everyone's a comedian these days," commented Cody as he handed her the paddle and climbed up on the wing beside her. Sliding the middle part of the canopy back, he helped her get inside and seated without too much unnecessary physical contact and showed her how to buckle herself in. He also showed her how to put on and adjust the old, World War 2 vintage American flying helmet and googles. Cody had rigged up a good intercom system in the plane and the pilot and passenger could actually speak and be heard quite clearly with the remodeled helmets. After showing her the 'push-to-talk' button on the floor he had her slide the canopy forward and latch it before he slid open the pilot's canopy, climbed in and situated himself.

Eventually, after setting up the digital avionics, Cody fired up the upgraded Mitsubishi Mk8 engine, did the magneto checks and so forth and began taxiing out of the submarine pen. At the far end of the harbor, Cody swung the Jake to port and guided the old plane into the long calm stretch of water behind the breakwater that paralleled the shore. Closing his canopy, he did one more instrument check before starting his take-off run.

Taeng was howling with delight as they got light on the pontoons, skipped off a few small waves and got into the air.

"How did you like that, Ms. Skeete?"

"Exhilarating! We should do this again sometime."

"We will. Now just sit back and enjoy the trip. You can unlatch your section of the canopy and slide it back if you want the convertible experience. We'll be flying on the leeward side of Canouan, Mayreau, Union, Carriacou, Rhonda and Grenada before coming in from the south. It's only about a half hour or 45-minute flight."

"Bummer, this is fantastic. Maybe on the way back we can joyride a bit longer?"

"No problem. We at Pala Island Airways aim to please."

A minute later Taeng asked, "What about oxygen? Will I need oxygen back here?"

"We won't be flying high enough for oxygen to be a concern. Any other questions?"

"Now that you ask, yes. You mentioned that you found this old plane in Thailand, have you been to Thailand often?"

"I was there a lot when I was negotiating to buy this aircraft," answered Cody.

"I'm half Thai myself, but I've never been there."

"I could tell that your non-Bajan half was something Asian, just couldn't determine which part of Asia that half hailed from. Thai is interesting."

"Is that good or bad?"

"Good, as long as you get the best of both halves."

"That being the case, how'd I do in the DNA sweepstakes?"

"From what I have been able to see, you lucked out on the good physique, skin tone, lips, eyes and black, curly hair DNA. I haven't been able to get a good look at the rest of the package yet, so the jury is still out on those bits."

"'Yet' being the operative word," laughed Taeng.

"Touché," replied Cody as they both revisited the conversation earlier in the morning about Cody not knowing her well enough 'yet' to discuss her choice of underwear, or lack thereof.

A few minutes later, Taeng hit the 'push-to-talk' button again.

"What do you remember most about Thailand?" she asked.

Now knowing that Taeng was definitely half-Thai, Cody couldn't pass up the opportunity to wind her up about it.

"I was young at the time, but what got my attention the most were the incredibly sexy women with that beautiful teak skin, almond eyes, silky black hair and their unbelievably casual attitude towards physical relationships."

"Nice try, but you are really pushing your luck, Mr. Morgan. Probably best to quit while you're ahead."

After passing Quarantine Point, Cody asked Taeng to close and latch her canopy and to make sure that she was buckled in tightly. Swinging the old Aichi to starboard, Cody took the plane about five miles out to sea off the western end of the Maurice Bishop International Airport and contacted the tower to let them know that he was in the area and would be swinging around the southern tip of the island to make a water landing in Mount Hartman Bay before tying up at the Secret Harbour Marina. They just told him to hold at 5,000' until he was 2 miles out to the south of the runway and then to drop down to 500' before he made his run into Mount Hartman Bay. The winds were onshore to the north at five miles per hour.

Cody made a pass down the length of the bay to check the sea state there as well as to check the position of boats either at their moorings or underway before going back out to sea to set up his approach. Coming in at the mouth of the bay, Cody lined up with the Secret Harbour Hotel, reduced throttle, lowered his flaps and just kissed the surface of the bay before setting the old Jake down properly. Powering the remaining 200 yards to the marina, he coasted to the narrow end of one of the t-shaped piers before he climbed out of the plane and onto the port pontoon. An employee of the hotel tossed him a mooring line and yelled, "It's a beautiful day for flying, Mr. Morgan!"

"That it is, Francis," replied Cody as he reeled the plane in toward the pier.

While Francis and Cody secured the plane, Taeng climbed out of the middle canopy in her cut-offs and t-shirt, which caused Francis to stop and take a look and a few wolf whistles were heard from some of the boats moored at the pier. Without missing a beat, Taeng curtsied while standing on the wing before climbing down onto the pontoon. The geometry was much different at the mooring than it had been in the sub pen, and she could step directly off the pontoon onto the floating dock.

When the Aichi was secure, Cody climbed back up on it to retrieve his Oakley knapsack and his Ray-Bans before climbing back onto the dock and slipping Francis a $100 bill for his help and for him to keep an eye on the plane. The plane had been painted in the livery of the 553 Kokutai: dark green on its upper half and hemp on its underside, and always drew a crowd. Before Francis departed, he whispered to Cody to watch himself, women like his passenger could only be trouble.

With that in mind, Cody and Taeng walked down the docks and to the Secret Harbour Hotel concierge where they ordered a taxi to take them to Seasons, a store on Melville Street, across from the Republic Bank that, according to Taeng's phone, would allow her to get what she needed.

When the cab stopped in front of Seasons, Cody handed Taeng his Visa card and warned her that if she didn't behave herself with it, she'd be walking home. He said he'd meet her in front of Seasons in two hours, and they would figure out what to do next. Taeng grinned as she stuck the card in the back pocket of her cut-offs, theoretically forcing them marginally tighter on her posterior thought Cody, and got out of the cab almost running into the store.

Cody admired the marginally snugger shorts before getting out himself and walking back down Melville Street and hooking a left onto Grandby Street. Crossing to the other side of Grandby at the intersection with Young Street, Cody walked the half block to the WeCare Pharmacy to pick up a new toothbrush, shaving cream, razor blades for his safety razor and some toothpaste. He'd need to up his game if he was going to have a fairly appealing houseguest for the foreseeable future. While paying at the counter he claimed that he'd forgotten something and rushed over to get a few bottles of the foul-tasting original Listerine as well.

With that done, he ambled over to Bryan's Bar across Grandby Street from the pharmacy to down a few Carib Blues while Taeng spent his money. He was hoping that it was worth it, which it probably was since the girl could likely put on a plastic trash bag and still look stunning.

At the appointed time, Cody was waiting outside of Seasons, and being a woman, Taeng did not show up for another 15 minutes. She came out of the doors carrying three large bags and grinning like the proverbial Cheshire Cat. Reaching into her back pocket she handed Cody back his Visa card.

"Anything left on this card?"

"I think so, but it was money well spent, I assure you."

"Show me, don't tell me," Cody said with a smile.

"Later perhaps. Can we do lunch? I'm starving."

"Shopping is such hard work," agreed Cody as he flagged down another taxi.

Cody directed the driver to the 61° West Restaurant and Beach Bar on Grand Anse Beach where Cody had the fish and chips and another beer, while Taeng had the lobster mac and cheese and a beer as well.

They eventually retired to the lounge for a few more beers. Cody thought that this was as good of a time as any to fish for information.

"Taeng, at some point you're going to have to tell me why somebody tried to blow you up. Depending on what you tell me, we may need to make some other plans while you're playing dead."

"Let me give it some thought. If I do, I may be putting you in danger as well."

"You are talking to a guy that flies an 80-year-old Japanese seaplane for grins and giggles, with no formal training on the type I might add. Danger is my middle name, sweetheart."

"Let's hold off on the 'sweetheart' thing and you are not giving me a warm fuzzy feeling about the flight home tonight," admonished Taeng.

"About that flight home, I think that we should postpone it until tomorrow."

"And why is that?"

"First, I've had a few beers. Second, I don't like to make water landings in the dark. Third, I need to go by CK's and put in an order to be delivered to the Secret Harbour Marina tomorrow morning."

Taeng didn't relish the idea of her fraudulently licensed personal pilot attempting a night landing on water either, it seemed like a bad idea even to a non-pilot type. This raised other questions.

"So where are we staying this evening if we aren't going back to the island tonight?"

"I took the liberty of booking us a room at the Secret Harbour Boutique Hotel while you were shopping for underwear and stuff."

"It wasn't just underwear, clown. Did I hear you right and you have only booked one room for the two of us?"

"Apparently, they only have one deluxe cottage available this evening, everything else is fully booked. Logistically it makes sense to stay there: we are close to the plane, we can leave early in the morning, and the room comes with a two-course meal, a bottle of sparkling wine and a free breakfast."

"How many beds?"

"Just one, but it's a big one."

"Mr. Morgan, since I don't seem to have much choice in the matter, I think we'll need to set some ground rules. The first and foremost is that there will be no hanky-panky. We would need to know each other much better before any hanky-panky is even considered. Secondly, you will stay on your side of this big bed and will not make any adolescent moves toward my side. We have been thrown together by circumstances and I am getting the feeling that you may be trying to take advantage of, or worse perhaps be attempting to manipulate, these circumstances. Do you agree to these rules?"

"I agree with the rules as stated. I can't believe that you think so poorly of my character. This is the second time you have impugned my reputation today."

"The fact that you don't seem to be able to keep either your hands or your eyes off of my butt is indicative of your more primal instincts."

"They are not primal instincts; they are simply healthy urges. That said, we need to head over to CK's so that I can place an order for some groceries before they close."

After paying their tab, they walked over to Grand Anse Main Road and hailed another cab to take them to CK's Food Depot at the southern end of the Main Road, just before the Sugar Hill Roundabout.

Getting out of the taxi, they walked into the depot and Cody put in an order for some items which he had been running short of on his island to be delivered to the Secret Harbour Marina at 9:00 in the morning before they grabbed another taxi to take them to the Secret Harbour Boutique Hotel.

Pulling up to the hotel entrance on Mount Hartman Drive, Cody paid off the cab before he grabbed his bag of toiletries and one of Taeng's large bags from Seasons while she snagged the other two and they walked into the foyer and up to the registration desk. The very attractive young lady at the desk seemed to know Cody, so the check-in process did not take long and 10 minutes after they arrived Cody had the card key in his possession and they were strolling down the outdoor path that led to their cottage, which just happened to be between the outdoor pool and the harbor itself. While Taeng threw her loot on the bed and began to check out the cottage, Cody strolled back to the marina and onto his plane to retrieve his go-bag which he'd left in the plane since he had not planned on staying the night. Essentially the go-bag held a change of clothes, toiletry articles and anything else he may need if he had to overnight somewhere.

Walking back to the cottage, he walked into what looked like an explosion of women's clothes on the bed while Taeng was in the shower. Dropping his knapsack on the floor on what he was claiming as his side of the bed, he thought it would be a fine opportunity to check out Taeng's choice of apparel.

There were wide leg light denim jeans, denim shorts, crop tops, t-shirts, a jersey, socks, a pair of black Converse sneakers, a pair of Havaianas red floral design flip-flops and what really caught his eye was a Venus floral pattern scoop bottom halter bikini and several pairs, in a variety of colors and prints, of Venus lace back bikini panties with matching bras.

Needless to say, this had Cody's imagination running in overdrive when he heard somebody clear their throat in the open bathroom door off the open plan bedroom slash living room of the cottage.

"See anything you like? I don't think much would fit you," asked Taeng leaning against the bathroom door jamb as Cody turned to face her.

Taeng was wearing a new pair of cuffed denim shorts over a skin-tight, hot pink, one-piece swimsuit. It took Cody a minute to take in the incredibly sexy girl in her incredibly sexy outfit, but he finally managed to croak that he was simply checking that his money had been well spent.

"And has it?"

"If the rest of it looks as good on you as what you're wearing now, the money was very well spent."

"Good to hear. I'm going up to the pool, you want to go with me?"

It has been said that there is no such thing as a stupid question, at this instant Cody would beg to disagree.

"Let me put on some board shorts and I'll be right with you."

Cody went into the bathroom and changed out of his cargo shorts and into his foggy palms patterned board shorts before he and Taeng walked out of the front door of the cottage, which was on the opposite side of the cottage from the side facing the harbor, and crossed a section of manicured lawn to the hotel's outdoor pool. An older yachting couple was already there catching the afternoon sun, but there were several empty lounge chairs on the opposite side of the pool. Taeng selected a pair with a patio umbrella between them and with absolutely no consideration for Cody's weak heart, simply kicked off her Havaianas, unbuttoned her shorts and wriggled out of them while her back was toward Cody, who was watching the performance in stunned silence. Taeng's skin-tight, hot pink, one-piece swimsuit was also from Venus and was advertised as a 'one-piece bandeau with high-leg cut and midi coverage. This suit is made to highlight your figure in every way and includes a cutout in back to keep things interesting', which it did in exceptional fashion from Cody's point of view.

Taeng's Thai blood took primacy where her figure was concerned. As mentioned earlier her silky black hair was not straight as it is on most Thai women, but wildly curly. Her lips were fuller than your typical Asian woman and her posterior was ever so slightly more rounded than the Asian style. Both her facial features and posterior had benefited from her Bajan blood. After that, she was all Asian with a slim but very fit body, with long, toned limbs. She had a long, graceful neck and high cheekbones under her almond eyes. What she was, was simply fit and feminine. There was only enough fat on her to round off the edges and give her a much more feminine look than your typical female gym rat. Her breasts were not over-stated, and some men might think they were on the small side, but they were pert, proportional and fit her figure well. The package, taken as a whole, could make a freight train stop on a dime. She was not beautiful in the classical sense, especially with her slightly Roman-style nose. A more accurate description would be captivatingly entrancing or bewitching.

In any case, Cody was almost drooling when she turned around and asked him if he was going to get into the pool. Her front profile was just as alluring as her rear profile, and a team of wild horses could not have held him back from getting in the pool with her. Once in the pool, they swam around for a while before sitting on the steps leading down into the pool, with the water lapping around their waists to keep them cool, which wasn't really working out too well for Cody. He feared that his somewhat unwholesome thoughts might be causing him to experience a physical reaction that would definitely be embarrassing if it were to be witnessed by the root cause of his tainted stream of consciousness.

Taeng was blissfully unaware, supposedly, of the uncomfortable position which she had, through no fault of her own, placed her pilot in and started interrogating him about his past and how he enjoyed life on his island. He managed to field her questions for an hour or so before he suggested that they might want to return to the cottage and shower up before going to dinner in the restaurant for the two-course dinner included with the room.

"Good idea, but I think I should probably go on ahead and wait for you. You might need some time to deal with that problem in your board shorts that you keep trying to cover up," suggested Taeng as she jumped up laughing and ran to their lounge chairs to dry off and wrap a towel around herself. Cody told her to go on by herself as it might be a while before he could get out of the pool with dignity.

Eventually Cody's condition improved, and he walked back to their cottage. Walking through the front door he found Taeng already dressed in her wide leg jeans, a yellow V-line hem cropped top and her new black Converse low-top sneakers. He didn't even bother to contemplate if she was going commando or not after the embarrassing debacle at the pool.

"Hurry up, Cody! I'm starving," prodded Taeng.

"How can you be starving? You just ate a few hours ago," replied Cody as he went over to his knapsack and pulled out a fresh t-shirt and some old, but clean Levis and headed to the bathroom.

"I have the metabolism of a hummingbird."

"And judging by your performance at the pool, at my expense, the sense of humor of a hyena."

Taeng was laughing uncontrollably as Cody closed the bathroom door to shower up.

After a nice dinner of seared mahi-mahi, they retired to the lounge for a few drinks before retiring to their cottage. Now the game got interesting.

Once back in their cottage, Cody went into the bathroom first to brush his teeth and prepare for bed since everybody knows that men are much quicker at this than women are and he didn't want to rush Taeng. When he was finished with his ablutions he walked out and told Taeng that it was her turn.

When she was finally finished, she opened the bathroom door, took a step out and jerked to a halt.

"What do you think you are doing?" she asked Cody, who was laying up against the headboard on his side of the bed reading a Lee Child novel clad only in a pair of Fruit-of-the-Loom Y-front briefs.

"What?"

"You are only wearing underwear, and you haven't even bothered to pull the duvet over you. This is unacceptable."

Cody grinned, "I sleep in my skivvies. This is not a 'come on'."

"Good to know, I sleep in my skivvies as well," and with that she dropped the Secret Harbour supplied bathrobe revealing that all she had on was a white t-shirt and a pair of her new Venus lace back bikini panties. She quickly climbed under the duvet and reached over to turn off the bedside light on her side of the bed. Reluctantly, Cody did the same with his light.

"You could have at least taken your time getting into bed before you turned the light off."

"Sweet dreams, Mr. Morgan."

CHAPTER 5

DURING THE NIGHT, CODY HAD gotten up to visit the restroom and just happened to 'misplace' the bathrobe that Taeng had shed on her side of the bed the previous evening before she got under the covers. He figured two could play that game.

In the morning, Taeng woke up supposedly before Cody, but he was faking sleep so that he could watch the show. Taeng looked over the side of the bed and searched for her bathrobe but couldn't find it. Looking over to make sure that Cody was still sawing logs, she climbed out of bed and tip-toed over to the dresser to grab a fresh pair of denim shorts and a new crop top before heading to the bathroom to get dressed. As she turned around, she found Cody looking at her like the cat who got the cream.

"Misplaced your bathrobe, did you?"

At this point Taeng knew that she'd been had. "What goes around, comes around, Mr. Morgan. You should be looking over your shoulder from now on. I will have my revenge," she informed Cody curtly before she casually sauntered into the bathroom in her knickers and t-shirt.

Cody felt that it was worth it. Those Venus panties were a snug fit, and that lace back accentuated the package it was supposed to be concealing. The vision was seared into Cody's retinas. All in all, Cody figured it was worth whatever payback Taeng had in mind, and it was a stimulating start to his day.

After they had the breakfast in the hotel restaurant which came with the room, they collected the trolley from the concierge that held the two fairly large boxes of stuff from CK's Food Depot which had been delivered earlier, and wheeled it onto the pier extending out into the marina, and then over to where their old floatplane was moored. Cody climbed onto a pontoon and Taeng passed the boxes from CK's to Cody from the pier, along with their knapsacks which now held their original gear as well as Taeng's haul from Seasons and the toiletries which Cody had purchased.

Taeng then hopped onto the pontoon while Cody climbed up on the wing, she passed everything up to Cody, who stowed it in the old gunner's compartment at the aft end of the extended cockpit and strapped it down. Cody then got Taeng situated in the old observers compartment in the middle and strapped her in as well before getting back on the pontoons and untying the mooring ropes attached to each pontoon. Grabbing the paddle he'd used in the sub pen earlier, he paddled the aircraft away from the dock before he climbed back onto the wing, stowed the paddle back in the gunner's compartment from whence it had come and buckled himself back in the pilot's seat.

Firing up the old Mitsubishi air cooled radial engine, Cody deftly threaded the Jake between the boats moored out in the harbor until he had an open take off run before he hit the throttle and they got airborne.

"How was that?" Cody asked his passenger.

"Not too bad for a voyeuristic, unlicensed pilot."

"You're not still mad that I saw you in your underwear, are you? I'm thinking that one-piece suit you wore to the pool was just as revealing," asked Cody as he climbed to 2,000 feet and made a sweeping turn to port so that they could travel up the eastern side of Grenada for a change.

"The jury is still out as far as holding a grudge, but I'm still going to pay you back. What route are you taking back to your island?"

"Since we aren't in a hurry and the weather is clear, I thought we'd take the scenic route and go up the eastern side of Grenada and the Grenadine Islands. When we get to Battowia I'll cut east to your home island then circumnavigate Barbados before heading home. What do you think?"

"Sounds nice, if you've got the gas."

"The Japanese built their planes with long legs. It'll be about a 350-mile trip, but even with our jaunt to Grenada, that's only about half a tank in a Jake. Why don't you just kick back and enjoy the ride."

As they were flying along, Taeng had a question for Cody. She hit the intercom button with her foot and asked, "Why does a guy who doesn't seem to worry about financial issues and owns his own island fly around in an old propeller plane. Can't you afford a Lear jet or a Gulfstream like your garden variety rap stars or climate activists?"

"As you so aptly described, every noveau riche dirtbag on the planet has a personal jet. I find personal jet ownership to be ostentatious and lacking in good taste. Furthermore, those elite morons never even learn to fly, they hire someone else to do it for them and totally miss out on the joys of flying," explained Cody.

"So basically, you just want to be the token rich guy flying around in an 80-year-old Japanese crop-duster."

"You know not of what you speak. This aircraft is technically a long-range reconnaissance seaplane and not a crop-duster, there's also the fact that I couldn't land a jet on my island without destroying its natural beauty by building a runway on it, which I refuse to do."

Cody asked Taeng to slide her portion of the canopy forward. Once she had, and Cody had slid the pilot's section back, he got back on the intercom and said, "One other thing, in a jet you can't fly convertible." Taeng was loving the open cockpit flying and was beginning to see the benefits of an old warbird seaplane as opposed to a $20 million Gulfstream G550.

Cody dropped down to 500' so that Taeng had a good view of the coastlines of the islands they flew past. They passed alongside the Grenadine coast, then that of Caille, Carriacou, Union, Canouan, their own little island, Baliceaux and Battowia before banking to starboard and heading east to Barbados. Taeng hadn't said another word in the past half hour it had taken to fly to that point; she was just engrossed in the adventure of cruising the Windward Islands in a World War Two vintage Japanese reconnaissance plane.

As they headed out over the Atlantic Ocean to Barbados, Cody asked her if there was anything particular place on the island she wanted to see.

"Can we fly over Crab Hill? I'll show you where I live."

"Your wish is my command. We'll fly in toward Bridgetown then circle the island counter-clockwise and fly over Crab Hill just before we make a beeline for home."

Cody brought the old Aichi in toward Barbados on a heading of due east at about 5,000' and about three miles off the southern point of Barbados to stay out of the traffic pattern going into or coming out of Grantley Adams International Airport located in Seawell, Christ Church. Staying three miles off the coast he banked the old seaplane to the northeast and dropped back down to 500' once he had passed Foul Bay. From here on, he remained at 500' or so as he flew the coastline in a counter-clockwise direction and throttled back to about 100 knots to give Taeng a better viewing experience. They flew up to Kittridge Point before turning northwest and flying past Ragged Point and on up to Cove Bay, Little Bay and River Bay before turning due west toward Crab Hill.

"Pilot to crew, you'll need to guide me in from here. We're about three miles out from Crab Hill."

"Crew to pilot, keep going until you see four large white poultry barns, that's the Bright Hall Poultry Farm. At the chicken farm, veer slightly to the west-southwest. You'll see two more poultry barns, fly by the south side of them and look for a house with a blue tile roof, that's mine." Sure enough, at the intersection of Crab Hill No. 1 Road and Grape Hill-Salmond Road, Cody spied the only blue tiled roof in the village.

"That's it! That's my house!" exclaimed an excited Taeng.

Cody circled around it a few times, then flew out over Granny's Bay and came in over the house from the north and circled it again a few times before flying back out to sea and taking a southwest heading back to Pala Island.

"I wonder if I will ever live in it again," muttered Taeng.

"Well, I can't answer that until you tell me what the heck is going on and why somebody wanted to blow you up."

"Fair enough, I'll tell you tonight while you fix me dinner."

"Already thinking about food again?"

"I told you; I have a hummingbird metabolism."

"I'm guessing that having that sort of metabolism would also make you a little bit frisky, for lack of a better term, wouldn't it?"

"Just fly the plane, Bozo."

CHAPTER 6

THEY GOT BACK TO CODY'S island around 2:30 in the afternoon. Cody was making his second circuit around the island when Taeng pushed the 'push-to-talk' button on the floor with her foot and asked him what he was doing.

"Looking for visitors."

"You get visitors?" she asked.

"I keep hoping that the Swedish women's beach volleyball team will show up again, but usually it's just the CIA or the NSA. I like to know ahead of time."

"Don't they call or something before they arrive?"

"Haven't so far."

There was a moment of silence before Taeng asked, "What would you do with the Swedish women's beach volleyball team if they did show up?"

"It would be better to show you than to tell you, it is more of a physical, tactile experience. Now be quiet and make sure that you're buckled in tight, the water looks a little choppy."

"Have you ever done this before?"

"What, landed on choppy water?"

"Yes."

"Often."

"Then why did you bring it up?" exclaimed Taeng.

"Because I have never landed this thing on choppy water with a chick in the plane before."

"I am not a chick!"

"Au contraire, mon chéri. From what I have seen, you are definitely chick material. Now be quiet while I try to put this thing down in one piece."

Cody lined up west to east aiming towards the calmer water just behind the breakwater that paralleled the shore on the north side of the island. They got lower and lower, and slower and slower before the plane skipped once off a wave before settling down into the water on the pontoons. Taeng gave a shriek when they bounced but managed not to wet herself.

Cody coasted to the end of the breakwater before hanging a right into the opening of the small harbor, then another right to line himself up with the opening to the sub pen. Pulling close to the cement wall on the left-hand side of the pen, Cody cut the engine off and let the pontoons nose into the bumper. Climbing out, he used the paddle to snag the float on the end of one of the mooring lines bobbing in the water and used it to reel the float plane into the wall before securing it to the cleat on top of the pontoon. Grabbing the 2' x 6" board off the top of the bumper, he crossed over and snagged the other mooring line, pulled it tight and tied it off to the cleat on the other pontoon. Scrambling back across, he tightened up the first line. Putting the paddle and the board back on top of the bumper, he told Taeng that she could get out now and to put their loot out on the wing.

While she was doing this, Cody climbed up the rusty ladder and grabbed the controls for the bridge crane that was racked on that side of the pen. The controls just hung free from the ceiling on their electric cables, so he could position the crane from just about anywhere on the dock. Swinging the hook over to him and lowering it to the cement deck, he went into a utility room built into the wall of the pen and carried out a small cargo net. Dragging this back over to the hook, he dropped the loop at each corner over the hook then picked it up with the crane and gently lowered the net onto the port wing near the fuselage where Taeng placed all their stuff inside and gave Cody the 'thumbs up'. He picked up the net and brought it back to where he was standing on the dock before unhooking the net and moving the bridge crane back in its original position.

As Taeng came up the ladder, Cody gave her a hand and pulled her onto the dock before he went back down to the aircraft, made sure that everything was secured and as it should be before he closed all three canopies: pilot, passenger and storage area, and scampered back onto the dock.

Loading their knapsacks, the boxes from DK's and their other purchases onto a trolley that was sourced from the same utility room he'd gotten the little cargo net from, Cody led the way to an old cage elevator hidden in the corner of the pen. Punching the button beside the elevator door to summon the elevator, they waited patiently for the old elevator to arrive and for the doors to slide open and admit them. Cody pushed the trolley inside followed by Taeng. Cody reached around her and pushed the upper button of a set of two beside the door and they rode the elevator to the shop above.

Once they and the trolley were out on the shop floor, Cody went over to the roll-up garage door beside the man door which they had used to enter the shop earlier that morning and used the chain hanging beside it to roll it up. Asking Taeng to stay put, Cody went wandering behind a row of machinery toward the back of the shop before Taeng heard a small gas engine fire up and start working its way towards her.

A few moments later, Cody came around the end of the row of shop equipment on a little Gator utility vehicle pulling a small two-wheeled trailer.

"Your chariot arrives," grinned Cody. While Taeng threw their knapsacks and the shopping bags from Seasons and the pharmacy purchases into the bed of the Gator, Cody put the boxes from CK in the trailer. Once they had loaded up, Cody got into the driver's seat while Taeng rode shotgun and they pulled the Gator outside the shop. Cody then got out, rolled the Kawasaki dirt bike inside from where they had left it out that morning then rolled the door back down before coming out of the man door and getting back into the Gator.

They slowly made their way back up the meandering crushed oyster shell path to the house and unloaded the loot into either the pantry or the respective bedroom of the purchaser. Cody suggested that they shower up after their long day and he'd meet her in the kitchen afterwards to figure out dinner.

Since women take forever to shower up and get ready for anything, Cody changed out of his flying clothes and already had the spaghetti bolognaise well in hand before Taeng walked into the kitchen freshly scrubbed and dressed in some, and there is no other way to describe them, form-fitting, crotch-hugging, black, high waisted yoga shorts and a black, snug, cropped top tank top worn above them.

Cody forgot what he was doing for a moment. "You clean up very well indeed, Ms. Skeete. Like the outfit."

Taeng blushed, but while attempting not to appear too concerned about his inspection of her close-fitting attire, she replied. "Thank you, but the same cannot be said for you. Isn't that the same pair of shorts that you had on when we met?"

Cody looked down at his shorts and said, "They are, but I'm slaving over a hot stove, and this is perfect attire for this type of work."

"What about a shirt of some type?"

"Superfluous to requirements, but if it makes you feel better, I'll grab one before dinner."

Taeng thought about what was on display for a moment, then replied, "Don't go out of your way on my account."

"Okay then, if you'll set the table and grab us a couple of beers out of the fridge, the spaghetti will be ready in a minute."

After dinner and a few beers to loosen up, Cody suggested that they retire to the couch along the far wall of the open plan living room and dining room. It was an L-shaped couch with the long leg extending along the full length of the exterior wall under wooden louvered windows, while the short leg was along the inboard wall that separated the living room and kitchen areas from the open courtyard where the bedrooms were located.

Taeng made herself comfortable along the short leg while Cody grabbed them another round of beers before perching himself on the long section of the couch with the corner of the couch separating them.

"Okay, Taeng, time to come clean and let me know why somebody tried to blow you up and what I might be getting myself into."

"You don't have to get involved. You could graciously let me play dead on your little island, let the storm blow over, then return me to Barbados with my thanks and walk away."

Appearing to think this over for a moment, Cody replied, "Nah, where's the fun in that? Tell me what's going on and we'll take it from there."

"Are you sure?"

"Not really, but I can't make that decision until I know what is actually going on and what I may be getting myself into, can I?"

"Fair enough, but don't say that I didn't warn you."

And with that, Taeng described to Cody what he may be letting himself in for.

"Have you heard of the Chinese Belt and Road Initiative, or the One Belt One Road as it is known in China?" asked Taeng.

"Peripherally, I really don't follow any of that sort of thing unless it affects the supply chain of a project I happen to be working on," answered Cody.

"Some background then. The Belt and Road Initiative, commonly known as BRI is a development strategy adopted by Xi's Chinese government in 2013 to boost China's leadership role in global affairs in step with her rising power and status. To facilitate this, China invested heavily in infrastructure projects, mostly in Africa and Asia. China would have you believe that BRI is altruistic in nature and is a benevolent way to increase global trade with developing countries thereby decreasing global friction while at the same time boosting the global GDP.

"The fact is that this is simply a cleverly disguised power and influence grab to facilitate Chinese domination in Africa and Asia as well as a mechanism to control the natural resources of the nations which fall for it. BRI has resulted in debt-trap diplomacy by China as well as neocolonialism and economic imperialism.

"In Uganda, the Ugandan government secured a loan for $325 million from China through the Exim Bank to finance and expand Entebbe International Airport. The Chinese knew full well that the Ugandans could never hope to service this debt. The grace period to repay the loan expired in 2022 and the Chinese essentially, for all practical purposes, seized ownership of the airport as payment for the loan. It is speculated that an identical situation occurred in Zambia regarding a loan made to refurbish and update the Kenneth Kaunda International Airport. It is a known fact that the Chinese set up the Sri Lankans when they provided loans for the Hambantota Port facility. In 2015, the Sri Lankan government struggled to make payments on the debt and finally handed over the port and 15,000 acres of land around it for 99 years.

"During the past 10 years or so, developing countries in Africa and Asia have gotten wise to the BRI scam, so China had to look elsewhere for their marks and the Caribbean seemed like fertile ground, so to speak. In Cuba, their primary technology providers for the country's internet are Huawei, TP-Link and ZTE; all Chinese. The Chinese are also heavily involved with the military-controlled tourism sector. In 2022, both governments signed a memorandum of understanding to solidify tourism cooperation. As of 2021, China has invested over $2.1 billion in Jamaica. Guyana has purchased the Safe City Surveillance System that utilizes Huawei facial recognition technology. In the Bahamas, Chinese backed companies are building a $3 billion deep-water container port as well as a four-lane highway and the Baha Mar Resort. The Dominican Republic received a $6 million loan to expand that country's electrical grid as well as a $3.18 billion investment and loan package in exchange for diplomatic recognition at the expense of Taiwan. The list goes on and on."

Taeng was obviously passionate about this topic. After taking a healthy swig from her beer, she continued. "This is where I came in. I am, or I was, an investigative journalist for the Caribbean News Agency based in Barbados. About a year and a half ago I was working on a project concerning Chinese influence and investment in the region and was doing research on a story that was focused on the re-emergence of the BRI on Barbados.

Although Barbados joined BRI in 2019, along with 19 other countries in Latin America and the Caribbean, the emerging accusations of debt-trap diplomacy, neocolonialism and economic imperialism, coupled with the collapse of the tourism industry due to COVID had caused the newly elected President and Prime Minister, as well as the majority of the Cabinet, to delay the construction of several offshore wind and onshore solar farms being pushed by the Chinese as 'green' alternatives to fight climate change. Needless to say, the Chinese were not very happy with this.

"A group of people in the present Cabinet; specifically the Deputy Prime Minister who is also the Minister of Foreign Affairs and Foreign Trade, the Minister of Lands and Maintenance, the Minister of Environment and National Beautification which oversees the Green and Blue Economy, and the Minister of Economic Affairs and Investment, all of whom have been bought by the Chinese, were extremely upset about the delay in construction of these farms and they are now actively planning to overthrow President Griffith as soon as they believe they have enough support to do so.

"About a year ago I received an anonymous phone call which told me that it would be in my best interest to take a good look at the Regimental Sergeant Major of the Special Operations Company of the Barbados Regiment based at The Garrison at St. Ann's Fort in St. Michael. I was told to specifically look at his contacts within the Chinese Embassy in Bridgetown. This sounded interesting, so I looked into it.

"Since I usually worked from home in Crab Hill, I decided that it would be better if I relocated to Bridgetown, so I took a room at Gratitude House, about half a mile as the crow flies from St. Ann's Fort and started shadowing Warrant Officer Class 1 Gabriel Collins, the Regimental Sergeant Major. During the day Collins seemed to go about his business as usual, although he did seem to make an inordinate number of detours to the Chinese Embassy several times a week when he was returning from the Barbados Coast Guard Headquarters, known as BCGS Pelican in Bridgetown. At night, it was a different story. Two or three times a week, Collins would leave St. Ann's Fort, drive back to his apartment in Howells, change out of his uniform into something smart casual and then drive back into town, usually to one of the resort hotels along the beach to have dinner and drinks with friends. The interesting thing to me was that all his friends appeared to be Chinese."

Taeng polished off her beer and asked Cody if she could have another, so he got up, walked to the kitchen to get her one and returned to his place on the couch. He didn't say a word as he didn't want her to lose her train of thought. Popping the top off the Carib bottle with the Swiss Army knife he routinely carried in one of his cargo pockets specifically for this task, Cody handed it to her. After she took a few swigs to wet her whistle, she continued.

"Apparently Collins was the go-between for the various disloyal ministers and the Chinese. I tailed Collins to several one-on-one meetings with the various ministers and documented the meetings with photographs taken clandestinely, or so I thought at the time.

"Eventually 'Deep Throat', which is how I referred to the voice on the other end of the phone who had initially suggested that I watch Collins, revealed himself to be Wilfred Duguid, the Minister of Energy and Business. The Chinese had approached him for support, but he wanted no part of what they were offering. Wilfred reported the approach to his friend, Ian Gooding, the Deputy Commissioner of Police, who decided to put together a small, trusted group within the police force to investigate the allegation. Needless to say, these people had to be seriously vetted to make sure that they hadn't already been approached and corrupted by the Chinese. Ian asked Wilfred to play along with the Chinese in an effort to find out what the end game was. When Wilfred asked the Deputy Commissioner if he was asking him to act in the role of a snitch, Ian had replied that this was a crude description of exactly what he was asking Wilfred to do. Wilfred then asked the Deputy Commissioner how he would describe the role. He replied that although he had said the term snitch was crude, it was not inaccurate. So, Wilfred became our snitch.

"Eventually, the group consisted of Deep Throat, three members of the Barbados Police Service, two people from the Caribbean News Agency, my photographer, my editor, and myself. What we failed to realize at the time, was that the Chinese were already on to us, which is not surprising since none of us had been trained to be spies and we were just operating like cops on a stakeout, and that the Chinese were tailing us as we tailed their people and the tainted Bajans.

"Eventually, Wilfred was invited to a meeting at the Hilton Barbados Resort one weekend where the tainted Bajan ministers met informally with Ms. Qu Ching, the Economic and Commercial Counsellor of the Chinese Embassy and a few other Chinese without portfolio. Once the conference room had been swept for bugs, the plan was revealed verbally, but nothing was put in writing. The Chinese were going to support a coup in Barbados on Independence Day, November 30.

"For their support of the coup, the windmill and solar farms would be approved, and the Bajan government would adhere to the One China policy and not recognize Taiwan as a separate entity. The Bajan ministers and military personnel involved would receive substantial contributions to their campaigns as well as their personal bank accounts. If the coup was successful, they would also become the ruling elite of Barbados.

"At some point, the Deputy Commissioner of Police became aware of a plan to get rid of our little group before the coup so that we could not reveal the plan or form any opposition to it. I'm not sure how he found out about the plan, but that is immaterial. The threat was real.

"We decided to go hide out on St. Vincent. Wilfred, the Minister of Energy and Business, had friends in Camden Park who would put us up and help us hide out for a while. This is where we were headed when the Caribbean Queen blew up, and here I am."

CHAPTER 7

TAENG LOOKED AT CODY EXPECTING him to have something to say after her epic tale, but all he did was stand up, deep in thought, as he made his way to the fridge to get them another round of beers, since they had both finished the last round while Taeng told her tale. Coming back to the couch, he sat back down, and after popping the tops off, he handed one to Taeng still without speaking.

Eventually, Cody looked at Taeng and said, "Typical journalist, you poke the hornets' nest then you run away." He was grinning as he said it. "You've apparently managed to not only piss off a number of Bajan politicians, but the Chinese Embassy as well. If the Chinese diplomats, and I use that term loosely, are annoyed, then you were probably brought to the attention of the Chinese Ministry of State Security. From what I've been led to believe, the MSS can be very nasty, and I would be willing to bet that they were the ones following you guys around and they probably blew up the Caribbean Queen as well.

"It would probably be a good idea for you to hang out here for a while and let the Chinese think you are dead until things blow over. What do you think?"

"Cody, I can't just sit around and do nothing. I need to get in touch with my friends on Barbados and figure out a way to let President Griffith know about the coup and see if there is anything that Ian and the Barbados Police Service can do to try and stop it."

"Why don't you sleep on it tonight and tomorrow I'll show you the comms system here so that you can get in touch with your people."

They collected their empty beer bottles before walking back to the kitchen to throw them in the trash. Cody made sure that he followed Taeng back into the little courtyard where their bedrooms were located. While doing so, he decided that those high waisted black yoga shorts hugged the back just as tightly as they hugged the front. From what he could see, Taeng had to be going commando this evening. There was absolutely no way she could have worn anything under those shorts without those unsightly panty lines being visible.

As Taeng turned to open the guestroom door, and without turning to face Cody, she asked, "Were you looking at my butt?"

"'When opportunity knocks' and all that, so yes, I was."

"Good, I guess I still got it then. Good night and I'll see you in the morning," said Taeng as she entered her room and closed the door.

As Cody went to his room, he was thinking that if Taeng had actually lost it at this point, he'd have liked to have been around to see her when she still had it. This kept his imagination in overdrive until he fell asleep.

The following morning they enjoyed a breakfast of scrambled eggs, toast and link sausage. After they had cleaned up the kitchen, Cody led Taeng back through the living room area, through the open courtyard to his bedroom door. While he was opening the door and ushering her through, Taeng commented that this seemed a bit forward and asked Cody if he was always so presumptuous with his female houseguests.

"Hey, if you want to toss me on my bed and have your way with me, don't let me stop you. I've had similar thoughts cross my mind concerning yourself the past few days as well and at some point, we should probably address that issue. In the meantime, you indicated last night that you needed to get in touch with your friends and this is the shortest path to my communications center."

With that out of the way, Taeng followed Cody across his bedroom, which was large and combined with the ensuite bathroom, took up the whole back side of the house. Opening the exterior door, which was on the opposite side of the bedroom from the entry door, Cody led the way about ten yards down a landscaped path, bordered by red fountain grass and shaded by large sea grape trees, to a building built to match the house. The communications center was located at the bottom of the antenna tower behind the house.

The door to the comms building was of solid steel construction with a handwheel in the center. It looked like something you would find on a Level 7 gun safe. There was also a backlit keypad to the right of the door. Fairly serious security on a private island, thought Taeng.

Cody punched an 8-digit code into the keypad before spinning the handwheel and pushing the door open and ushering Taeng inside. The inside of the comms building was completely out of step with Cody's house and its location on a remote Caribbean island. The interior of the building was square in shape, about 30' x 30'. The entry door was located off-center to the left on the wall facing the house. As they walked in, Taeng noticed that the building was windowless and that the back half of the room was caged off in heavy duty steel mesh with a mesh door built into the center of the cage wall. This door sported a Model 8077 High Security Combination Padlock.

The building was air-conditioned down to a cool 68 degrees Fahrenheit, which was necessary due to all the electronic gear in the place. This morning it also had the beneficial effect, from Cody's point of view anyhow, of causing Taeng's womanly nubbins to poke out of the papaya-colored V-necked tank top she had chosen to wear. Apparently even with the additional coverage and support of one of her new bras underneath the tank top, her attire was failing to suitably restrain these perky female attributes. Taeng seemed to be blissfully unaware of her condition, while Cody, on the other hand, was very much aware of her condition and decided that the air-conditioning not only protected expensive electronic equipment, but now also provided a form of lizard brain entertainment. He'd need to mentally file this tidbit of cause and effect for future consideration.

After getting over Taeng's physical response to the relatively chilly environment, Cody explained that behind the mesh was the CIA and NSA signals intelligence equipment. Not being a communications geek, Cody assumed that all the blinking lights and stacks of equipment were the servers, routers, switches and so forth required to spy on the Caribbean Basin as well as the communications system to relay what was found. Cody was not allowed to access the cage, which was not a problem as he wasn't interested in doing so.

The front half of the comms room was Cody's half. This consisted of a state-of-the-art computer system along the right-hand wall with everything he would possibly need concerning communications with the outside world: high-speed internet routed through a variety of VPNs to hide his location as well as satellite, radio and cell phone communications. If Cody had a pressing project that did not require the manufacturing or testing of some component or compound, he'd do his research here at night, but he actually preferred to work in his full lab and shop built on top of the submarine pens.

"But check this out!" Cody asked Taeng as he went over to the large desk built against the left-hand wall. Sitting in the office chair in front of the desk, Cody 'woke up' the four 50" external monitors mated to the MacBook Pro on the desk and typed on the keys for a second before pointing to the monitors. The four monitors now showed the view from the island along the four cardinal compass points, obviously from high resolution cameras mounted somewhere high on the antenna tower. Playing with his mouse, Cody could pan any camera in any direction.

"Interesting, but why?" asked Taeng.

"Since I live here alone most of the time, I sometimes get too caught up in whatever I'm working on at the moment and forget that this is a secure installation. This makes it easy to see who is coming to the island or, in the worst case, who is already here. I really don't need it since the NSA and CIA crowd monitor the island 24/7, but it does give you a good view of the island."

"So, the Yanks know that I am here?"

"Yep, I'm sure they do. They called me and asked me to put a camera in your shower, but I'm a gentleman."

Taeng thought about this for a second. "Did you put one in or not? Being a gentleman doesn't mean that you did, or you didn't."

"I am tempted to ask you to see if you can find it, but that would be caddish. I promise you that there is not, and never has been, a camera in your shower. I'm enjoying your company and I don't want you running off to Barbados when you are supposed to be playing dead."

Taeng was standing close behind Cody as he sat in his office chair, so she slapped him on the back of his head. "If I do find a camera in my shower, it will be you who is dead, and you won't be playing."

As Cody spun the handwheel to re-lock the door as they left the comms building, he informed Taeng that he needed to go down to his shop for the afternoon to get back to the project she had so rudely interrupted when she washed ashore. Since the comms system could be accessed from the shop, he suggested that she come with him and contact her friends while he worked.

As they walked back through the house, Taeng went to the refrigerator to grab a few beers, but Cody told her that he had cold beer down in the shop. He did suggest that she grab some of the mustard he'd bought in Grenada, he'd run out in the shop, but he had all the other makings for ham and cheese sandwiches down there.

Since the Gator was still parked in front of the patio at the front of the house where they'd left it after coming back from shopping in Grenada, they hopped in and took it and the little trailer back to the shop. Once at the shop, Taeng hopped out and went inside to roll up the garage door and Cody pulled the Gator and its trailer inside and drove it back to wherever he'd originally gotten it from. Coming back from behind the row of shop equipment, Cody walked with Taeng across the shop floor to another air-conditioned room at the far side of the building in the front corner of the shop, where he did his research.

The room was set up like an office space. The wall opposite the entry door was obviously the 'business' part of the office, with a wide desk-high shelf extending across the entire wall, which actually acted as a desk. This shelf held three workstations spaced equally along the length of the shelf with six large external monitors arranged in pairs in front of each workstation.

To the left as you entered the room was a huge L-shaped, brown leather couch, with the short leg facing the wall where the desk shelf was mounted. There was a coffee table made out of what looked like a solid core oak door in front of the couch, sitting on a tropical motif area rug. On the opposite side of the coffee table from the long-leg of the couch was an old Lay-Z-Boy recliner in chocolate colored microfiber. On the righthand wall, which would be toward the front of the building, was another shelf, this time about the height of a normal kitchen counter, with a built-in double sink and a cut-out for a Maytag 25 cubic foot French door refrigerator. There were also several tropical potted plants placed around so that the place didn't feel so much like someone's garage.

Cody noticed that the air-conditioning in the office, although not as chilly as in the comms room up at the house, was still having a similar and much appreciated effect on Taeng's anatomy. He'd have to put this physical reaction to the back of his mind if he really wanted to get some work done today.

"Well, this is my home away from home and where I do the bulk of my research. I'll set you up at one of the workstations so that you can contact your people and then I need to get back to work."

Cody got Taeng set up at the workstation on the far left while he set up on the one at the far right. Cody told Taeng that if she needed anything to just give him a shout.

Taeng got busy on her end of the desk while Cody did the same on his. She was busy typing emails and making the occasional WhatsApp call while Cody was silent as he worked his keyboard, peered at his monitors, then typed some more. The hours passed quickly and eventually Cody stood up and stretched before announcing that it was lunchtime.

Taeng stood up and stretched as well. Cody happened to notice that the air-conditioning was still working its magic before he walked over to the refrigerator and took out all of the makings for proper ham and cheese sandwiches: thick sliced ham, wholemeal seeded bread, mature cheddar cheese, mayo, butter, cracked black pepper and Dijon mustard.

As Cody made the sandwiches, Taeng found the paper plates and napkins and put them out on the coffee table before going to the refrigerator and getting out a couple of Cokes to wash the sandwiches down with. Once Cody had finalized his culinary masterpieces, he brought them to the table on a cutting board along with two packets of sour cream and onion potato chips he'd gotten from somewhere.

Sitting side by side on the couch they had their lunch. Taeng related what she had been able to find out from her sources. First, her friends and associates were thrilled that she hadn't been blown up with the Caribbean Queen. Everyone else, including the authorities, the tainted Bajans and the Chinese were still certain that she had been. The Chinese and the corrupt politicians were convinced that their secret was still safe and that the coup was still on for Independence Day, November 30.

Those that were aware of the coup had been laying low since the Caribbean Queen had met its demise and were still trying to come up with a plan to approach President Griffith and make him aware of what was afoot. Now that they were aware that Taeng was still alive and in hiding, they agreed to stay in touch as they continued to try and find a way to thwart the coup.

"You didn't happen to tell them where you were playing dead at, did you?" asked Cody.

"I may have failed to mention that, moron. I may not be an engineering savant, but I didn't just fall off the mango truck yesterday. You said that your comms are routed through a bunch of VPN's, so nobody should have any idea where I'm at."

"Don't get your knickers in a knot, I was just checking."

"Theoretically the only way that I could get my knickers in a knot is if I was actually wearing knickers, and no, you cannot check to see if I am going commando today or not," Taeng teased.

Seeking to avoid any further conversation concerning her knickers or lack thereof, Taeng asked Cody what was keeping him so occupied at his end of the shelf-like desk.

She could see Cody instantly switch from his lizard, knicker obsessed brain back to his frontal lobe, and he got serious.

"Are you familiar with the North American XB-70 or the Lockheed SR-71 aircraft?" asked Cody.

"Nope, can't say that I am."

"Both projects were begun in the late '50's and first flew in 1964. The XB-70 was designed as a supersonic strategic bomber while the SR-71 was developed as a reconnaissance aircraft. Both were designed to fly at Mach 3 or greater, which was a quantum leap in technology at the time. One of the issues they had was that at those speeds, the friction due to air moving across their surfaces would create temperatures up to $1,000^{\circ}$ Fahrenheit over the engines and an average skin temperature of 600° Fahrenheit. Proper panel alignment was only achieved once the airframe heated up and expanded several inches. Because of this, and the lack of a fuel-sealing system that could handle the airframe's expansion at extreme temperatures, the aircraft leaked fuel on the ground prior to takeoff. There were no seals that were flexible and durable enough to deal with those kinds of temperatures and the contraction-expansion cycles. As a result, the plane would leak fuel while on the runway, but it would stop leaking once the aircraft came up to temperature.

"The problem with finding a material that was both durable and flexible enough to handle the thermal cycles was never resolved, and it is still a problem when developing hypersonic aircraft or missiles. I'm working on that issue."

"And how's that coming along?" asked Taeng.

"I've had some promising results with the Viton F-type fluoroelastomers, which are a new generation of terpolymers with good resistance to various fuels as well as significant improvements in processing, rheology and physical properties."

"Well, that went straight over my head." Wanting to use this as a lead into a more interesting topic, interesting to Taeng at least, she asked, "Are you really happy on this island? You have no social outlets here and as they say, 'all work and no play makes for a dull boy'. Don't you ever just want to go out and party, dance, get a little wild? Am I missing something here?"

"Who says I don't ship in the wine, women and song when I get the urge? Didn't I mention the Swedish women's beach volleyball team earlier?"

"That could be, but I haven't seen a single sign of a past female presence on the island: no lingerie fallen behind the dresser drawers, no lady-like stuff left in the bathroom cabinet, no wine in the refrigerator, and the couches, both here and back at the house, have only one depression worn into them. Only one depression indicates that only one person uses it and sits in the same place over and over again. As a woman, I see things that you men would not, and I would know if another woman had been here."

"The truth is that I have the same urges and desires as any other man and when I feel the need to socialize, I fly to either Martinique, St. Lucia, St. Vincent or Grenada for a week to relax and knock the edges off. I then fly back to my hermitage and get back to work."

"So, a woman in every port?"

"I am fairly discerning when it comes to women. I've had my share of 'one-night stands', but I'm looking for something a little more permanent, relaxing and intimate these days. That said, living on a private island like this and doing this kind of work, makes it kind of difficult to find a 'real woman' if you know what I mean. It just is what it is."

Being a real woman, Taeng just had to ask. "Interesting. So hypothetically where would I fit into this picture now that I'm basically stuck here playing dead for a while?"

"Hard to say," Cody replied as he pensively studied the ceiling. "I've never had an annoyingly attractive island girl wash up on my island before, emphasis on annoying. I'll need to research this further and get back to you on that."

"So, you think I'm attractive?" This, to even the most casual observer, was a leading question that needed to be handled delicately.

"The term 'attractive' is very subjective. That said, don't they have mirrors where you come from?" responded Cody as he stood up and suggested that they get back to work before he could get interrogated further.

They continued working on their respective projects for a few more hours. At one point Cody left the office for about an hour to go do something out in the shop. When he returned, he announced that it was time to close up shop and go have dinner. Taeng had actually done as much as she could do as far as reestablishing contact with her co-conspirators, before lunch and had just been surfing the internet since then, so she was ready and willing to get out of the windowless, concrete office.

After ushering Taeng out of his workplace, Cody turned off the lights and closed the door before they made their way back across the shop to the man door beside the rollup garage door and exited the building after Cody again turned off the lights in the shop proper. Locking the door behind him, Cody motioned Taeng over toward the Kawasaki dirt bike that had brought them there. It had been parked inside when they had come down earlier but was now sitting outside the rollup garage door.

Cody showed her the new passenger foot pegs on the bike, which is what he'd been fabricating and installing on the bike during his afternoon absence from the office. Once they were on the bike, Cody informed Taeng that just because she had foot pegs now did not mean that she had to stop rubbing up against him and that she should hold on as tight as possible for her own safety as well as his entertainment.

While Taeng was trying to figure out how to properly utilize the foot pegs for stability while still being able to rub up against Cody's butt without looking like a tramp, Cody dumped the clutch and went scooting straight up the hill, off the crushed-oyster path, like an AMA professional hill climber at the Devil's Staircase event in Ohio. Taeng had to hold on for dear life while the back of the bike yawed left and right trying to find traction, exactly how Cody had planned it. The 'crotch-to-crack' separation was essentially non-existent during the run up the hill, even with the new foot pegs.

As they dismounted the bike in front of the house, Taeng was rubbing her inner thighs and accused Cody of doing that on purpose. Cody just grinned as he followed her up the steps, across the patio, and into the French doors leading into the house.

The options for dinner were shrimp scampi or seared mahi-mahi. They did rock-paper-scissors to decide, and the scampi won out. So, while Cody got busy on the scampi, Taeng worked on a green salad to go with it.

Cody melted the butter in a large skillet over medium heat while adding garlic, shallots and red pepper flakes while stirring frequently for about two minutes. Adding in the shrimp, Cody seasoned the mix with some salt and pepper and cooked the concoction until the shrimp were cooked through and pink. Stirring in some parsley, lemon juice and zest, Cody announced that dinner was ready.

Taeng had set the dining table for two and placed the salad and some bleu cheese dressing on the table, so when Cody hollered that the scampi was ready, she grabbed the two plates and brought them up by the stove to be served. Once they were both back at the table, they dug in.

When they were finished with their meal, Cody informed Taeng that the house rules stated that when more than one was residing in the house, if one person cooked, the other washed dishes. There was no reason to have a dishwasher installed in the kitchen if there was only Cody in residence, so washing dishes was a hand job.

"Have any of the other guests managed to avoid washing the dishes?" asked Taeng.

Cody thought about this for a moment before admitting that two guests had in fact avoided doing the dishes.

"And how, pray tell, did they manage that?"

"By agreeing to play strip poker with me. Do you want to get out of doing the dishes, Ms. Skeete?" asked Cody with a lecherous grin.

"That sounds like a win-win situation for you, Mr. Morgan. You would possibly get to watch me slowly undress with the end game being somewhat of a foregone conclusion and eventually the dishes would still get washed. Do you mark the cards?"

"Of course! What kind of an engineering savant would I be if I didn't try to engineer the outcome? For you, I may even mark them twice just to be sure."

"I think that was sort of a left-handed compliment, but I believe that I'll just wash the dishes and keep my clothes on this evening," replied Taeng as she strolled over to the kitchen sink with what Cody thought was a little more swagger in her strut than what was actually called for. Taeng figured that if Cody could tease her, the least she could do was to return the favor. The game was on.

They stayed up a few more hours just shooting the breeze and getting to know one another better before they decided to call it a day and went to their respective rooms.

CHAPTER 8

THE FOLLOWING MORNING, TAENG CAME out of her room dressed in Cody's old Toots and the Maytals t-shirt and not much else that Cody could see. Not a bad start to the day, he thought.

While he busied himself at the kitchen counter putting the finishing touches on the scrambled eggs and toast, Taeng took a seat at the island and placed her rope handled, Rastafarian flag motif, canvas tote bag on the floor beside her. When Cody was bringing their plates to the table, Taeng bent down to rummage around in the tote bag, which caused the t-shirt to ride up high enough that Cody could see that she did in fact have something on under her t-shirt. The article of clothing appeared to be the bottom half of some type of floral-patterned bikini. This was the swimwear that Cody had seen on the hotel bed in Grenada while Taeng was in the shower. He felt that he could give it the appreciation that it deserved if he was given the chance to see more of what little there was of it.

While they ate, Cody asked her what she planned to do that day. She replied that as she was still waiting to hear back from her associates on Barbados and some of the other Windward Islands, she thought that she would just lay out in the sun today on one of the lounge chairs on the front deck.

"What are your plans for the day?" asked Taeng, returning the favor.

"If I didn't need to go back down to the shop and run some tests, I think that I might join you. Just to see what is under that Toots t-shirt if nothing else."

Taeng let Cody know that she didn't feel like being ogled while catching rays and that he should probably just go to work. She indicated that the hormonal overload of seeing her in the new bikini she had picked up in Grenada might cause him to lose focus.

While Taeng cleaned up the kitchen, Cody got on the dirt bike and headed down to his office in the shop. After grabbing a bottle of water out of the refrigerator, Taeng went out on the front sundeck, arranged one of the lounge chairs to take full advantage of the morning sun, then stripped off her t-shirt, put on her Oakley HSTN Metal shades, with the black frame and lenses, recently purchased in Grenada, and laid down on the lounge chair exposing herself to the sun, and unwittingly to other things as well.

Cody was slaving away at his workstation when he received what appeared to be a WhatsApp call on his monitor. The call was actually coming through a cleverly disguised encrypted NSA spoof of WhatsApp. Cody answered the call while continuing to work since he assumed it was just the joint NSA/CIA listening post located in Puerto Rico, at the highest elevation on the island in the hills above Santa Barbara, calling to check up on him.

"Yeah, Mike, what can I do for you today?" Mike was a friend of Cody's and was a senior NSA signals analyst. They had met while the NSA and CIA were rigging Pala Island 'for sound'. Cody flew up to Ponce on Puerto Rico every few months just to hang out, drink beer and bullshit with Mike.

"It's not so much what you can do for me, but what I can do for you. I think that you may have been keeping something from me."

"What the heck are you talking about?" Cody was a bit confused by the conversation.

"Go to a workstation other than the one that you are presently working on and open up the camera link for the camera facing north at the top of the mast behind your house."

"Why?" demanded Cody.

"Just do it, you'll thank me later."

Cody rolled his office chair over to the middle workstation and did as instructed. What he saw was a high resolution shot of the desalination plant across the small harbor from the shop he was presently in above the submarine pens.

"Looks like the desalination plant to me, am I missing something?"

"Just keep watching."

The view on the camera started working its way from the desalination plant south and up the hill toward the house. The camera could be controlled remotely from Puerto Rico.

"Boring," sighed Cody.

"Keep watching, dickhead."

The top of the comms tower, where the high-resolution camera was located, was high enough so that when the camera was rotated as far down as it would go, it had a good view of most of the sundeck. As the sundeck came into view, so did Taeng in her new Venus floral pattern scoop bottom halter bikini. The view was outstanding.

"Forget to tell me about your new houseguest, amigo?" asked Mike.

Cody had other things on his mind at the moment and was preoccupied. He also knew that the camera had zoom capability as well as high resolution.

"Can you zoom in and slowly pan down from head to foot?"

"Already done it a few times myself, but I'll gladly repeat the process. This girl is not a beginner's model. Where did you find her?"

"Long story, keep panning!"

As the voyeurs slowly panned up and down Taeng's sleek and sensuous form, she casually reached down to adjust her bottom before she took her time to rearrange her top, causing a sharp intake of breath from both Cody and Mike. While they watched, she got up and dropped the back of the chair down flat before she laid down on her stomach, exposing what was probably one of the most magnificent bikini-clad female backsides in human history.

"If that bikini bottom goes any further between those phenomenal butt cheeks, it'll become a thong," observed Mike.

Almost as if she'd heard him, Taeng, while still lying flat on her stomach, reached behind her with both hands and pulled her scoop-front cheeky bottom back into its originally intended orientation on her butt.

"Turn that off before I have an aneurism," demanded Cody.

"I've already had three, so that's probably a wise idea," replied Mike as he shut down the video feed.

"Where did you find that unbelievable specimen of feminine pulchritude?" Mike waxed eloquent when he was excited.

"Honestly, she just washed up on the island one morning."

Cody then told Mike the whole story including the part about the anticipated coup in Barbados, although there was no proof of that yet.

Hearing this, Mike got serious. If the Chinese were going to be involved in a coup in the Caribbean, both the NSA and CIA would be very interested in stopping it and keeping the status quo in the region. Mike asked Cody to keep him up to date and that he would pass the information up the ladder to both Fort Meade and Langley and get back to him. Before he signed off, he told Cody not to overexert himself and to call if he needed any help with his new houseguest.

By the time Cody called it a day and got back to the house, Taeng had long since finished her tanning session and had showered and changed into a pair of cuffed denim shorts and a loose fit long-sleeved t-shirt. She was sitting on the couch and had a Carib beer waiting for him. She must have heard the Kawasaki coming up the hill.

Sitting down beside her, Cody took a long pull on his Carib before he started to wind his guest up.

"Liked your new bikini. It shows you off to good advantage and the floral pattern highlights your unique complexion."

"And how would you know that? If I remember correctly you left for work before I went out to get some sun."

"Remember the high-resolution cameras mounted on the comms tower?" asked Cody.

Taeng could see where this was going and started blushing appropriately. "I do, now that you mention them."

"Well, those cameras are monitored 24/7 at a so-called 'listening post' in Puerto Rico by our friends in the No Such Agency and the Citizens In Action, better known as the NSA and the CIA, respectively. While I was working this morning, I received a call from my buddy Mike at the listening post and he suggested that I access the feed from the cameras, which I did, and there you were, scantily clad in your new bikini, sunning yourself. It seems that when the camera is tilted down to the lowest extent of its panning capability, it has a good view of the sundeck, which I never knew. I should also mention that it has fantastic zoom capabilities as well."

Taeng was going full scarlet now, well as scarlet as one could get with her particular skin tone and coloring and asked what the two voyeurs did next.

"Well, for 15 minutes or so we played with the pan and zoom features of the camera, but when you flipped over on your stomach and had to readjust your bottom to a more comfortable arrangement, we left you to your privacy."

"Really? You decided to stop being perverts after I pulled my bottoms out of the crack of my butt? That seems like odd behavior for lechers."

"The decision to stop our voyeuristic enterprise was based on our health. We felt if we kept watching that we'd both have had hormonally induced myocardial infarctions, that's heart attacks to you of the non-medical persuasion."

Taeng grinned at Cody. "It's nice to be appreciated. Lucky for you deviants I wasn't going topless or trying for a full body, no tan lines, tan. What's for dinner?"

Cody was speechless as he drew a mental picture of Taeng laying out in the altogether with all her naughty bits on display. Taeng eventually smacked him on the shoulder and pointed toward the kitchen.

CHAPTER 9

THE NEXT MORNING, AFTER A quick breakfast of Honey Nut Cheerios and coffee, Cody and Taeng once again mounted the Kawasaki dirt bike and headed back down to the shop and then back into the office to get some work done.

They were both enjoying the 'close encounters of the dirt bike type' now, though neither would openly admit to it.

About an hour into the work session, Taeng received a WhatsApp call on the encrypted system and talked for about half an hour with one of her colleagues. After hanging up, she turned to Cody and asked if it was possible to get to Kingstown on St. Vincent that evening. She needed to get up there to attend a clandestine meeting of her little group.

"Sure, no problem. When would we be coming back?"

"Probably tomorrow sometime."

Cody thought for a moment, before asking, "You do realize that you still need to remain dead for your own safety, correct?"

"Yeah, obviously."

"That means we can't take the old Nipponese seaplane; it stands out like a sore thumb and it's too easy to get a look inside and see who's in it. We'll need to take old Shag McNasty."

"What, pray tell, is a Shag McNasty?" asked a confused Taeng.

"My old torpedo boat parked down behind the fuel barge; I showed it to you earlier."

"Right, nobody will notice an old torpedo boat," Taeng observed sarcastically.

"Unless you look closely, it can be mistaken for a variety of pleasure or fishing boats, such as an HCB Speciale or Suenoa, maybe even a Pursuit OS 405, or an old Post 43 Sportfish, if they don't look too closely. Without its guns or torpedoes, and in its storm gray paint job, it can go most anywhere without attracting attention. How many people are in your group?"

"Five, no more than that," replied Taeng.

"Okay, call back and ask to meet them at the end of the pier at Barrouallie, there's only one, at 9:30 tonight. They can come aboard, and I'll go back out to sea and cruise around while you guys chat, then I'll return to Barrouallie. You'd better describe old Shag to them, or they might get nervous."

Taeng called back and made the arrangements, then hung up. "Why did you name your boat Shag McNasty?"

"Well, first off, it is an old Nasty boat, which is what the US Navy called the Tjeld class Norwegian patrol torpedo boats when they bought them. Second, Shag McNasty's was the name of a pub I frequented while I was working in Aberdeen, Scotland. Lastly, I like the term 'shag'. At some point I'll likely need to show you, as opposed to tell you, what shagging is."

"Mr. Morgan, I know exactly what shagging means in the British vernacular."

"Okay, that saves me the trouble of having to define it for you. What are the chances of any shagging occurring on the Shag McNasty while we are out this evening? It will be a nice night out on the water and the motion of the ocean should be an asset. The opportunity really shouldn't be wasted."

Taeng turned back to her monitor. "I guess you can ask the others tonight, there will be two other women, but I intend to remain shag-free while aboard the Shag."

"Does this mean that there may be an opportunity for some shagging while you are not onboard the Shag?" asked Cody hopefully.

"When pigs fly some offboard shagging may be possible, but not probable," Taeng informed him.

"On it," said Cody as he turned back to his own monitor.

"On what?"

"I am going to engineer, design and build a flying pig."

"You are impossible," laughed Taeng.

Once again, they rode belly to backbone up the hill to the house and packed up what they thought they would need for the run up to Barrouallie that evening. Cody changed into some old cut-offs with a Hootie & The Blowfish t-shirt under an old denim work shirt. Taeng, still in teasing mode, especially after the shagging conversation, chose to wear the crotch-hugging, black, high waisted yoga shorts and a black sports bra, just to keep things interesting. In a nod towards modesty, and the possibility that it might get cold out on the water, she also wore one of Cody's old work shirts over the sports bra as well. Totally unbuttoned, of course.

With everything covered so to speak, they hopped back on the bike with Taeng holding on to their knapsacks, one in either hand, and rode slowly back down to the shop. Pulling the bike inside, Cody shut the door, and they both shouldered their respective knapsacks and took the old cage elevator down to the submarine pen. Cody got on board his Nasty boat with the knapsacks, while Taeng stood on the dock and waited to release the bow and stern lines.

Cody fired up both of the twin supercharged Napier-Deltic diesel engines, checked the gauges to make sure they were running in the green and that all the electronics he'd installed were working as advertised before reversing to get some slack in the stern line so that Taeng could get the loop off of the bollard and toss it onboard. He then pulled forward to put some slack in the bow line so that Taeng could do the same with it.

When Taeng jumped onboard, Cody slowly moved out of the pen and into the small harbor while she coiled and stowed the mooring lines before joining Cody on the bridge. Cody maneuvered the boat out of the harbor and into the passage behind the breakwater and then out to sea. Once clear of the breakwater, Cody throttled up to 20 knots and headed north so that they could pass up through the Windwards, keeping the islands of Savan, Petite Mustique and Mustique off the starboard side. The seas were calm, the winds were gentle, and the trip was relaxing. Taeng got bored and carried their knapsacks down through the starboard side access hatch on the bridge and took the opportunity to check out the accommodations below. Cody had remodeled the crew's quarters under the forward deck of the boat where the M2 .50 caliber machine gun had originally been mounted. It now consisted of a small galley and a nicely appointed stateroom. The original head, or bathroom for those not nautically astute, nestled in the bow had been remodeled as well so that it no longer resembled the basic head you would expect to find on a military patrol boat and leaned more toward what you might find on a mid-range yacht. Taeng thought that the queen-sized bed bolted to the deck looked very comfortable, but she would refrain from mentioning this to Cody so that he would keep his mind on driving the boat as opposed to other, perhaps more carnal pursuits such as shagging.

After taking off her old work shirt to enjoy the breeze, at least that is what she told herself, she went back up the ladder and onto the bridge. Nestling into a corner of the port side of the bridge, she just enjoyed herself and watched Cody handle the boat. He seemed confident and comfortable and was enjoying himself as well. He caught her watching him and asked her if she could handle a boat.

"I'm basically a Bajan girl, I can handle anything with a mast or a motor. Scoot over and I'll show you." Cody explained to her the layout of the instrumentation and showed her how to work the throttles before he handed the helm over to her.

Cody was fairly impressed. Taking control of an 80-foot, 71-ton, 6,200 horsepower boat was much different than taking control of some 43', 1,400 horsepower sport fishing yacht, but Taeng took to it like a duck to water, and before long she was enjoying herself as well.

"Alright Captain Jack Sparrow, keep us on a heading of north by northwest so that we pass between Pigeon, Quatre, Petit Nevis and Bequia islands to port and Baliceaux and Battowia to starboard. I'll take over again once we clear the northern tip of Bequia."

While Taeng drove, Cody went below to check on the engines since they had sat for a while before today's outing. The original, fully armed, Vietnam-era version of the Nasty boat required a crew of 17 to both man the weapons and handle the boat, but without weapons and with modern automation and engine control systems, the old boat could be run with a crew of two. Going back up to the bridge, he parked himself in the corner recently vacated by Taeng and just watched her work the boat. He thought that this was an excellent way to spend his time.

About 30 minutes later, they had just cleared Bequia, when Taeng exclaimed, "What the heck is he doing out here?"

Cody looked where she was pointing and saw what looked like an old oilfield crew boat, not a common sight in the Lesser Antilles.

"Who is that? Do you know that boat?"

"Yeah, it's the Scantily Clad, my father's boat."

"What!"

"Yeah, he smuggles on his off time." As they closed on the vessel, Taeng explained.

"Mom teaches English at the Coleridge & Parry School in Douglas on Barbados. She met Dad while he was working as the head chef at the Zen restaurant in Saint Philip Parish. Once I was out of the house and on my own, he eventually became part-owner of the restaurant and only works in the kitchen when he wants to now. His whole life he wanted to be a pirate, but the closest he could come to that in the Caribbean these days was as a smuggler. So, when he wants to get away from the restaurant and wants a little excitement in his life, he gets on that old crew boat he had rebuilt and smuggles stuff, mostly untaxed cigarettes, booze and auto parts around the islands. Mom kind of likes the arrangement as it gets him out of the house and it surprisingly generates a decent secondary income.

"He's a little out there and he takes a while to get used to," she added.

As Cody pulled up alongside the old crew boat, he told Taeng that she had an odd family and asked her if she had any of that pirate-smuggler DNA in her.

"Oh yeah, I can be a little out there as well sometimes," she replied with a wink.

Upon closer inspection, the crew boat appeared to be an old 65' aluminum hulled Swiftship, which to Cody's knowledge ran two GM12V71 engines and would have a top speed of around 18 knots. The waters were calm, so Cody pulled alongside while Taeng dropped some fender buoys over the starboard gunwale to keep the hulls from scraping together. As the two boats slowly lost steerage, Taeng stood on the deck just starboard of the Shag's superstructure and waved at her father on the crew boat's bridge. The boats finally came to rest and Taeng's father came out on deck to help her tie the boats together using the mooring lines from the Nasty boat. He was a nut brown, weather-beaten, skinny little guy in his late fifties dressed in old, faded khaki dungaree shorts and a wife-beater t-shirt that had once been white. His hair and beard were shading from grey to white and scruffy although his eyes were alight and lively.

"Dad, what are you doing out here?" asked Taeng.

"Smuggling, what else would I be doing out here. Your mother wanted me out of the house, so I thought I'd run some vodka and some of them nasty black cigarettes to those rich Russian assholes on St. Lucia, they're always good for a 200 per cent markup. Who's the hippie you're running around half naked with and how did he get an old Nasty boat? I'm jealous."

"I am not half naked."

"Really, my eyesight is not what it used to be, and I can almost see every cleft, crack and crevice that you were born with."

"Dad!"

"Okay, just joking. Who's the dude?"

Cody had put the boat in neutral and had walked up behind Taeng.

"Dad, I would like you to meet Cody, a friend of mine. Cody, meet my father, Tanawat."

Although Cody thought it was a bit odd that Taeng's father hadn't said a word concerning his daughter's recent near-death experience, he still waved and told Tanawat that it was nice to have met him.

"Yeah, yeah, yeah," said Tanawat as he waved aside the compliment. "What are your intentions toward my daughter?"

This sort of social interaction, immediate interrogation, was not something that Cody was prepared for. "I'm just giving her a ride to Barrouallie, sir."

"Really? Haven't you taken a good look at her, especially dressed as she is? A real man would be interested in giving her a ride of another sort. Are you a real man or one of those lady boys?"

Cody couldn't believe that Tanawat seemed to be pimping his daughter, which really wasn't what he was doing at all, he was simply trying to get the measure of the man his daughter was cruising around the Lesser Antilles with, and perhaps to gauge if Cody might be suitable son-in-law material. Taeng, on the other hand, knew exactly what her dad was up to.

"Dad, Cody and I are going up to Barrouallie so that I can meet up with some associates. We are trying to stop that Chinese coup that I told you about a few weeks ago, and would you stop trying to marry me off. I'm not going to fall for some throwback to the Grateful Dead." Cody, in his defense, clarified that he was a really smart throwback, and that the Grateful Dead had been inducted into the Rock & Roll Hall of Fame back in 1994.

After this piece of trivia, Tanawat got serious as Taeng brought him up to speed on the situation concerning the coup. She'd given him the CliffsNotes when she'd seen him just before she boarded the Caribbean Queen and had brought him up to date once she had access to comms on Pala Island, but she filled in the details now.

"You be careful, daughter, those uncivilized Chinese are worse than us Thais, they have no moral compass whatsoever."

After saying that, he asked if he could come aboard and take a look around Cody's Nasty boat. Cody agreed and took him on a tour of the boat with Taeng following close behind to make sure that her father didn't make any promises to Cody that she couldn't keep. There was no telling what sort of deal he'd make with Cody concerning her. Tanawat made no secret that he wanted grandchildren, whether Taeng wanted to provide them or not.

After taking a tour of Cody's boat, Tanawat offered to show Cody around his boat. Cody wasn't too interested in having a guided tour of an old crew boat, but boating etiquette demanded that he accept, so he did.

Once in the engine room, Cody noticed that the engines were not the original GM12V71's supplied by Swiftship.

"You have a good eye, Mr. Cody. Not many people would have noticed that. These babies are the GM16V71TA's giving me 4 more cylinders per engine and they are turbocharged. I'm getting 760 horses out of each plant now," boasted Taeng's father.

"What top speed does that give you? I believe this crate was originally rated at 18 knots."

"Running full tilt, she'll make 25 to 30 knots now. Just because I am a curious man, how many horses are you running in that old Nasty boat, and how fast is she?"

"The two Napier-Deltic turbocharged diesels are cranking out about 6,200 horses. With the weight of the guns, ammo and torpedoes removed, and only a crew of two, I can get up to 50 knots fairly easily."

Going back on deck, Tanawat told his daughter that her inconsiderate ferringhi would not agree to trade boats and that she should use her feminine wiles to convince him to do so, Cody agreed. With that said, Tanawat told them to be careful and to give him a shout if they would require his services. Cody got back on his bridge and kicked the Nasty into gear while Taeng and her father released the mooring lines holding the boats together. As Tanawat eased his boat away from Cody's, Taeng coiled the mooring lines back up and hauled in the fenders before going up to the bridge where Cody was throttling up and getting back on course for Barrouallie. As Taeng got comfortable in the corner of the bridge again, Cody asked her if she would be willing to use her feminine wiles on him to get him to trade boats with her father.

"Depends, ferringhi. How's that flying pig project of yours coming along?"

CHAPTER 10

AFTER LEAVING THE UNEXPECTED RENDEZVOUS with Tanawat, Cody set a course of 320° until he was roughly 2 miles off Barrouallie before turning hard to starboard and bringing Shag McNasty smoothly alongside the end of the pier. It was dark now, which had been the plan, and five people materialized at the shore end of the pier and sprinted the 50 yards to the boat and hopped on without ceremony. Once everyone was present and accounted for, Taeng held up her hand and with the twirling of her index finger signaled that it was time to get the show on the road. Cody slowly pulled away from the dock before he headed back out to sea. When he was a mile or so offshore, Cody pointed his boat north until he was due west of the extinct La Soufrière volcano before pulling close into the steep, rugged coast and dropping anchor.

At this point, Taeng brought her associates up to the bridge to meet Cody before they all climbed down through the hatch in the bridge to the stateroom under the forward deck where they would get down to business.

There were two women about Taeng's age, roughly mid-20's: A'lynn and Lacy. A'lynn was a chunky little thing about 5'5" or so, with an attractive face framed by an impressive afro. For a conspirator, Cody thought that she had a great sense of humor and a beautiful smile.

Lacy was about the same height as Taeng, and absolutely stunning. Her hair was braided tight against her head with the end of the braids falling well past her shoulders. Combined with her long, elegant neck she looked like a Nubian princess. Her bust was larger than Taeng's pert 34B trending toward C endowment, but the rest of her was extremely fit and built more for speed than comfort. She also seemed to be a flirt and winked at Cody as she was introduced. Cody couldn't keep his eyes off her until Taeng, with maybe a tinge of jealousy, punched Cody in the shoulder with what he thought was just a little too much gusto as she informed him that it was impolite to stare.

The men: Gideon, Marcus and Rommel, were all about 6' tall with short, cropped hair and were well muscled, but with ropy muscles molded by manual labor as opposed to muscle attained by lifting weights. They were dressed identically in cut-offs and t-shirts, and they looked like men who could take care of themselves if they had to.

All the conspirators headed down the ladder to the stateroom leaving Cody on the bridge to stand watch. Lacy was going down the ladder with Taeng being the last to go. Just as Lacy stepped on the ladder, Cody asked her how she had gotten her name, and did it have anything to do with her preferred style of undergarment. Lacy laughed; Cody got a slap on the back of the head from Taeng as she went past him to go down the ladder.

Before Taeng's head passed below the deck level of the bridge and down into the accommodation area, Cody said, "What? It was a reasonable question! They probably call you Ms. Granny Panties."

"Actually, they used to call me Dental Floss," Taeng told Cody as she dropped below the bridge deck. Cody spent his time on the bridge forming various mental pictures of Taeng arrayed in a dental floss, what the Brazilians call a fio dental, bikini. It was an extremely stimulating mental exercise.

After about two hours or so, the Bajans came back up the ladder and down to the main deck in the same order they had gone down to the stateroom earlier. As Lacy came up and walked past Cody she said, with a straight face, that they had decided to call her Lacy because Crotchless just sounded too risqué. Taeng, not to be outdone, just commented that the problem with dental floss is that it sometimes gets stuck in your teeth.

On the way back to Barrouallie, Taeng took a call from an unidentified vessel on VHF channel 9 telling them to go to the channel that corresponded to 'twice your bra size plus 9'.

"Who was that and how many people know your bra size?" queried Cody.

"That's my father. Not many, and if you had to guess, which channel should I be going to?"

Cody took a good look as Taeng stuck out her chest, which was snuggly clad in that black little sports bra. After some intense study, Cody once again decided that her breasts were slightly larger than a handful, about the size of a grapefruit, likely a B-trending toward a C-cup. Which had actually nothing to do with the band size, which was the important measurement at the moment. After taking a last look at Taeng's chest, he decided that she probably wore a 34-inch band size and that they should go to channel 77.

Taeng laughed, "Good eye, sailor!"

Switching to channel 77, Taeng broadcast, "Scantily Clad, this is the Shag McNasty, what can we do for you?"

"More like, what I can do for you. You know that little headland just south of Barrouallie, below the Leeward Highway, where it runs along the coast?"

Cody nodded that he did, so Taeng replied that they did.

"Well, I was just cruising back from St. Lucia and noticed a blacked-out Viking 65 anchored in the little cove just south of that headland. Since I was curious as to why a blacked-out Viking 65 would be sitting there and thinking that maybe someone was trying to horn in on my smuggling action, I throttled back and got out my night vision binoculars and took a look. There were a few Bajans onboard, who I didn't recognize and a couple of Chinese looking guys, who I also didn't recognize.

"So, I says to myself, 'Self, who is out on the water this evening that would be of interest to a mixed bag of Bajans and Chinese?', and all I could think of was my half-dressed daughter, her hippie boyfriend and a few other Bajans that want to stop a coup instigated by Chinese people. You with me here?"

"Yeah, Dad, I'm with you. I wonder how they found out about our meeting. This is not good."

"No, it isn't. You know as well as I do that you can't keep a secret in these islands."

"What do you think we ought to do?" asked Taeng.

"And this is why you are fortunate to have a skilled smuggler for a father. Is your hippie listening in?"

"He's not 'my hippie', but yes."

"Okay, I am going to make a big loop out to sea and come back into the north of where they're anchored. I will meet you in Wallilabou Bay, where we will cross deck your friends and I will take them the long way around the north of the island and drop them off near Jimmy Rock's Bar & Mini Mart in Biabou. Have somebody collect them there on the Windward Highway. I could take them back to Barbados, but I think it best if they just lay low for a while.

"Now comes the fun part. Cody will need to run past that Viking 65 and let them chase him while I go around the north of the island. Hey, hippie! Think that old Nasty boat can lose that Viking? She's a lot sleeker than an old Nasty and she's packing about 3,600 ponies in the stern."

Taeng passed the mic to Cody. "Listen, old timer, I can run circles around that fancy piece of fiberglass. Want to put some money on it?"

"Not really, just wanted to wind you up a bit. Heck, you've got them by 2,600 horsepower! Even a long-haired throwback to the Grateful Dead should be able to outrun those clowns with that advantage. Give the mic back to my daughter, I need to ask her something."

Taeng just rolled her eyes as she took the mic. "Yes, Father."

"Now don't take this the wrong way, Taeng, but I was just thinking that maybe if you just show a little more skin and let him take a good look at what you've got to offer, maybe the hippie would re-consider trading his boat for mine, what do you think?"

"Dad, if I did that right now, he would die of a stroke, and we'd need to rethink the plan which you have just finished outlining. Do you really think that's a good idea?"

"Point taken but keep it in mind for the future. Once I drop your friends off, I'll run over to Barbados to fuel up and see your mother. I'll see you two at Pala Island tomorrow sometime. Do you need anything?"

"If you stop by my house, could you get Mom to pack me up some clothes and toiletries? It seems like I'll be staying with the hippie for a while."

"That's my girl! Does your hippie need anything?"

Cody said he could use a resupply of beer and some toothpicks.

"What?" asked a confused Tanawat.

"Never mind, Dad. The hippie has visions of something getting stuck in his teeth. See you tomorrow."

CHAPTER 11

SINCE THE SHAG MCNASTY WAS already underway to the south along the west coast of St. Vincent towards Barrouallie when Tanawat got on the radio, Cody made a U-turn and headed back to the north past Barrouallie. The Shag and crew arrived in Wallilabou Bay about 20 minutes before the Scantily Clad showed up. During this time, Taeng had briefed her other conspirators on the situation, and the plan that Tanawat had come up with. They were also concerned as to how the Chinese had tracked them, but they could disappear on St. Vincent and would organize a pick up at Jimmy Rock's Bar once they were ashore.

When Tanawat arrived, the two boats came alongside each other again and the five Bajan conspirators hopped from the Shag to the Scantily Clad. As Lacy was about to hop over to the old crew boat, she looked at Cody and with a sly smile told him that if he ever got tired of Ms. Dental Floss, he should look her up.

"How can I get tired of a meal I've never had a chance to eat?" he exclaimed.

Once Tanawat and his new crew were underway, Taeng and Cody got back on the bridge so that they could get the Shag underway and start trolling for the Viking 65. While slowly making their way out of Wallilabou Bay, Taeng told Cody that she had heard what he'd said to Lacy, and she thought that he needed to work on his adages. "To refer to me as a meal which is to be eaten could have very vulgar connotations."

"Sorry, I was caught off guard, and my lizard brain took over for a second, besides vulgarity is in the eye of the beholder," Cody grinned.

After a few moments of silent contemplation, Taeng asked, "Hypothetically speaking, if you were to become tired of me, not that we are romantically involved in the slightest, would you look up Lacy?"

Cody took a few moments to consider this before replying. "Well, your friend Lacy is definitely a head-turner, and her body could make a preacher cuss. I would be tempted to look her up in the event that I was ever in a position to be tired of someone that I've never had the chance to really get to know. That being said, and regardless of the vulgar connotations, I would need a meal not a snack, and from what I can see, you would be a veritable feast whereas Lacy is more of an appetizer. Hypothetically speaking, I don't think that I could tire of you, but since we are not romantically involved, this is simply a mental exercise in futility, correct?"

"Correct. Don't you think that you should play with the throttles and get this old crate moving? You've got less than half a mile before we pass the cove that Viking boat is hiding in," suggested Taeng.

"Maybe you should play with my throttle before we…"

Taeng cut him off before he could finish the thought. "Just drive the boat, Cody."

Cody ran both of the throttles up about halfway and the old Nasty boat came up on plane. Before long they passed the headland that formed the northern edge of the cove that the Viking was hiding in going about 25 knots. It took a minute for the Bajan skipper of the Viking to notice the old Nasty boat flying by his starboard beam before he could fire up both of his MTU 16V2000 1,800 horsepower diesels to give chase.

The top speed of a Viking 65 is about 40 knots, while the lightened Nasty, with no torpedoes, gun mounts, or extraneous crew could get up to 60 knots, and probably higher, but Cody had never tried to top-end her and didn't know for sure. The thing was, he wanted to drag out the chase as long as possible just to keep their pursuers busy while Tanawat was running around the north side of St. Vincent and dropping off his passengers at Jimmy Rock's Bar before he ditched the Viking. Cody had the Nasty running about 45 knots as he sped along the coast of St. Vincent before heading southeast into open water. While Taeng kept a watch on the Viking, Cody worked the throttles to keep the Viking about half a mile behind him.

Still keeping their pursuers in tow, Cody positioned himself for a run down between Bequia, Petit Nevis and Quatre to starboard, while keeping Bettawia, Baliceaux and Mustique to port. Swinging around the southern tip of Mustique, Cody led them between Mustique and Petit Mustique. This had been a good 35-mile run so far, but Cody didn't want to lead them any closer to Pala Island. He also wanted them to believe that the conspirators were still onboard and that he was going to drop them in Barbados, which is what they would have been expecting.

With all of this in mind, Cody took a heading of 80° for the 105-mile run to Bridgetown. About halfway to Barbados, Taeng and Cody felt that they had played around long enough and Cody pushed the throttles up until they were scooting along at 55 knots. Since they could assume that the Viking had radar, they needed to get far enough ahead to put Barbados between them and the radar so that the Chinese and their cohorts would not see where the Shag put the conspirators, which he supposedly still had onboard, ashore.

Cody had increased the distance between the boats to 15 miles before he turned east and ran around the southern tip of the island and up the east coast. Still running at 50 knots, he ran past the northern tip of the island before heading west into open water. He could not risk running back down the west coast and running into the Viking again, so once back in open water Cody set a course of 248° and made a beeline for his island.

It had been a long afternoon and an even longer evening on the water. The sun was just coming up as Cody pulled into the channel behind the breakwater. Pulling in behind the fuel barge, Cody worked the throttles while Taeng looped the mooring lines around bollards fore and aft. They were both so tired that neither one could really appreciate the motorcycle ride back up to the house the way that it should have been. As they headed into the little courtyard in the house to go to their respective rooms, Taeng grabbed Cody's butt and said with a grin, "Not a bad night's work for a white guy."

They were both exhausted, but Cody could not pass up the opportunity. "You ain't seen a good night's work from me yet, but hold that thought," replied Cody with a lecherous grin.

CHAPTER 12

THE NEXT MORNING, TAENG WAS up first and was the one preparing breakfast for a change when Cody finally strolled out of his room and into the kitchen. Much to his chagrin, although Taeng was wearing one of her little cropped top t-shirts, her bottom half was concealed by a pair of common, unenticing, loose fitting sweatpants in bog standard gray.

"Have a seat, squire. The pancakes will be ready in just a minute. Is that the attire you plan on wearing today?" Taeng wasn't really complaining as all that Cody had on was a tattered, sun-bleached pair of khaki cargo shorts which had seen better days. No shirt and no shoes. There was a lot of Cody on display for her to inspect, and she was making the most of it and decided that she liked what she saw.

"Yep, today is maintenance day. I need to do the maintenance on both the Aichi and the Nasty, then fuel them both up. You just never know when you might find a hot little mixed-race Caribbean girl washed up on your island that needs a shopping spree in Grenada, or a boat race around the Windwards. What is your unflatteringly dressed self going to get up to today?"

Taeng looked down at what she was wearing. "You don't like the sweats?"

"No! They hide roughly half of what I look forward to seeing first thing in the morning."

"I'll see what I can do to rectify the situation after breakfast," said Taeng mischievously as she brought the platter of pancakes to the table. "As far as my schedule for today, I need to use your fancy communications system to check on my friends from last night, to make sure Dad got home okay, and see what the others have planned in regards to the upcoming coup. We may need some outside help."

"You guys get your plan together and tell me what assistance you think you might need; I think I may be able to help you out in that department. I have many friends in low places, as Garth Brooks used to croon about."

"Why doesn't that surprise me?" needled Taeng as she placed the pancakes over on the island.

While Cody cleaned up the dishes and the kitchen, Taeng went back to her room to brush her teeth, brush her hair, and re-attire herself. Coming back out 15 minutes later she was now dressed in form fitting, mid-rise, 3" inseam Nike biker shorts and a neon pink halter top.

"Better?" she asked as she pirouetted in the kitchen.

"Much, now I can actually tell if you are wearing a weapon, a wire, or basically anything else. My day has now gotten off to a much better start," Cody said as he perused Taeng's new attire.

"Okay, pervert, let's get down to the shop and get busy."

After the usual 'bump & grind' on the dirt bike as they went down the hill, Cody parked the bike by the door, and they went inside. While Taeng went back to the office, Cody rode the elevator down to the sub pen and got to work on the old seaplane. After climbing down onto a pontoon, he did the obvious stuff: he checked for loose or missing inspection plates, panels and fairings, and for any missing screws used to attach them. He checked that all the cowling fasteners were latched and tight and then just did a full visual inspection of the aircraft.

After he was satisfied that he had not bent, spindled or mutilated anything on the outside of the aircraft during the trip to Grenada, he opened up the cowling and pulled the dipstick to check the oil level before he pulled each and every spark plug and checked them for fouling. Everything looked good, so he buttoned the cowlings back up and climbed into the cockpit.

Once in the pilot's seat, Cody ensured that all electrical switches were off, and that all pullable circuit breakers were pushed in. Turning on the master switch, he checked the bus voltage to make sure the battery voltage was correct. The ammeter was showing a very small discharge, which was fine.

At this point Cody fired up the old, air-cooled Mitsubishi Mk8 14-cylinder engine to make sure that the oil pressure came up into the green within 10 seconds and that the engine idled smoothly with the throttle all the way back. Verifying on the modern EGT display that all cylinders were firing properly, he let the engine idle until he could see the oil and cylinder head temperatures starting to rise then leaned the engine out to maximum RPM. While doing this, he powered up all his modern avionics to ensure that everything was lighting up properly and that nothing smelled wrong, like burnt wiring. Before he shut everything down, he cycled the control stick and worked the rudder just to make sure that all the control surfaces were working smoothly.

After shutting down the engine, Cody climbed back onto the pen's dock and went over and unrolled the hose from the fuel bowser he kept against the wall in front of the Aichi before climbing back aboard the plane to fuel it up. After getting back on the dock and reeling in the fuel hose, Cody reached under the electric motor that drove the pump on the bowser and pulled out 2 quarts of Phillips 25W-60 engine oil and climbed up again and topped up the oil tank.

With the aircraft maintenance complete, he walked around to the other side of the pen where the Nasty boat was berthed just aft of the fuel barge. Going down through the bridge access, he made his way to the engine room aft and did some routine and preventative maintenance to the big Napier-Deltic diesel engines before climbing back up through the bridge access and going on deck to fuel up both of the 2,700-gallon saddle tanks mounted on either side below deck just forward of the engine room.

After checking the oil levels in both sumps, Cody went up on the bridge and fired up both engines. He watched the gauges until he was satisfied that both engines were running well before he fired up his electronics suite and made sure that everything was working as advertised before he shut everything back down and decided that it was a good time to go check on Taeng and see if maybe the planets had aligned and she needed her oil level checked as well.

Alas, it was not to be. Taeng was deep in conversation with some people in Barbados and didn't seem the least bit interested in having her fluid levels checked. With nothing better to do, Cody made a couple of ham and cheese sandwiches, put them on plates with some potato chips and carried them over to the coffee table in front of the couch before going back and getting some napkins and two Cokes out of the fridge. Setting everything on the table, he waited for Taeng to get off the phone and tell him what was going on.

Once Taeng had signed off, she came over to the couch and sat beside Cody and gave him an update while she ate her sandwich.

"Wilfred Duguid, the Minister of Energy and Business, is still our only inside source within the coup elements, both Bajan and Chinese. As far as he can tell, the coup is still on, and the Chinese are fine tuning the plan continuously.

"Gabriel Collins, the Regimental Sergeant Major is still busy organizing the coup sympathizers within the Special Operations Company of the Barbados Regiment. They plan to hit the Voice of Barbados radio station on Fairchild Street. Once inside, they'll put their own people on the air. At the same time, another group will be hitting the presidential residence at Government House. They will not assault the residence, but plan to surround and lock down Government House before forcing President Griffith to capitulate. This will all take place at around 2:00 in the morning on Independence Day, November 30th.

"The 1,400-man Barbados Police Service still seems loyal to the President, and a plan is being developed to have them stop the coup before it can gain traction by interdicting the insurrectionist before they can leave the Paragon Army Base near the airport and The Garrison at St. Ann's Fort in St. Michael.

"At 2:00am, we will have our people start broadcasting from the radio station and will inform the nation that a coup is taking place and give them as much detail as we can on how it is unfolding.

"The problem is that although both the police and the army both have similar small arms and light machine guns, the Chinese are supplying the insurrectionists with Chinese small arms, heavy machine guns, and mortars for indirect fire. Hopefully, the element of surprise will be enough to offset the heavier weapons.

"We really don't have much choice. We have to make a stand and just hope that the people rise up. What do you think?" asked Taeng after letting Cody know the plan.

"What I think," he replied, "is that you are all going to get yourselves killed! The Chinese are past masters of the coup and political intrigue. They'll have shipped in more, better, and heavier weapons than the police will have access to. The Chinese Ministry of State Security will be running the show, not the Bajan Special Operations boys. The Chinese will have war gamed the whole thing from start to finish and the poor Bajan police will get slaughtered, and the coup will be successful.

"The Chinese will simply storm into the radio station once you start broadcasting and slaughter everyone inside and put Bajans who are supporting the coup on the radio to tell people to shelter in place until the 'situation' is under control.

"If they can't get in to stop the broadcast, they'll simply blow the place up. You guys need the radio station, they do not.

"They may initially just surround Government House and try to negotiate for 10 to 20 minutes, then they will assault the president's house and either force him to capitulate and broadcast his capitulation on equipment the Chinese will have brought along with them, or they will simply 'disappear' the President. That's what I think," replied Cody.

Taeng was chewing on her lower lip and looking frustrated. Cody thought it was kind of sexy although now was probably not the time to mention it.

"So, what do we do? We have to do something!" exclaimed Taeng.

"Lucky for you, as I may have mentioned earlier, I have friends in very low places. Let's give Mike, the pervert in Puerto Rico that caught you on camera sunbathing in your cheeky little bikini, a call and you can tell him everything you and your friends know about this coup and see what he can come up with."

"How can a voyeuristic pervert in Puerto Rico possibly help us out in Barbados?"

"He has friends in even lower places than I do, friends who are not enamored with the Chinese. I've grown very fond of your little butt and would hate to see it get shot off, it would ruin the proportionality of the package as a whole," informed Cody.

"You are only fond of my butt?"

"Actually, I am very fond of the whole package, but I tend to look at the package as a life support system for your amazing butt."

"That's not very romantic," said Taeng as they got off the couch and made their way over to Cody's workstation to call Mike.

Cody dialed up Mike on the double-secret NSA spoofed WhatsApp app on his computer. Mike answered after a few rings.

"Are you still hanging out with that stunner that was toasting her tush on the patio?" Mike asked in a totally unprofessional manner.

"I am. She's right here and she has a story to tell you."

"She heard what I just said?" asked a chastened Mike.

"Dammit! I just stepped on my crank again. It's no wonder I can't get a date without calling an escort service. Okay, what does the lovely lady have to say?"

Taeng had pulled a chair over beside Cody. "First off, my name is Taeng, and I would like to start off by saying that I don't appreciate you watching me while I sunbathe on your silly little camera up at the house. I want that to stop. Is that understood?"

"Yes, ma'am," replied a suitably chastened Mike.

"Okay, we've got a problem brewing in Barbados," and with that introduction Taeng gave Mike a rundown on what her and her friends had uncovered concerning the upcoming coup and the Chinese involvement in it.

Mike, serious now, asked a couple of probing questions before telling them that he'd need to run this by a few people back in the States, but that he'd get back to them the following day.

As Cody clicked off the app, Taeng leaned back in her chair and revisited their previous conversation before they contacted Mike.

"So, what about my boobs? Don't they get any attention?"

Cody thought carefully before replying, he was on thin ice here. "Although pert, balanced and well-proportioned, they may be a little on the small side for the taste of most guys. Personally, I feel that anything over palm sized, say the size of a medium grapefruit, is wasted."

"Fair enough but do you find the overall package worthy of your attention?" She was fishing for compliments now.

"I personally think you are hotter than a two-dollar pistol. That said, I couldn't possibly say more without seeing the rest of the package. Just saying..."

"You are a sexist pig!"

"Not true. I am that rare man who is simply in touch with his emotions."

"I hope you enjoy your emotions, Mr. Morgan, since that'll be all you are going to be touching." Taeng could play the game as well.

CHAPTER 13

ABOUT THAT TIME AN ALERT sounded on Cody's workstation. This particular alert was tied to a light beam intruder alert that was triggered when a specific light beam was broken for a certain amount of time. This particular beam was located at the open end of the sheltered strip of water behind the breakwater.

Calling up the particular camera which oversaw the beam, they noticed Tanawat's old crew boat making its way into the small harbor outside the submarine pens. They'd both forgotten that Tanawat had told them he'd be visiting them sometime today. They hurried to the elevator and took it down to the pen. Tanawat was skillfully maneuvering the crew boat alongside the concrete dock behind the Nasty boat when they walked up, so he threw them the mooring lines and dropped some fenders over the side as they snugged him up to the dock.

Going back inside the covered portion of the aft deck, where the crews would have sheltered in foul weather, he started stacking cases of Carib beer along the starboard gunwale. Cody hopped over and started handing the cases over to Taeng, who had remained on the dock. Once the last case of beer had been handed over to Taeng, Tanawat came over to Cody and handed him two small boxes of toothpicks, which Cody had jokingly mentioned when he had placed his beer order.

"I don't know why you wanted these, but I assume you have a reason."

"I do, but you really don't want to know what it is."

"I'm guessing it has something to do with her old nickname, doesn't it?"

"You know about that?"

"I do. It used to drive the local boys crazy. Almost everything that God had given her was on display when she wore one of those little Brazilian dental floss bikinis. It was shameful, but it made me proud that something that hot had sprung from my loins. She's got you going, doesn't she?"

Before Cody could answer, Taeng barked from the dock, "Dad, would you please shut up! You're leading him on!"

Tanawat and Cody were both grinning as they jumped back up onto the dock. While Cody was going to get a handcart to haul the beer to the elevator, he heard Taeng berating her father for embarrassing her in front of Cody.

"Well, daughter, if you are not going to lead him on then I'll have to do it for you. He seems like a nice enough guy, for a white guy, and he does have a nice little island here. You need to give this some thought, you aren't getting any younger, you know."

Taeng just put her head in her hands and gave an exasperated sigh.

Once they had the beer in the elevator, they rode it back to the shop level and unloaded it by the garage door and Cody trotted off to fetch the Gator and the 2-wheeled trailer. After the beer had been loaded in the trailer along with Tanawat's seabag and the garage door had been pulled back down, they piled into and onto the Gator, Cody and Taeng in the front and Tanawat on the back cargo area, and they made their way up the hill to the house.

After getting the beer unloaded and stored in the pantry, Tanawat threw his seabag into Taeng's room, her room had two double beds in it, before everyone migrated to the living room. While Taeng took her father around the house and showed it off, disturbingly like the lady of the house thought Cody, Cody began preparing dinner, which consisted of pan-seared red snapper and asparagus.

Tanawat made the point to Taeng that it was a rare thing to find a man as comfortable in the kitchen as Cody seemed to be, and that she should keep this in mind as well, to which she replied that elderly fathers should be seen and not heard. After the meal was finished, Taeng and Tanawat washed dishes and cleaned up the kitchen before everyone grabbed a beer and retired to the living room and Taeng briefed her father on the situation on Barbados and Cody's friends in low places.

Tanawat had heard rumors about the Chinese people who had recently been relocating to Barbados from the shady people he occasionally ran with, and he had heard the rumors of a coup. What he hadn't known was that the coup planning was far enough advanced as to become a reality on Independence Day. Being a bit bored with smuggling cigarettes and booze to Russian jackasses, and with time on his hands, Tanawat wanted in on the action.

CHAPTER 14

AFTER EVERYONE HAD A FEW beers on the couch and relaxed a bit and Cody got to know Tanawat a bit better, everyone got a good night's sleep and were up early the next morning. Cody was up before his guests so that he could get started on a breakfast of Belgian waffles. The waffles were meant to reinforce Tanawat's remarks to Taeng regarding the fact that good men who could cook were as rare as hen's teeth and that she should be paying attention.

Tanawat and Taeng came out of their room in a hushed, but heated debate. Tanawat seemed to be of the opinion that his daughter should be wearing something more revealing that showcased what God had given her, and Taeng, dressed provocatively, in Cody's opinion anyway, in Daisy Duke cut-offs and a 'The Real McCoy' Barbados rum t-shirt, was saying she was not going to act like a tart just to get a man.

"Stop looking at it as acting like a tart, it is simply using the tools you were given, in the manner they were intended to be used, to snag a man. If you really like this hippie then he'll eventually see what you've got on underneath those rags anyhow," lectured Tanawat.

"Dad, not all men are as shallow as you, some men like a capable, independent woman as a companion," replied Taeng.

"Not exactly, daughter. Real men want a capable, independent woman on their arm in public, and a real, down to the bone home wrecker, in the privacy of their own home. One does not necessarily negate the other."

"You just want his boat," suggested Taeng.

"There is that," agreed Tanawat as they walked into the kitchen.

After breakfast, and after the Skeetes had cleaned up the dishes and the kitchen, they all made their way to the communications building under the tower at the rear of the house. Tanawat was suitably impressed and thought that there may be more to this Cody fellow than met the eye.

Cody sat down at the console in his half of the communications hut and dialed up Mike in Puerto Rico to see what his partners in the CIA wanted to do regarding the upcoming coup on Barbados.

"Your information regarding the upcoming Chinese sponsored coup on Barbados has really rattled some cages back in Langley. They had an idea that something was going on, but no idea that a coup was planned and that it was about to become a reality. They want you up here to brief them face to face. When can you and Ms. Skeete get up here?"

Cody thought about it for a minute. "We can fly up in the old Jap seaplane and be up there this afternoon. Where should I tie it up and what is the dress code?"

"Tie it up at the San Juan Bay Marina and I'll have someone meet you and clear the paperwork. He'll then drive you up here for the meeting. You can wear whatever you want, I would ask Taeng to wear that hot little halter bikini she had on the other day when we caught her on camera, but I'm afraid that nobody would be able to concentrate on the issue at hand if she did."

While Tanawat was giving his daughter the 'I told you so' look, Taeng informed Mike that there was no way that she was going to wear a bikini into a meeting with a bunch of horny old intelligence officers.

"Fair enough," Mike replied, "but really anything tight and revealing would probably work. Us horny old intelligence types are harmless; we just tend to ogle and drool."

"Would it help the situation in Barbados if I did sport my bikini at the meeting?"

"If you did, I think we'd have a fair chance of getting the Joint Chiefs of Staff to send a Marine Expeditionary Brigade simply in an effort to rescue nubile Bajan girls such as yourself from the clutches of the nefarious Chinese."

"I'm only half Bajan," Taeng pointed out.

"Okay, maybe we'd only get half a brigade. But we wouldn't necessarily have to bring that up."

"Are you trying to tell me you didn't video me while I was sunbathing? I find that hard to believe. Haven't you already shown this to whichever other perverts you associate with in Puerto Rico?"

"Actually, I did and I have, but I was going to save that for the kicker in case we needed to push the powers that be over the top during the meeting. Anyhow, call me from the plane when you are about 30 minutes out so I can get my guy down to the marina," Mike informed them as he signed off.

"See, I told you, showing a bit of skin always pays dividends, either with the hippie here or with the US Marine Corp," scolded Tanawat.

"Dad, remember what I told you about old smugglers being seen, not heard." Turning toward Cody, she continued, "I'll pack a bag and see you in the living room in 10 minutes. What do we do with my paternal pimp?"

"He can stay here and watch the fort. There's plenty of food and beer, and not much else to get him in trouble. We'll likely only be gone for a day or two."

"Do you have Netflix?" Tanawat wanted to know.

"I have every channel known to man; I'll get you set up before we leave."

With that, Cody and Taeng got geared up for the flight while Tanawat got comfortable on the couch to watch movies and drink beer. Taeng came out of her room carrying her backpack, dressed in a pair of cuffed denim shorts over a black tank top style bodysuit covered demurely with another of Cody's unbuttoned old denim work shirts. She felt this was more appropriate for the upcoming meeting than her Daisy Dukes. Okay, it wasn't the requested floral patterned halter bikini, but Cody figured the outfit was still worth a squad or two of Recon Marines.

They took the Gator back down to the submarine pen, opened the garage door to pull the Gator inside, then pulled the door back down before getting into the elevator and taking it down to the pen itself. Going through the routine that they had done previously for the shopping trip to Grenada earlier, Cody slipped the Jake out of her moorings and guided the old seaplane into the little harbor and then into the calm water just inside the breakwater before hitting the gas and getting airborne.

Leveling off at 1,000 feet, Cody took a heading of 320° for a straight shot across the Caribbean and the 500-mile trip to Puerto Rico. It was a pleasant three and a half hour trip at the Aichi's cruising speed of 138 miles per hour, but when Cody called Mike while he was passing over Cidra, Mike told him that there was a change in plans and that Cody was now supposed to tie up at the Catano Park Pier on the little peninsula jutting out into the Bahía de San Juan opposite the Isla Grande container yard. Since time was of the essence, a helicopter would be waiting there to fly them to the listening post at Cerro de Punta, the highest point in Puerto Rica.

While they were tying up to the pier, an unmarked black Bell Jet Ranger came in and landed at the shore end of the T-pier and sat with the rotors turning while it waited for them to get finished tying down the Aichi and to walk down the pier with their backpacks. As they were taking off, a Jeep full of Puerto Rican soldiers stopped at the end of the pier to guard the plane, which Cody thought was a nice touch.

Since it was only about a 40-mile flight from the pier to the listening post at the top of Cerro de Punta, they were only in the air for a short time before they dropped onto the helipad at their destination. Once the rotors stopped turning, they hopped out and were met by Mike. Taeng had never met Mike and was somewhat impressed by the 30-something guy who met them. She had developed a mental image of Mike as a short, leering, toadlike creature who would be drooling as he stared at her breasts. As it was, Mike was a fairly good-looking guy, around 6 feet tall, reasonably well built with hazel eyes. Although he wasn't drooling, he was staring at her breasts. Understandably since they were somewhat highlighted and defined by the bodysuit she was wearing, in this instance, she decided that the staring was forgivable.

After Cody introduced Taeng to Mike, they all made their way into a low building festooned with satellite dishes and geodesic radomes. Once inside, Cody and Taeng were issued visitor badges before being escorted by Mike into a conference room. As Mike turned to close the door to the room, the two men who had been sitting at the conference table rose and came over to meet their guests. Mike made the introductions.

"Taeng and Cody, I would like you to meet Mr. Smith and Mr. Doe, not their actual names you understand, who are associated with either the Central Intelligence Agency or the National Security Agency, or both. They would like to hear what you have to say concerning the coup presently being planned on Barbados. Please take a seat, get comfortable, and just go at your own pace."

Everyone took a seat: Mike, Mr. Smith and Mr. Doe on one side of the table, and Cody and Taeng on the other. Mike nodded to Taeng to start when she was ready, so she took a deep breath and began at the beginning giving an almost verbatim recital of what she had told Cody earlier.

"About a year ago it became obvious that several people in the present Barbadian Cabinet were becoming upset with the delays in the construction of the offshore windfarms and onshore solar farms which the Chinese had proposed and were prepared to fund as part of their Belt and Road Initiative in the Caribbean. These Cabinet members included the Deputy Prime Minister, who is also the Minister of Foreign Affairs and Foreign Trade, the Minister of Lands and Maintenance, the Minister of Environment and National Beautification which oversees the Green and Blue Economy, and the Minister of Economic Affairs and Investment, all of whom have been bought and paid for by the Chinese, and are actively planning to overthrow President Griffith as soon as they believe they have enough support to do so.

"A few months ago, I received an anonymous phone call suggesting that I take a good look at the Regimental Sergeant Major of the Special Operations Company of the Barbados Regiment based at The Garrison at St. Ann's Fort in St. Michael. It was also suggested that I specifically look at his contacts within the Chinese Embassy in Bridgetown. This sounded like an interesting story, so I did.

"Eventually I took a room at Gratitude House, about half a mile from St. Ann's Fort and started shadowing Warrant Officer Class 1 Gabriel Collins, the Regimental Sergeant Major. During the day Collins appeared to go about his expected business as usual, but at night it was a different story. Several times a week, Collins would leave St. Ann's Fort, drive back to his apartment in Howells, change out of his uniform into civilian clothes and then drive back into town, usually to one of the hotels along the beach to have dinner and drinks with friends. The interesting thing to me was that all his friends appeared to be associated with the Chinese Embassy.

"It soon became obvious to me that Collins was acting as the cut-out between the various Cabinet ministers and the Chinese. I tailed Collins to several one-on-one meetings with the corrupt ministers and documented the meetings with photographs taken clandestinely, or so I thought at the time.

"Eventually the person who had called me and asked me to look into the Sergeant Major revealed himself to be Wilfred Duguid, the Minister of Energy and Business. The Chinese had also approached him for support, but he didn't want anything to do with them. Wilfred reported the incident to his good friend, Ian Gooding, the Deputy Commissioner of Police, who decided to put together a small group within the police force to investigate the situation. Needless to say, these people had to be seriously vetted to make sure that they hadn't also been approached or compromised by the Chinese. Ian asked Wilfred to play along with the Chinese to find out what their goal was. When Wilfred asked the Deputy Commissioner if he was asking him to act as a snitch, Ian had replied that this was a crude, yet accurate description for what he wanted Wilfred to do. So, Wilfred became our confidential informant also known as a snitch. I called him Deep Throat after the informant who gave information to Bob Woodward in the Watergate Affair.

"Eventually the core group consisted of Deep Throat, three high ranking members of the Barbados Police Service, two people from the Caribbean

News Agency, my photographer, my editor, and myself. What we didn't realize at the time was that the Chinese were on to us, not the Police Service members, but those of us in the press. None of us had been trained to be spies and were just operating like cops on a Hollywood stakeout. The Chinese were tailing us as we tailed their people and the corrupt Bajans.

"Wilfred was invited to a meeting at the Hilton Barbados Resort one weekend where the subverted Bajan ministers met informally with Ms. Qu Ching, the Economic and Commercial Counsellor of the Chinese Embassy, and a few other Chinese without portfolio. Once the conference room was swept for bugs, the plan was revealed verbally, but nothing was put in writing. The Chinese were going to organize and support a coup in Barbados on Independence Day, November 30.

"In return for their support of the coup, once the windmill and solar farms were approved and the Bajan government signed on to the One China policy and would not recognize Taiwan as a separate entity, the Bajan ministers and ranking military personnel would receive substantial contributions to their campaigns, their personal bank accounts, or both. If the coup was successful, they would also become the ruling elite of Barbados.

"At some point, the Deputy Commissioner of Police became aware that the Chinese were on to us and planned to take us 'out of the picture', whatever that meant. I'm not sure how he found out about the plan, but the threat was real.

"We had decided to go hide out on St. Vincent where Wilfred had friends in Camden Park who would put us up and help us disappear for a while. This is where we were headed when the Caribbean Queen blew up. I washed ashore on Cody's Island, and here we are."

As Taeng sat back, Mike asked Cody and Taeng if they wouldn't mind leaving the room for a moment while he, Mr. Smith and Mr. Doe discussed what Taeng had just described. Mike showed them to a small coffee room where there were sandwiches and soft drinks in a refrigerator, pastries on the table and an urn of fresh coffee, before he returned to the conference room.

"You did well in there. I hate speaking in public, but you pulled it off like a pro," Cody commended Taeng.

"Part and parcel of being a journalist, I suppose. You have to be comfortable speaking with others, and you need to be able to organize your thoughts before you put them down on paper."

Taeng was pensive for a moment before she asked, "I thought that you were just an engineering savant and a lecherous hippie. I really do not think that people who are in, unless I miss my guess, the Special Activities Center of the CIA, or whatever the equivalent is in the NSA, generally agree to meet with lecherous hippie type engineers on short notice. Would you care to enlighten me?"

"No, I would not."

"Even if I promised to make it worth your while?" asked Taeng remembering her father's suggestion that morning regarding using the tools you were given, in the manner they were intended to be used.

Cody looked around the coffee room. "I don't think that this venue is suitable for that sort of blackmail. I see no acceptable horizontal padded surface and unless I am mistaken, the door does not lock from the inside."

"I didn't say now, jerk."

"When, then?"

"I'm thinking after we successfully stop the coup would be a more appropriate time to consider suitable remuneration. It could be seen as a form of celebration as well."

"It definitely would be for me, but I'll need a preview, you know, something to keep me on the hook until we get this coup thing sorted out. What have you got?" Cody smirked.

Taeng thought for a moment, then stood up, turned around and slowly and seductively took off her work shirt before she undid the button on her cuffed denim shorts and apparently, Cody couldn't be sure as her back was to him, slowly ran the zipper down. She then bent over to untie her sneakers, placing that gorgeous posterior just out of reach but close enough to appreciate it in all its denim covered glory. Kicking off her sneakers, she turned around and leisurely yet seductively wiggled out of her denim shorts. Stepping out of them and kicking them to the side, she performed a slow pirouette, attired solely in her skintight black bodysuit which appeared to Cody to be more akin to body paint than the thin cotton covering that it was. Taeng turned around again before bending over and making a production out of slowly pulling her shorts back up over her taut little derrière.

While she was performing, she explained to Cody that bodysuits were meant to be slowly peeled off like the skin of a grape, gradually exposing the juicy flesh inside, which instantly had Cody mentally picturing him performing the procedure on present company.

"That is cruel and unusual punishment, with tinges of blackmail mixed in," said Cody as she zipped up her shorts and put her work shirt back on.

"All true. Are you now going to fill me in? Wait... I'd better rephrase that, are you now going to tell me how you managed to get an audience with CIA's Special Activities Center in such short order?"

"Alright, I'll give you the CliffsNotes version with the understanding that you will be required to make it worth my while at some point in the near future. Do you agree to these terms?"

"Agreed, now get on with it."

"Just after I earned my degrees from Rensselaer, I became bored with academia and wanted to do something a bit more manly. I didn't think I had what it takes to be a Navy SEAL, those guys are nuts, but I liked being on boats and out on the water, so I tried out for the SWCC, the Special Warfare Combat Crewman program. Although I had a few technical degrees and could have gone in as an officer, it would have been counter-productive since Special Boat Teams are generally commanded by Navy SEAL officers, not Navy SWCC officers, but I wanted to be on the boats as opposed to commanding from shore. Provisions were made for me to join the Special Boat Teams as a Master Chief Petty Officer, an SBCM, if I somehow managed to pass the SEAL Orientation course, the Basic Crewman Selection process, the Crewman Qualification Training regime and finally the Basic Crewman Training course. I managed to do all of this and became a Special Warfare Boat Operator.

"I did three years of this and was having a blast, when one night, while we were hauling ass down a river in a 33-foot Special Operations Craft-Riverine, in a country which shall remain nameless, I hit a crocodile, an extremely large crocodile. The boat went airborne and flipped ass over tea kettle. Everyone else managed to get out okay, but I ended up with cracked ribs, a punctured lung and other assorted injuries, and my career as a boat driver came to a screeching halt. Apparently SBCM's are supposed to be able to detect and avoid large crocs while travelling at speed at night.

"The fact is, the Navy never wanted a dual-degreed engineer playing with the SEALs. The smart guys were supposed to go the Surface Warfare route and end up in the blue water Navy commanding ships, not boats. I took the option of being medically discharged and re-entered the private sector. Since I was actively being scouted by Lockheed Martin to work in their Skunk Works program, there I went. So, Ms. Skeete, there you have it."

Taeng looked at Cody with a thoughtful look on her face before asking, "So, you really aren't just your typical long-haired, unshaven, pencil necked geek?" asked Taeng with a thoughtful look on her face.

"I'm not sure what qualifications or skills are required to qualify as a long-haired, unshaven, pencil necked geek, but I probably qualify for that as well. Let's get this coup out of the way and I'll show you some of my more alluring talents. I think you'd be rather impressed," replied Cody with a salacious grin.

Mike walked back into the coffee room about this time and asked them to step back into the conference room, as Mr. Doe and Mr. Smith had some more questions. Once they were settled back into their original chairs opposite the SAC men, Mr. Doe asked Taeng if she would be willing to put him in contact with her friends and sources on Barbados so that they could form a more up-to-date picture of the situation on the island, since Taeng had been away for a few weeks.

"Can you guarantee their safety? A bunch of fit white guys running around looking for my not-so-white associates is bound to raise some eyebrows."

"Ms. Skeete, we cannot guarantee anything. What I can tell you is that the people we put on the ground have done this sort of thing many times, and believe it or not, not all of us are fit white guys, we even have some fit black and brown guys and gals working with us. We are an equal opportunity employment agency. We'd probably use them on Barbados since, as you say, us white folks would stick out like a sore thumb," interjected Mr. Smith.

"Could you pull my friends out if things went sideways whenever your plan takes place?"

"We'd pull them out before things got noisy. We'd want them safe and out of the way. We need them to go back once the noise dies down and tell the people what they know about the coup and win some hearts and minds. Nobody else would have the credibility," answered Mr. Doe.

Taeng pondered this for a moment before asking, "If any of my friends or associates get damaged during whatever it is that you mutts are planning, can I shoot Mike? He took some liberties with one of his camera at Cody's place while I was sunbathing awhile back and I'm looking for some retribution."

Mr. Doe and Mr. Smith looked over at Mike, who had his hands up with the palms out saying, "Whoa! Hold on a minute! That was an equipment failure and the tilt and zoom functions simply did their own thing while Ms. Skeete was sunbathing!"

Mr. Doe and Mr. Smith conferred amongst themselves for a moment before Mr. Smith replied, "I can fully appreciate how the tilt and zoom functions could possibly malfunction while Ms. Skeete was sunbathing, but we in the intelligence community have a reputation to uphold. If any of Ms. Skeete's friends or associates are harmed during the coup attempt, we agree that she can shoot Mike, as long as it is not fatal. Does this meet with your approval, Ms. Skeete?"

Taeng just shot Mike an evil grin before she replied, "Perfectly."

With that out of the way, Mr. Doe and Mr. Smith ended the meeting with the understanding that further meetings may be necessary prior to the coup attempt, and that Mike would be the liaison between Langley, Fort Meade, Puerto Rico and Pala Island. They would be back in touch within the week.

Once the SAC boys had left the room, Mike asked Taeng if she would really shoot him.

"Only a flesh wound kind of shot. It seems that you still have some value to your bosses." Turning to Cody, she asked if shooting Mike in the groin would be fatal.

"Usually, I'd say yes. There is usually a lot of blood flowing around a guy's dangly bits, but since Mike doesn't seem to be getting much use out of his package these days and that they have probably atrophied, he'd probably survive a groin shot."

"Atrophied is a bit harsh, hibernating would be more accurate. Are you two clowns ready to chopper back to your antique seaplane now?"

They were, so they did.

On the trip back to Pala Island, Cody and Taeng were just chatting on the aircraft intercom when Cody asked Taeng if she would really shoot Mike in his nether regions.

"Nah, I just wanted to embarrass him in front of his bosses and get him to stop his adolescent voyeurism."

Cody thought about this for a moment before asking, "Do I have to stop mine?"

"Of course not! A girl needs to feel appreciated, but she likes to have some control over that appreciation. That said, if the appreciation is mutual, it should be acted on sometime before the next Ice Age, don't you agree?" Cody couldn't see the impish smirk on Taeng's face when she said this.

CHAPTER 15

AFTER GETTING BACK TO PALA Island and tying the Jake up in the old sub pen, they made their way up to the shop level via the service elevator and threw their kit into the Gator, backed it out of the shop, closed the garage door and headed up to the house.

The first thing they saw when they walked through the front doors was Tanawat sprawled on the couch watching a replay of the 2005 Rugby Union qualifier when Barbados played the Bahamas in the play-off match and beat them 52-3. Although there were a few beer bottles on the table, Cody was surprised that Tanawat was not knee-walking drunk. When you considered the fact that he was a smuggler, with cases of beer at his disposal, and that he tended to act like a reprobate, Cody felt that this was a reasonable expectation.

Tanawat saw the look of surprise and said, "What? You expected to find me passed out on the couch?"

"Yep," replied Taeng and Cody in unison.

"I'll have you know that I am a reasonably disciplined individual when left alone, do not let the tag 'smuggler' mislead you. Historically speaking many smugglers have been fine, upstanding members of society."

"Name one," prompted Taeng.

"I've never been good with names. What did you two lovebirds find out in Puerto Rico?"

Cody gave Tanawat a rundown on the meeting in Puerto Rico and the promise that the CIA et al would be getting back to them within the week. Until then they'd just have to hang loose. In the meantime, the powers that be would be getting in touch with Taeng's associates to get an as up-to-date picture of the situation on Barbados as possible prior to planning a suitable response to the Chinese instigated coup. At this point, Cody told Tanawat about his daughter's promise to shoot Mike in the nuts if any of her associates came to harm if they were outed to the opposition by the black and brown agents of the NSA or CIA, whoever was going to run the recon show. Tanawat indicated that this showed character and was likely a result of her superior DNA, and Cody should keep this in mind at all times.

"I assume that as a fairly successful smuggler and an expert at navigating in these waters, that I will be playing a part in anything that the CIA or NSA may be planning. Is this correct?" asked Tanawat.

"Let's wait and see what the plan is first. There is a good chance that none of us here may be involved," suggested Cody.

"It is a bad idea not to employ local talent when countering a coup," opined Tanawat.

"Really, Dad? How many counter coups have you been involved in?"

"None, but I read a lot. Is anyone going to prepare dinner?" replied Tanawat changing the subject.

The following morning, after Tanawat had eaten his fill of the leftover macaroni and cheese that Cody had thrown together for dinner the night before, he boarded his old crew boat and sailed off to wherever old Thai smugglers sail to in the Caribbean, leaving Cody and Taeng alone on Pala Island. Although they had become fairly good friends since she had washed up on the breakwater, the situation was becoming tense since they both seemed to want something more out of their relationship, but neither had any idea how to accomplish that in a proper, dignified manner. Also, the upcoming coup and the yet to be defined response was weighing on them.

Five days after the meeting in Puerto Rico, while they were replacing the spark plugs in the old Aichi seaplane, Cody's cell phone rang, and Mike suggested that they get up to the office in the shop for a video call. So, after they buttoned up the Jake's cowling, they did just that.

Back in the office, Cody got on the encrypted WhatsApp and opened up the conference call. Mike, Mr. Doe and Mr. Smith were online and after everyone had said hello to everyone else, the conference got started in earnest.

Mr. Doe led off and said that all of Taeng's associates had been approached and interviewed. They had been able to fill in some blanks in the information obtained by the NSA and the CIA, and it was confirmed that the Chinese were still in the process of organizing a coup attempt for Independence Day, November 30th, three weeks from today.

At this point, Mr. Smith took over and related that the Chinese had brought in at least 10 CSK-131 armored reconnaissance vehicles: eight armed with the 12.7mm heavy machine guns and 35mm automatic grenade launcher package, and two with the four-pack of TL-4 fire-and-forget anti-tank missiles. Since neither the Barbados Police Service nor the Barbados military had any sort of armored vehicles, these heavily armed Chinese versions of the Humvee gave the conspirators a game changing advantage which would need to be dealt with before the coup gained traction.

The CIA proposed to air drop six FGM-148 Javelin man-portable anti-tank missile systems, complete with the Command Launch Units (CLUs) and the necessary training aids and live rounds, as well as other weapons onto Cody's island. Along with the Javelins, a dozen ex-military operatives from the CIA's Special Operations Group (SOG) would also parachute onto Pala Island ten days before the planned coup.

Furthermore, ten Bajan loyalists would need to be identified, vetted and brought to the island so that they could train with the SOG operatives. On the night of 27 November, three nights before the coup, Cody in the Shag McNasty, and Tanawat in the Scantily Clad, would each transport half the team and weaponry to different points on Barbados where loyal Barbadians would meet them and stash the two integrated SOG teams in safe houses: one close to the radio station and the other close to Paragon Army Base near the airport.

On the night of the 28th, the SOG teams would make contact with the Barbados Police Service to go over the counter-coup response which would take place early in the morning of 30 November.

Needless to say, there were a lot of moving parts and a lot to get done prior to the morning of the 30th. The Special Operations Group would organize the air drop to Pala Island as well as the necessary liaising with the Police Service on Barbados to select ten suitable candidates for training. In the meantime, Cody, Taeng and Tanawat would need to prepare for the arrival of the SOG teams and their loyalist trainees so that they could keep them fed and watered while the actual weapons and tactics training occurred. They would also need to make a plan to go collect the loyalist trainees from Barbados and bring them to Pala Island. Finally, they would need to transport the SOG personnel, the trainees and all their equipment to as yet to be defined locations on Barbados on the 27th.

At this point, Mr. Smith asked if there were any questions. Nobody had any questions, but Taeng had some comments.

"I think that I should go ashore with the teams," she said.

"Why would you want to do that? There is going to be a lot of shooting at some point and you'd be safer out on one of the boats," said Mr. Doe.

"Barbados is my country, Mr. Doe. I know the people, I know the country, and I have been involved with this little operation from the start. I should be the one liaising between the teams and the Police Service and I want to be the one broadcasting from the Voice of Barbados radio station during the coup attempt. The listeners know who I am and will trust me."

Mr. Smith and Mr. Doe put their mikes on mute for a short discussion before coming back up on audio and agreeing with Taeng, which surprised the heck out of Taeng, she'd expected some serious pushback.

"All good points, Ms. Skeete, we hadn't thought that far ahead as of yet. Anything else?" asked Mr. Doe.

Cody put in his two cents worth. "If she goes, I go. I'm ex-military with combat experience. I am familiar with the Javelin missile system and leaving me out on my boat is wasting a resource in place."

Again, Mr. Doe and Mr. Smith conferred off mike before coming back and telling Cody that although he would be valuable in a firefight, he was also a Yank and if things went pear-shaped he would be another finger pointing back at the US.

"Just like the twelve SOG operators you'll be putting onshore," Cody argued.

"The SOG operators will have nothing on them to identify them as Americans, you, on the other hand, are a known entity in the Grenadine and Windward Islands. Furthermore, we need you and Tanawat on your vessels standing by in case things go belly up and we need an escape route. You are more valuable to the mission on your boat as opposed to being in the fight onshore. I hope you can see the sense in this," said Mr. Smith.

Cody didn't like it, but the logic was irrefutable. Even a reclusive engineering savant could see this, so he grudgingly accepted his role, similar to that of his Special Warfare Combat Crewman days, of delivering the players to the field but not getting in the game. That said, sometimes getting to the field could be just as exciting as the game.

The next few days went by in a blur. Before the SOG operators and the ten Bajan loyalists got to the island, Cody and Taeng had to prepare a place for them to stay as well as getting enough provisions to keep them fed and watered while they were there. All without raising any eyebrows in the neighboring islands.

The day after the conference call, Cody and Taeng took the Nasty boat up to Fort-de-France on Martinique to start the shopping spree. Tying up in the Baywatch Marina, they walked over and booked a room at the B&B Hotel before catching a taxi to the old Army Navy surplus store located on the west bank of the Canal Levassor, on the Boulevard Amiral de Gueydon, just below the Passerelle Gueydon pedestrian bridge. Here they purchased 22 old French Army cots that were still in very good condition, 22 blankets, 22 pillows, and had arranged to have it all delivered to the B&B Hotel the following morning.

Making their way back across the Canal Levassor, they visited the Carrefour Market on Rue Victor Sévère where they stocked up on canned goods and freeze-dried items and also arranged to have it delivered to the B&B Hotel the following day as well.

By the time they had finished dinner at the Think Tank des Berges restaurant on Boulevard Soweto, night had fallen and they were beat. Getting back to the hotel, they didn't even consider moving their relationship further along the romance scale even though they were sharing a room and a bed. They were just too tired for that foolishness.

The next morning, they had breakfast in the hotel before collecting their cots, blankets, pillows and non-perishable food items from the concierge. They crammed this all into a hotel van and hitched a ride back to the boat at the marina.

On the way home, they stopped by the Rodney Bay Marina on the west side of St. Lucia, just inland of Reduit Beach and tied up again before heading over to the Cocoville Marketplace to stock up on bottled water and soft drinks. Due to the sheer volume of the order, it was also delivered to the marina before storing it on the boat. They were spreading out the purchases just in case.

At a comfortable 30 knots, it was still a three-hour sail from St. Lucia to Pala Island, which put them back at home in the late afternoon. By the time they had taken the cots, blankets, pillows and the food and beverages from the boat to the elevator, then from the elevator into the shop, it was well past dark. Back up in the house, while Taeng showered, Cody made them a light dinner of chicken fajitas. Taeng came out of her room dressed in leggings and a cropped t-shirt and wandered into the kitchen while vigorously drying her hair with a towel. When she looked up and saw the fajitas she was impressed, and she discovered that she was also starving. Cody, on the other hand, was thinking of the old adage, 'Leggings don't lie'.

While they ate, they discussed the preparations for their SOG and Bajan commandos. They'd have to set up a barracks down at the shop and stock the place with the purchases they'd made over the past two days.

After helping Cody clean the kitchen, Taeng said goodnight and began walking back towards her room. Cody couldn't help but notice that when covered in leggings, Taeng's taut, perfectly formed backside had roughly the same shape and proportions as a ripe Georgia peach, complete with the crease down the middle.

And with that tantalizing thought dancing in his head, he turned off the light in the kitchen and made his way toward his own room.

CHAPTER 16

AFTER ANOTHER HEARTY BREAKFAST OF sugar infused Honey Nut Cheerios, Cody's favorite energy food, and coffee, they jumped into the Gator and drove back down to the shop above the sub pen to set up the barracks for their impending visitors. The office was too small to arrange all the cots in, so they decided to line them up in the aisle between the two rows of equipment and machinery tools that ran back across the shop floor toward the garage door and the elevator. Figuring that the guests would be squared away military types, they lined all 22 cots up exactly in the middle of the aisle with exactly 5' between each cot. On each cot, precisely in the center, Taeng placed a pillow on top of a folded blanket. The canned goods and freeze-dried foodstuffs were placed in the office where running water, a stove and range, a refrigerator, toilet facilities and an industrial sized coffee maker could be found.

That done, they made their way down to the sub pen and onto the Nasty boat to fuel it up and service it since at some point they would be making a nighttime excursion up to Barbados to drop off some of the SOG personnel and their equipment, as well as half the vetted Bajans. Once that task was completed, they went back up to the office to touch base with Mike. No plan had yet been approved, so they took the Kawasaki dirt bike up to the house. They had both forgotten just how exhilarating the old bump-and-grind trip up the hill on the Kawasaki could be.

Back in the house, Taeng got busy with making lunch, grilled cheese sandwiches with bacon, while Cody just sat at the kitchen island and admired the view of Taeng's form while clothed in old cut-off jeans and a Midsummer's Night Dream 1983 concert t-shirt featuring Peter Tosh on the front and his 1983 concert schedule on the back.

Without turning around, Taeng asked if he was looking at her butt again. Since he didn't see any sense in denying the obvious, he replied in the affirmative. After a few minutes spent transferring the sandwiches to plates, Taeng brought their lunch over to the kitchen island and sat down across from Cody. After a few bites, Taeng looked over at Cody and asked him why he had never propositioned her. She was used to being propositioned and had been propositioned almost non-stop since she'd hit puberty. She didn't necessarily enjoy being propositioned but it was a sort of left-handed compliment in its own way. She knew that Cody watched her when she supposedly wasn't looking, but the guy had not once made a serious attempt to get physical with her and she just thought that this was odd, and she wanted to know why.

Cody finished his sandwich before he answered. "The thing is, Taeng, I am an engineering savant. I like what I do, and I am very good at it. This has made me very financially secure, and I even ended up with my own little island. The problem with being good at what you do and being wealthy is that you either end up alone, and you get comfortable with that, or you end up essentially paying people to be your friends or for female companionship.

"As I told you before, I do occasionally fly over to Martinique, St. Lucia, St. Vincent or Grenada for a week to relax and knock the edges off, but it is a pointless exercise. I have no real friends in the islands, I have no authentic social interaction except when I visit Mike in Puerto Rica, and I am smart enough to realize that paying for sex is no substitute for a healthy relationship.

"We've had a lot of fun and some memorable adventures since you washed up, we seem to be getting along fairly well, and now and then we seem to be testing the waters of a relationship, and truth be told, it frightens me somewhat. I have no experience with serious relationships. Even when I was in the Navy hanging out with the guys when we weren't required elsewhere, I never picked up girls in bars because I was dancing on the edge of the autism syndrome, which is fairly common with savants.

"In a nutshell, from my point of view you are way out of my league and even if you weren't, I have no idea as to how to move forward from where we are at the moment. I'm guessing that we'll get this coup sorted out, you'll be a hero, you'll go back to Barbados and pick up where you left off and I'll just carry on with my projects here and life will go on."

Taeng thought about this for a while and as she got up to collect their plates and clean up the kitchen area, she started in on Cody.

"You're an idiot, you realize that, don't you? How can you be so smart and so stupid at the same time?" she asked in frustration as she washed their plates and utensils and placed them in the drying rack. Turning back to face Cody, she leaned back against the counter, crossed her arms under her breasts and continued lecturing him. "I've probably been hit on by every narcissistic prick on Barbados. They've been hitting on me since I was in high school. It was fun for a while, until it became obvious that they were all only interested in a 'hit & run'. I haven't had a serious relationship for probably the past 10 years since I refuse to become someone's trophy girlfriend or mistress, and secondly, I value my independence and my career as a journalist. I'm good at it, I like the work, and I don't need someone to support me.

"When I first washed up here and you came walking down the breakwater yelling at me, I figured you were just another egocentric white guy who was thanking his lucky stars that some half-naked, helpless island girl had washed up on the rocks and that with any luck he'd get lucky playing her knight in shining armor. I was wrong, you haven't made a serious move on me since I've been here, although I've teased you often enough to warrant it if you had.

"Basically, I find you nominally attractive and a whole lot of fun, but your apparent lack of interest is disturbing, it is almost as if you don't find me desirable enough to even hit on me, which is very damaging to my fragile ego. Any comments?"

"I'm only nominally attractive? What about my fragile ego, Ms. Skeete?"

"You jerk! You're deflecting. Spit it out." This was said while trying to keep a straight face.

Cody took a moment to compose himself before delivering his reply. "Well, it seems we find ourselves in a conundrum: I can now justify giving you the attention which you deserve thereby reinforcing your faith in your womanhood, but if this would go sideways at some point, the rejection, from my point of view, would be disastrous. On the other hand, if I continue to keep you at arm's length, we might never know just how well we may have fit, in a manner of speaking.

"I suggest that we let nature take its course, perhaps at a more accelerated rate than before, and once we sort out this coup thing, and you become rich and famous, that we revisit our budding relationship and see where it goes."

"Fair enough, but I will be expecting some serious flirtation and perhaps even some light petting while this coup thing is getting sorted out just to keep my engine idling. Think you can manage that?"

"I'll probably need to do some research on the flirting and petting, but I'm reasonably certain that I can keep your engine turning over," Cody said with a randy grin.

Taeng suggested that he revisit her comment about him being a jerk, but she did so with a smile.

"I do have one question, why does your father seem to want to pimp you out all the time? That does seem a bit weird."

"It is weird! I've never seen him do that before and I'm not sure that he even knows that he is doing it. He is generally harmless and likes to play the smuggler and run around the Caribbean in his boat, but he's never, ever tried to pawn me off to someone who was essentially a stranger. He may think that you are just off center enough to be a kindred spirit, or he may just simply want to get me hooked up before I get too old to be marketable. Having a spinster as a daughter probably doesn't fit into his narrative. It could also be that he just wants grandchildren to tell his tales to or maybe he really and truly thinks I am worth your Nasty boat. It's confusing, he may just be a crazy old man."

"Well, for what it's worth, you could possibly be worth my Nasty boat, but women, like cars, need a good test drive before you make the trade. In the meantime, while you ponder the pros and cons of test driving, let's go out back to the comms room and see if anyone is trying to get ahold of us."

Taeng threw the dish towel at Cody before following him to the communications hut to get an update.

CHAPTER 17

ONCE THEY GOT HOLD OF Mike, he let them know that the powers that be in Langley were still working on a plan and that they should call him back the following morning to get read into it.

With nothing better to do for the remainder of the day, they cleaned up the house in preparation for their guests, then decided to watch the Guy Ritchie film 'The Ministry of Ungentlemanly Warfare' in an effort to get into the spirit of thwarting a coup. Somewhere during the movie Taeng had managed to scoot up between his outstretched legs on the couch and rested the back of her head on his stomach like a pillow. Cody felt that this could possibly be the beginning of the flirting and light petting mentioned earlier. If so, he reckoned that he could get used to it.

After the movie, they made dinner, fish and chips, before retiring to their respective rooms. As they headed back into the open-air courtyard with the water feature where the bedrooms were located, Cody wished Taeng a good night and turned to go to his room. Obviously, this did not meet with Taeng's approval, and she grabbed him by the shoulder, spun him around and planted a passionate kiss on his lips.

"And that, Mr. Morgan, is how you wish me a proper good night. You really do need to study up on this stuff," informed Taeng as she spun him back around, smacked him on the butt and shoved him toward the door to his room.

The next morning Taeng woke up to the smell of bacon frying and walked into the kitchen wearing a white t-shirt, with a likeness of Shabba Ranks appropriately showcasing his hit 'Housecall (Your Body Can't Lie to Me)', over what appeared to be a pair of sky blue, tight, minimal inseam, yoga shorts. The shorts probably would have been more attention riveting if the tail of the t-shirt hadn't kept getting in the way when she wasn't leaning on the kitchen island or bending over to set the table. Cody surmised that this may have constituted flirting on her part, and now that they had a better understanding of what was expected in their budding relationship, he was all for it.

After breakfast, Cody went back to his room to shave and brush his teeth while Taeng went back to her room to change out of what had apparently been her sleeping attire. They both met back up in the living room to figure out what to do with the rest of the day.

Cody missed the short yoga shorts but had to admit that the daisy duke cut-offs that Taeng now sported were pretty interesting as well. The curve of her butt just peeked out at the bottom, and the cropped yellow sleeveless t-shirt she now wore did not get in the way of the view at all.

"Well, the first thing we have to do is get back in touch with Mike and see what the plan is, and what our part in the plan consists of. Until we know the plan, we can't do much to prepare for it," said Cody.

Since Cody figured he may as well get some work in while they waited for instructions, they got back on the Kawasaki for another bump and grind session back to the shop. While Taeng inspected the cots, pillows and blankets for perfect alignment, Cody walked into the office and fired up his laptop and accessed the comms program. Taeng walked into the cave just as Mike answered on the first ring.

After the usual salutations, Mike got down to business.

"A C-130 just landed at the Muñoz Marin International Airport here in San Juan. The aircraft flew in from Hurlbut Field located at Fort Walton Beach, Florida. Prior to takeoff, 12 SAC/SOG operators boarded the aircraft while it was being loaded with a variety of weapons and munitions.

"These operators, weapons and munitions will be with you shortly. The aircraft will be making a night training flight to A. N. R. Robinson International Airport on Tobago, and it should pass directly over Pala Island around midnight tonight.

"The SAC/SOG team leader will brief you once he is on the ground."

"What! These bozos are going to parachute in at night? Why can't they take a boat like everyone else? If they drop something on my house, I will not be a happy camper," exclaimed Cody.

"Cody, this is the 4th Special Operations Squadron. It is part of the 1st Special Operations Wing, these bozos, as you referred to them, could probably drop everybody and everything onto your patio in a single pass. They've been doing this for a long time, quit whining!"

"Okay, fair enough. Who's leading this outfit, anyone I know?"

"Actually, I think you do. Remember when you ran over that crocodile a few years back and flipped your boat? Well, one of the SEAL's you so unceremoniously launched into the river was a certain Petty Officer First Class Martinez. Mister Martinez retired a few years later as a Chief Petty Officer in SEAL Team 2. He says he looks forward to seeing you again."

"Is that good or bad?" asked Cody.

"Can't tell you. I guess it all depends on if he ever forgave you for the broken nose he got when you ran over that big lizard."

"This adventure is not starting out well," muttered Cody.

"Well, it is what it is. Give me a call once everyone and everything is on the ground there. Talk to you later," and with that, Mike signed off.

Cody swung around in his chair to face Taeng, who commented, with an impertinent grin on her face, that running over crocodiles in Navy boats seemed to gather a lot of attention.

"It does. That said, what are we going to do with ourselves until our guests arrive?" asked Cody as he stood up and walked over to Taeng. He put his arms around her waist and said that some light petting was probably a good idea before they had company. She agreed but suggested that he might get a little frustrated with the limits of light petting.

"At this point, I'll take what I can get."

An hour later, an extremely frustrated Cody, and a very amused Taeng, mounted the dirt bike to run up to the house to have dinner and wait for their guests. They both agreed that after a light petting session, the bump and grind ride up to the house was sheer torture.

When they arrived at the house, they both went into their respective rooms and took cold showers to cool down their libidos before they decided on spaghetti carbonara for dinner. While Cody cooked, Taeng set the island for dinner. Once dinner was finished and the kitchen had been cleaned up, they took a cooler of beer out on the patio, positioned the pair of lounge chairs to face the little harbor, then just relaxed and prepared to watch the show.

A C-130J is a four-engined turboprop combat delivery aircraft. It makes a lot of noise, especially at low altitude. Cody and Taeng heard it long before they saw it coming directly at them at somewhere between 550' and 650' of altitude. Cody told Taeng that this was the usual altitude when making a LALO, low attitude low opening drop. This type of delivery for personnel or equipment was extremely dangerous since if the main chute fails, there is no time to deploy a reserve chute before you hit the ground.

The aircraft came roaring at them at 250 knots, directly over the northern shoreline, just to the east of the harbor and straight at the house. This only gave then about a 200-yard-long drop zone. As soon as the aircraft crossed over the rocky shoreline bundles started tumbling out of the aircraft, immediately followed by humans. The last human dropped out of the plane just before it roared directly over the house on its way to Tobago.

The last operative out of the plane landed about 10 yards in front of the patio. After gathering up his chute, he took off his helmet and walked up on the patio in front of Cody and Taeng. Giving an offhanded salute he said, "Agent Martinez reporting for duty!" Giving Taeng an appraising glance, he continued, "Doesn't look like you'll be running over any crocodiles here, Mr. Morgan."

By this time, Cody had gotten to his feet and reached out his hand to Agent Martinez, who ignored it and wrapped Cody up in a bear hug. "How ya' doing, Cody? The last time I saw you we had just unassed that 33-foot Riverine Boat after hitting that croc. How did you end up here, and how did you end up involved with a coup in the Caribbean, on your own little island with a Bond-girl by your side?"

Agent Martinez, often known as Tony, was a very large Hispanic man. He went about 6'2" and 250 pounds, all solid muscle. Once Cody escaped the bear hug, he introduced Taeng and then asked if Tony was still upset about the incident with the crocodile and the broken nose he'd suffered.

"Heck no, that was just part and parcel of special ops. Lucky for us the croc decided to die after you hit him or things could have gotten a whole lot worse with a pissed off croc in the water, that was one big-assed crocodile. Anyhow, it made me realize that I was getting a little long in the tooth for the SEAL games. I get to do the same sort of stuff now, but since most SAC/SOG agents are a bit older than SEALs, we tend to be more cerebral in our planning and operations, which makes it a whole lot easier on the body.

"Anyhow, let me get the boys, girls and equipment rounded up and show them where they'll be bunking and we'll catch up later."

"You've got girls on your team?" asked Taeng in surprise.

"You bet! Girls can gather intelligence where men often can't. Plus, when they get mad, they can fight like wildcats. I'll introduce you to them later, I imagine the boys will be making their own introductions personally," Tony said with a wink.

Cody thought about this for a second. "Be sure and tell the boys that they can read the menu, but if they try to order they can swim their asses to Barbados when the time comes." A lot of truth is said in jest.

As Tony went and rounded up his crew, Cody and Taeng got back on the dirt bike and scooted down to the shop to get the Gator and its trailer. Driving back to the drop zone they drove around and collected the equipment that had been dropped and took it back to the shop. This took several trips. Eventually, everyone and everything was back in the makeshift barracks at the shop. Cody made a final trip up to the house to get a cold case of Carib beer for his guests.

While Cody was making his beer run, Tony introduced Taeng to his crew. The eight men in the crew just stared at her and perhaps drooled a little, but the three women of the crew: two of African-American lineage and one of Hispanic heritage, bonded with her immediately.

CHAPTER 18

THE MEN OF THE SOG crew were all African-Americans, or black, depending on how someone chose to categorize them in this day and age, except for Tony and one other Hispanic guy. This made perfect sense when you considered that they would need to blend into the local population on Barbados. Not that there weren't any white folks on Barbados, but they only compromised about 3.5 percent of the population.

Tony introduced his crew, women first.

"Chiara, Cheryl and Cathy, the 3Cs, will be our infiltration package. These ladies are highly trained, highly skilled specialists tasked with getting in touch with the Police Service and the people in the Caribbean News Service prior to the coup. Once they contact the people we need them to contact, I'll meet with them, and we'll update the plan as necessary.

"The guys, please stand as I introduce you, are as follows: Autry, Booker, Dontrell, Emmett, Garlan, Isaac and Justus. Autry and Garlan are our Javelin missile system experts and will train our Bajan associates on the system when they get here. Booker, Dontrell, Emmett, Isaac and Justus are small unit tactics experts. They will also train our Bajan team members when they arrive. They'll focus on tactics as well as the weapons we've brought along to supplement the Javelins and the firepower of the police force.

"That just leaves the Hispanic contingent to introduce, which would be myself and the scrawny little Mexican over there hitting on the girls. Obviously, due to my dashing good looks and incredible intellect, I am the best choice for team leader. Carlos is our communications expert. My job is to keep this motley crew pointed in the right direction, while Carlos' job is to make sure that I can issue instructions to them before they go off the reservation and bring shame to SAC/SOG.

"Mr. Morgan, perhaps you can introduce yourself and that delectable young lady who for some inexplicable reason seems to enjoy your company."

Cody, who by now had returned with the beer and had walked up beside Tony while he introduced his crew had gotten into the spirit of things.

"My name is Cody, and through a variety of circumstances beyond my control, I own this island. I am a propulsion systems expert and the higher ups back in the States thought that it would be a good idea to shove me off in a corner and let me play with my toys, which you can see all around you. I am not currently in the military, and I simply got roped into this deal when Taeng, the hot little number in the daisy dukes over there by the 3Cs and Carlos, washed up on my shores a few weeks ago."

"Wish she'd washed up on my shores," muttered Garlan.

"Garlan, if she would have washed up anywhere near you, you'd probably be in the intensive care unit by now. I'm guessing that she's survived the attentions of many wannabe Romeo's like yourself in the past. Please, no more interruptions from the peanut gallery." Turning to Cody, Tony asked him to continue.

Before Cody could say a word, Autry asked the obvious question. "You said that you were not currently in the military. Does this mean that you have served previously?"

"Three years active duty as a Special Warfare Combat Crewman."

"That's some serious cred, man. Why only a 3-year tour?" asked Isaac.

"Well, I was running my boat down a little river somewhere in South America when I happened to hit a Boone & Crockett class crocodile. Those riverine boats were not built to run into 1,000-pound crocodiles at speed. My boat went airborne, and my career sank. You can address any further questions to Tony, he was there."

Getting back on topic, Cody continued, "Taeng was a journalist on Barbados. Her and her associates uncovered the coup plot. When she told me about it, I contacted the CIA/NSA listening post on Puerto Rico, which is why you guys are here."

Needless to say, this led to many questions from the SAC/SOG team.

"How did you possibly contact the listening post in Puerto Rico?" asked Carlos the communications expert. "Those comms are secure and encrypted out the wazoo."

"Well, I let them run a relay station up behind my house, so I have an encrypted WhatsApp direct to Puerto Rico as well as encrypted cell phone access."

"What is the deal with this little Saint-Nazaire sub pen set up? It seems a bit out of place in the Grenadines?" asked Dontrell.

"I inherited that. When the island was still owned by the British, they blasted out the harbor and built the seawall and this structure to operate two British Oberon-class submarines out of here. When the Oberons became obsolete, so did this base. I just repurposed it into a propulsion lab."

"Okay, enough questions for the evening. What are the sleeping and accommodation arrangements, Cody?"

"I'll let Taeng handle that."

Taeng looked a bit uncomfortable and said that she had not planned on any women being on the team.

"Don't worry about that, Taeng, they don't," assured Tony.

"Okay then, as you can see, we've arranged for you to all have a cot, blanket and pillow. The only place with enough room to set them up was here in the propulsion lab. Through that door in the corner is an office. We've stocked it up with canned goods and freeze-dried goods and snacks. There is also a sink, a refrigerator, a stove and range as well as a bathroom and a large coffee maker. It's all we could do on short notice, but we can make adjustments tomorrow if needed."

Tony assured Taeng that this would be fine. He then suggested that everyone get some sleep as dawn was only a few hours away. They would start prepping for the operation after breakfast and they all needed to be sharp. And with that, Cody and Taeng bid the crew a fond adieu before heading back up to the house on the dirt bike.

Once back at the house, Cody asked Taeng if she would like to pick up where they had left off in the office.

"Alas, I would, but we have a coup to stop and as Tony explained to Garlan earlier, it would probably put you in the hospital and then who would drive the Shag McNasty? Good night, Mr. Morgan."

CHAPTER 19

TAENG AND CODY GOT UP bright and early the next morning, they really had no choice since their new guests had gotten up even brighter and earlier and had been doing calisthenics for an hour before deciding to run up and down the hill from the shop to the house over and over again. Cody and Taeng, on the other hand, just sat on the patio, sipped their coffee and watched the show.

Eventually a sweaty Tony came over and suggested that everyone meet up in the living room at the house in an hour to run through the plan. Before he left, he asked if there were any shower facilities down at the shop. Cody and Taeng had totally forgotten about shower facilities, but the Brits had installed a locker room with showers when they built the pens. Cody was pretty sure that they still worked since he'd used them in the past when working on the seaplane or the Nasty boat on his own, but it was only a cold, seawater shower.

"Better than nothing," said Tony. "Especially if Ms. Skeete keeps dressing like she is at the moment," he added as he started back down the hill.

Cody looked over at Taeng in her signature sleepwear of short yoga shorts and a t-shirt and thought that it could definitely warrant a cold shower if you weren't used to seeing it on a regular basis. Taeng just grinned over the top of her coffee cup.

An hour later, with Taeng more appropriately attired and Cody still in his old board shorts and a ZZ Top Afterburner Tour t-shirt, the freshly showered SOG operators, Cody and Taeng had all grabbed a coffee before arranging themselves in the living room facing the kitchen island where Tony was preparing to go over the plan, such as it was at the moment.

"Guys and gals, we really don't have much to go on right now. All that we know is that the Chinese are prepared to support a coup on Barbados and we have been sent in to make sure that this coup doesn't succeed. We need more local intel and an update on the current situation. To that end, Cody will fire up his old gunboat this evening so that he can take the 3Cs up to the island to meet up with Ms. Skeete's associates. Ms. Skeete's associates will hopefully be able to bring our girls up to date on the present situation, which they will then transmit back to me and to Mike in Puerto Rico. Once they have given their update, they will make their way down the island to St. Ann's Fort and to the Paragon Army Base to scout around for further intelligence and to take some photos of the areas we plan to operate in.

"Once the ladies have completed their mission which will take roughly a week, they will give me a call and Cody will return to Barbados to retrieve them along with our ten loyal Bajan partners. Once everyone is back here, I'll debrief them before we finalize our plans. Any questions?"

"Yeah, I think I should go with the girls. I know the people and the territory, and that would give us two teams of two," suggested Taeng.

Tony thought about this for a little while before he responded. "Taeng, you are not a trained operator, and you have no military background to fall back on. This recon could get compromised and the Chinese Ministry of State Security will do whatever it takes to make this coup a success. What value do you think you could add to one of these teams?"

"I have no doubt that I'd be a liability to the girls if people started shooting at us, but I am a journalist trained to observe and see things that others might miss. I also know the area around St. Ann's Fort like the back of my hand. Two teams of two could cover twice the area in a week that one team of three could."

"Could you take orders, without question, from one of my girls?"

"Absolutely. This is not an ego trip for me, I think that I can add value, and I want to help out in any way that I can."

Tony thought some more. "Okay, you'll pair up with Chiara and you girls will recon St. Ann's Fort and the surrounding area while Cheryl and Cathy recon the Army Base. Once you ladies have fulfilled your mission you will give me a call, and we'll arrange for Cody to pick you up from somewhere out of sight and bring you and our ten trainees back here."

While Tony was finishing up his lecture, everyone turned toward the front door where a wizened, nut brown, weather-beaten, skinny little Asian guy, probably in his late fifties, dressed in old, faded denim cut-offs and an unbuttoned gaudy Hawaiian shirt was walking up the steps to the patio while tunelessly whistling a version of Bob Marley's 'Buffalo Soldier'.

When Tanawat finally realized he had an audience, which was about the time he crossed the threshold into the living room, he jerked to a stop. For a minute, everyone just stared at Tanawat while he stared back at them before Taeng took the reins.

"Everyone, I would like you to meet my father, Tanawat. Dad, this is the American crew that is going to give us a hand with what's about to happen in Barbados."

"I kind of figured that out on my own, daughter. Anyone within 50 miles of this island heard that Hercules fly over last night, and anyone with a decent pair of binoculars would have seen the bundles and bodies falling out the ass end of it as it came over the island. Anyway, with all that equipment I figured that you novices will need the use of me and my boat to get it where it needs to go. How come nobody has offered me a coffee yet? Today's youth have no manners."

Taeng just rolled her eyes as she got her father a cup of coffee and took it over to him as he sat down between Cheryl and Cathy. Tanawat thanked his daughter before turning to Cheryl and asking her if she possibly had a thing for old Thai smugglers.

Everyone had a good laugh before Cheryl replied that she only had a thing for old Thai smugglers with a strong heart that could possibly survive her affections for an entire evening. Cathy tapped him on the shoulder and when he looked around at her, she added, "Sometimes we tag team."

They thought that this might intimidate old Tanawat, but they had a lot to learn about him. "Girls, let's get this coup stopped in its tracks before we give this a shot. I don't want to hook up with you girls and inadvertently wear you out and sideline you before your other talents are required on Barbados. Don't fret, I'll give you a rain check, and you can cash it later." Everyone but Cathy and Cheryl thought that this was hilarious, the two women couldn't tell if the old guy was serious or not, but the grin on his face had them worried.

Tony meanwhile, had given some thought to what the old smuggler had said. Turning to Cody he said, "Mr. Skeete does have a valid point. We've got six Javelin missile systems with four rounds for each, we've got six 240B machine guns plus 500 belted rounds each, I also brought along eight M4 carbines with eight loaded magazines for each and 50 M67 fragmentation grenades. This is in addition to our own people and their personal loadouts. We'll need to split up the load and get them to Barbados and in place before the coup kicks off. The extra equipment alone weighs in at about 1,300 pounds total. Total number of operators plus loyalists that will be going ashore is 22, assuming that you, Taeng and Tanawat, stay on the boats. That's 11 or 12 people plus the boat driver on each boat plus about 650 pounds of kit plus my team's personal kit; say 11 people plus 1,000 pounds of equipment. Two boats would be handy, and we could insert both teams at the same time. The question is, is Mr. Skeete up to the task?"

Cody whistled and he motioned for Tanawat to come over to where he and Tony were standing next to the refrigerator. Cody explained the situation to Tanawat, then asked him if he thought he could help them out.

Before their eyes, the old smuggler in his worn-out attire transformed into the real deal version of the caricature that he put on display for the world to see.

"Mr. Martinez, I've been sailing these waters since you were knee high to a small duck. This would not be the first time that I've smuggled people or run arms around the Caribbean. I really don't need the income, although it helps, but it is just something that I do and I'm pretty damn good at it.

"You need to ask yourself how and why a guy who is supposedly a chef and part owner of a respectable restaurant in Saint Philip Parish came to own an old 65' aluminum hulled Swiftship oilfield crew boat, in an area with no drilling rigs or production platforms to service, and don't forget the uprated GM16V71TA engines. The only reasonable explanation is that the guy is a smuggler. My boat, in these waters, is a dead giveaway. Every law enforcement agency from Puerto Rico to Trinidad has been trying to bust me for years, yet here I am.

"I know every cove and inlet in the Grenadines and on Barbados. I guarantee that I can get you in and out of wherever you want to go, whenever you want to do it. A dozen people and 1,300 pounds of kit is nothing, my boat could easily handle twice that."

Tony looked at Cody and asked if he thought Tanawat was up to the task.

"I'm probably biased as I'm sort of dating his daughter. That said, we've already had a run-in with the Chinese when we ran into them while I was running Taeng up to Barrouallie on St. Vincent to meet up with her friends. We cross decked the friends from my boat to his and while I led them on a merry chase, Tanawat got them dropped off on the backside of St. Vincent with no one the wiser. I'd say he's good to go."

"Good enough for me," Tony said. "We'll give you a call when it is time to saddle up and get everybody and everything up to Barbados. Glad to have you onboard, Mr. Skeete."

Apparently Tanawat didn't hear Tony as he looked at Cody and asked if he was actually dating his daughter now.

"What can I say, Tanawat? She basically told me it was time to fish or cut bait. That said, she wants to put off the really interesting stuff until after we sort out this coup business."

"Smart girl. I raised her right. I guess you'll just have to wait and see what you're getting into, no pun intended. She, like her mother, can be a handful at times. Isn't it about time for a beer?"

Everyone but Cody, who was busy digesting Tanawat's last comment, thought this was good for a laugh.

CHAPTER 20

WITH THE TRANSPORTATION SORTED OUT, Tony and Cody left the others socializing in the living room and made their way out back to the communications hut behind the house to get an update from Mike.

It seemed that Ian Gooding, the Deputy Commissioner of Police, had selected and vetted the ten loyal Bajans that would be coming back to Pala Island with Taeng and the 3Cs after they had finished their reconnaissance mission: Nine men and one woman. The recon team would meet up with the Bajan loyalists in the Foul Bay Beach parking lot, about two and a half miles up the coast from the eastern end of the runways at the Grantley Adams Airport. Cody would collect everyone on the beach there at 2:00 in the morning, a week after he'd dropped them off far to the north at Stroud Bay, on the other side of the island, close to Taeng's house in Crab Hill.

Taeng was instructed to call one of her associates to arrange a pickup on the beach at Stroud Bay, and to come up with a way to contact them before the boat came in for the drop-off.

With that part of the plan decided, Tony and Cody retraced their route back into the living room and briefed the rest of the crew. Tony ordered the 3Cs and Taeng to go get their kit sorted out and have it on the dock beside the Nasty in an hour. They could then relax for a while and partake of the BBQ that Cody had suggested so that everyone had a decent meal before the game kicked off at 8:00 that evening. It was just over 100 nautical miles from Pala Island to Crab Hill on Barbados, so Cody figured a four-hour cruise at a comfortable 25 knots would put them off Stroud Bay at midnight.

Chiara, Cheryl and Cathy helped Taeng get her kit sorted out for their recon mission. They'd be wearing civilian clothes during the event, but they had to be able to carry cameras and comms equipment with them as well, so they would be carrying colorful, local made beach totes as well. Since Taeng would essentially just be acting as a guide and providing introductions for the other girls, she could get by just carrying her normal rucksack. She wouldn't be armed, but she noticed that the three recon specialists had shoved pistols, suppressors and extra magazines in their beach totes. Things started to get real for her at this point.

Cody rarely had as many guests as he found himself with that day, but after rummaging around the house, shop and sub pen he managed to locate three useable grills and a few sacks of charcoal briquettes. Dragging them out on the dock beside his boat, he set them up and got them going with the help of the SOG boys. After raiding his big Sub-Zero refrigerator in the house and the big 19.8 cubic foot Frigidaire chest freezer in the back of the shop, he finally found enough burgers, brats and hotdogs to feed the crew.

The boys and Tanawat got into the beer supply in the house, but the girls just had soft drinks since they would be on-call for later in the evening.

Eventually everyone had eaten their fill and Taeng, Cathy, Cheryl and Chiara loaded themselves and their kit onto the Shag McNasty. At the last minute, Tony invited himself aboard, just to get into the swing of things, he said.

Taeng and Tony cast off the mooring lines and Cody slowly eased them out of the pen and into the harbor before throttling up and getting them out past the breakwater and into open sea. Throttling up further, he got up on plane and running at 25 knots as he cleared Little Savan Island to port before taking a heading of 70 degrees direct to Crab Hill.

The girls eventually went down to the stateroom under the forward deck to get out of the wind and the spray, while Cody and Tony just got caught up on the bridge. Tony gave Cody the CliffNotes version of his career since the unfortunate collision with the crocodile and Cody let Tony know how he had ended up on an island in the Caribbean with its token Bond-girl while earning a paycheck by working on advanced propulsion systems for the US government.

Roughly four hours after leaving Pala Island, the Shag was approaching the Harrison's Point light house and Cody throttled back and turned to port so that he could follow the shoreline to Stroud Bay. By this time the girls were up in the blacked-out bridge with their kit getting ready to go ashore.

There is a small, isolated, sandy beach, no more than 20 yards wide, just below the bluffs where Harrison's Plantation Road peters out. This was where the girls were supposed to be picked up. Taeng made a call on her cell phone while Cody brought the boat beam on to the beach, about 200 yards out. Taeng then took a flashlight and pointed it towards the beach and sent out the Morse Code for the letter K, dash-dot-dash. From shore came the Morse Code for the letter R, dot-dash-dot. This was the correct recognition signal and the contact on the phone had not used any of the 'panic' words or phrases on the phone that would have indicated that they were under duress, so Cody aimed the bow at the beach and slowly made his way ashore until the bow crunched into the sand.

The girls, each carrying her own kit, went straight over the bow and across the beach before disappearing into the foliage at the base of the escarpment. Cody backed off the beach and took the Nasty out about a quarter of a mile and waited for the safe and secure signal from the top of the bluffs, the Morse Code letter G, dash-dash-dot. Scanning the top of the bluff with his Zeiss binoculars, he finally saw the correct signal then turned the boat around and headed back to his island.

CHAPTER 21

THE GIRLS CLIMBED TO THE top of the steep wooded scarp and looked through the edge of the foliage that grew on the bluff, they saw a middle-aged black guy leaning against the front of a 10-year-old Toyota Sienna mini-van, which may have been silver years ago, but now looked like the dust from the island's unpaved roads had been baked into whatever the original color was.

Taeng knew who he was and ran over to him and gave him a big hug. "Thanks for the lift, Neville! I didn't know who they would send, but I'm glad it's you. Do you know what you are getting into?"

"I know enough not to ask questions, Skeeter. I am supposed to stay with you and take you wherever you need to go."

Turning back toward the trees at the top of the bluff, Taeng waved to the other girls to let them know that the coast was clear and to come on over. Turning back to Neville, she asked him not to call her Skeeter in front of the company, saying it would not be good for her image.

"Oh, I see. Our little Skeeter is all grown up now and playing in the big leagues. Your secret is safe with me," replied Neville with a laugh.

As the 3Cs came up to the van, Taeng introduced them to Neville. Neville had been expecting rough, tough military men to be with Taeng, so when he saw three fit, attractive women dressed in shorts, T-shirts and flip-flops, his attitude changed to one of playful service.

"Well now, things seem to be looking up for me this evening."

Taeng had to nip this in the bud. "Neville, put it back in your pants. These girls would eat you up and spit out your bones. Let's just get over to my house and stick with the plan. People are counting on us."

"I could think of worse ways to go than that," said a chastened Neville as they got into the van and made their way through Crab Hill to Taeng's vacant house.

When they arrived at Taeng's place, everyone got out of the van and into the house as quickly and quietly as possible. Blackout curtains had been rigged over all the windows so once inside they could turn on the lights. Neville told them that although there had been no real interest shown in the place since the Caribbean Queen had been blown up, they could only afford to spend the night before heading south to take a look at what was going on at St. Ann's Fort and the Army base.

While Taeng and Cheryl quickly claimed the bed in the bedroom, Chiara and Cathy took the couch and the recliner. Neville got stuck with an old sleeping bag of Skeeter's and a spot on the throw rug in front of the coffee table by the couch.

Bright and early the following morning, they all took turns in the ensuite shower in the bedroom before having a quick breakfast consisting of coffee with slices of buttered toast prior to getting on the road for their next stop, Jo J's Hostel & Guest House in the Gall Hill area of Bridgetown, near Oistin Bay. Neville had booked two rooms in the guest house to use as a fallback location and his base of operations. The roughly 20-mile trip took them nearly 45 minutes due to the morning traffic and various road construction activities, but they were checked in and ready for business by 10:00.

Getting back in the van, Neville drove them to Lion's Palace Bar & Grill, which sits about 800 yards as the crow flies from the Paragon Army Base proper. Dropping off Cheryl and Cathy, who would appear to be having lunch at the grill while they got a feel for the surroundings, Neville then drove Chiara and Taeng to the Hilton Barbados Resort where Chiara booked a room on the top floor facing St. Ann's Fort. This gave them a clear view of the fort with the privacy to employ the powerful binoculars, cameras and zoom lenses that Chiara had packed into either her tote bag or her rucksack.

Taeng and Chiara had it easy compared to Cathy and Cheryl. All through their lunch the local guys hit on the fit young operatives. They played along for a while but really couldn't get anything done from the bar with all the attention they were receiving. Eventually they called Neville and explained what they needed. He did some research on his phone before driving them less than a quarter of a mile to the Ocean Ridge at Long Beach, where they took a room. Although they were now further from the base than they had been at the bar, they could now act like tourists and walk along Long Bay right up to the fence of the base. There were patches of sea grape trees along the beach that they could get into to photograph and observe the base, but it soon became obvious that someone was watching for just this sort of thing and within minutes an old khaki colored Chevy pickup came out of the base to chase them away. Some other tactic was called for.

The only way for Cheryl and Cathy to get the intel they needed on the Army base was a drone, but not just any drone. It had to be of Chinese manufacture to give plausible deniability and cause confusion if it went down on the base and was found. It also had to have night vision video capability since there was no way they could launch a drone over the base during the day with any chance that it would not be detected. Cathy gave Taeng a call at the Hilton Barbados Resort and explained the situation. Taeng gave her Tanawat's cell number and told her to give him a call. If anyone could find a suitable Chinese drone in the short time available, it would be her father.

Tanawat was doing general maintenance and changing out fuel filters on his boat in the sub pen when Cheryl called. After figuring out who was calling and asking her if she was ready to cash in her rain check, he became serious and asked her what the reason for the call was. She detailed what she and Cathy needed and Tanawat told her to stay by the phone, and he'd get back to her within the hour.

After making a few calls, Tanawat found a kindred spirit on Trinidad that for some unknown reason had a Chinese made DJI AIR-3 drone, complete with the video controller. The 1/1.3" CMOS cameras originally supplied with the drone had been replaced with compatible infrared versions. He was willing to part with this particular drone and all the accessories for the unreasonable price of $10,000. After relaying this information to Tony, Tony told him to buy it. Since the Scantily Clad was in the middle of having routine maintenance done on it, Tony told Cody to get ready to put the Shag to sea again as they needed to get to Toco Beach on Trinidad as soon as possible to pick up the drone and then get it up to the Oistin Fish Market south of Bridgetown in Barbados to drop it off with Neville so that he could then get it to Cheryl and Cathy as soon as possible. The trip to Trinidad and then up to Barbados was just over 300 miles. If they left now, they could be in Oistin Bay in six hours if they ran at 40 knots. This would have them handing off the drone to Neville at around 11:00 that night, giving the girls time to fly it that evening.

The Shag, with Cody driving and Tony along for moral support, arrived off Toco Beach at around 8:00 that evening. Tanawat's buddy met them in a skiff off the beach for the transfer, the drone for cash. Three and a half hours later they were alongside the pier at the Oistin Fish Market handing the drone over to Neville.

Neville immediately drove over to the Ocean Ridge and passed the drone and its associated equipment to Cathy. Cathy and Cheryl gave the instructions a quick read, which at their age was all that was required to understand the digital technology, before they made their way to a tree line that was about 250 yards from the base's perimeter fence. After letting the video controller run through its start-up diagnostics, Cheryl lifted the drone off, hovered just over the tree tops for a second, then flew it quickly to the base where she had programmed in a grid pattern to search the base, exactly like you would do with a side-scan sonar if you were looking for a sunken wreck on the seafloor. The drone stayed at 300 feet above the ground for the survey and was essentially silent and undetectable by those on the ground. The infrared cameras worked flawlessly and sent back continuous video of what the drone was 'seeing'. As the drone passed over the motor pool area, the girls hit paydirt: there were five of the new Chinese reconnaissance vehicles undergoing routine maintenance or having the weapons packages mounted on them. There were also six Dongfeng EQ2082 six-wheel drive troop carriers parked in the motor pool as well.

This is what the girls had come to find out, so they brought the drone back to the tree line, packed it up and walked back to their accommodation at the Ocean Ridge to forward the video to Carlos, the comms expert back on Pala Island.

The next morning, they checked out of their room at the Ocean Ridge where Neville collected them and drove them back to Jo J's Hostel & Guest House. They would wait at the guest house for Taeng and Chiara to join them after they had completed their part of the mission.

While Cathy and Cheryl were busy surveilling the Army base, Taeng and Chiara were having a much easier time studying St. Ann's Fort simply because their perch on the eighth floor of the Hilton Barbados Resort gave them a fairly unobstructed view into the interior of the fort. Although their line of sight was blocked in places by the abandoned tanks in an old oil storage tank farm between them and the fort, they still managed to identify five of the Chinese CSK-131 reconnaissance vehicles and two troop carrier trucks as they were shuttled between what appeared to be a maintenance shed on the south side of the fort and a walled-in parking area on the north side. After confirming the number and type of vehicles and passing the information to Carlos, the girls had dinner at Follow De Smoke on the beach just north of the hotel before calling it a day.

Early the next morning they checked out of the hotel and were collected by Neville and taken to Jo J's Hostel and Guest House where they met back up with their partners in crime and awaited further instructions.

Later that afternoon, Chiara received a message on her encrypted cell phone letting her know that the ten vetted loyalists, all of them ex-police or ex-military, would be making their way by ones and twos to the Foul Bay Beach parking lot at midnight the following evening. The girls were supposed to meet up with them at exactly 1:00 in the morning. Cody would collect them in his boat and bring them back to Pala Island. Several of the ex-policemen knew Taeng from their years of trying to bust her father, so no recognition signal or passwords were required when everyone met up in the parking lot.

The meet up in the parking lot went as planned, and to the best of their knowledge nobody was followed. Chiara, Cathy, Cheryl and Taeng were the last to arrive. Actually, they had arrived hours earlier and had gone to the Marco Polo Bar and Grill about 150 yards from the parking lot to blend in with the locals. Around midnight they left the bar and walked toward the parking lot but held back in the sea grape trees surrounding the parking area to make sure that all of the others arrived safely and that there wasn't a Chinese welcoming committee on hand.

When the girls walked out of the trees toward the group, the loyalists went silent and stared at them until one of the ex-cops recognized Taeng. After the necessary introductions were made, the group made their way down to the beach and 15 minutes later the Shag McNasty, crewed by Cody and Tony, nosed into the sand about 10 yards out from the beach and everyone waded out and were helped aboard.

As the last of the partisans were helped over the side of the boat, Cody had the Shag in reverse and was backing the old gunboat into deeper water before he spun her around and began the long cruise back to his island.

The Shag pulled back into the submarine pen about 4:30 in the morning, and after getting her tied up in front of the fuel barge, everybody disembarked and made their way up to the shop level via the elevator where the loyalists were given cots and shown where the food and facilities were located.

Everyone slept in until about 9:00 that morning before meeting up at the house for a simple breakfast of scrambled eggs, toast and coffee. Afterwards, Tony led the way back down to the shop where the SOG crew began breaking the partisans down into teams and training them on the Javelin missile system as well as familiarizing the Bajans with the 240B machine guns, the M4 carbines and the hand grenades.

The Bajans were quick study's and after two full days of training they were fairly comfortable with the guns but still needed a bit of work on the Javelins. This was not really an issue since the Special Ops crowd were tasked with killing the Chinese armor and the loyalists would only fire the Javelins if the SOG crews were no longer capable of doing so.

Once the SOG personnel and the Bajans were split into two crews: one to hit the column targeting the radio station and one to target the other element as it left the Paragon Army Base, each group huddled around a different monitor in the office and accessed Google Earth as well as classified satellite photos and began studying the terrain surrounding their objectives and making plans as to where they would be positioned and how to execute their missions.

About this time Mike called to ask for an update. Tony informed him that everything was good to go and that the full team, both loyalists and SOG, were ready to be inserted into Barbados on the 27th, a mere five days away. Mike said he'd pass the word on to Mr. Doe and Mr. Smith and suggested that Tony should start preparing an insertion plan and have it ready for review by the following evening. Before he signed off, Mike asked if any Bajans had been compromised or damaged in the operation so far. Tony reported that everyone was healthy and accounted for but asked Mike why he was asking that particular question.

"Ask Taeng," was all that he would say.

When Tony finally posed the question to Taeng, she simply said that Mike was simply protecting his package, which didn't make much sense to Tony, but he had other things on his mind and didn't pursue it.

Considering the number of people and the amount and type of equipment that needed to be put ashore clandestinely, Tony needed to find two remote locations with suitable piers and access to roads. After looking at maps and comparing what he saw there to what he could see on Google Earth, he finally decided to send one boat to the Arawak Cement Plant offshore loading facility at Fryers Well Point about three quarters of the way up the west coast, and the other into the little harbor at the Bridgetown Fish Market. Both would allow the boats to tie up while being unloaded and both were close to roads or parking lots where friendly Bajans could be waiting with transportation.

The team disembarking at the fish market would be within blocks of the Voice of Barbados radio station and could set up quickly to deal with the coup elements coming out of St. Ann's Fort. The crew unloading at the cement factory would need to take the Charles Duncan O'Neal Highway down toward the Mount Pleasant Cemetery before hanging a right onto the Highway 2A until they hit the D'Arcy Scott Roundabout. Coming out of the roundabout on the Errol Barrow Highway, they'd continue southeast until the Errol Barrow Highway morphed into the Tom Adams Highway at the Errol Barrow Roundabout. Staying on the Tom Adams Highway until they were just north of the west end of the Grantley Adams International Airport, they would turn south and take side roads until they could set up in the same tree line where Cathy and Cheryl had launched the drone from. This tree line was only about 150 yards from the front gate of the base and was guaranteed to be where the Chinese armor would exit the base on its way to secure Government House, the seat of government for Barbados.

There had been a lot of discussion concerning how to deploy the SAC teams along with the loyal Barbados police personnel during the coup attempt, and there were two schools of thought: hit the bad guys as they left their bases at St. Ann's Fort and the Paragon Army Base, or wait for them to arrive at their destinations and deal with them at the radio station and Government House.

In the end, in an attempt to limit collateral damage, the final plan was a combination of both options. It was decided to hit the coup element coming from the army base in the open fields where the two roads on the base converged at the front gate. Since the northern side of the base was constrained by the runway for the international airport which ran east to west, and the southern perimeter of the base was the ocean, the Chinese armor and personnel carriers could only leave by either the front gate leading toward Bridgetown proper or the eastern or back gate which would lead the vehicles directly away from their objective, Government House. The front gate was a sure bet.

On the other hand, the contingent of the coup based at St. Ann's Fort would exit the fort directly onto Bay Street, a major throughfare running along the beaches of Carlisle Bay. They would remain on Bay Street for about a mile before they would get on the H7 proper before hanging a right onto Fairchild Street for the final run up to the Voice of Barbados radio station.

It was decided to hit the St. Ann's contingent just after they had made the turn onto Fairchild Street. The Barbados Transport Board buildings and parking lot in the Granville area were the only structures across Fairchild Street from the radio station, and they would be unoccupied at the time the coup was scheduled to kick-off. The backside of the Transport Board area was hemmed in by the Constitution River. Hitting the Chinese armor and personnel carriers while they drove directly into the opposition was deemed about as good as it was going to get in regards to limiting non-target damage.

When Cody brought up the topic of a quick reaction force or air support for the coup, Tony told him that this had been looked into back at Langley. The Barbados Air Wing, a component of the Barbados Defense Force, had been formed back in 1979 and it had consisted of one Beech Queen Air and a Cessna 402C. As of 1985, both of these aircraft had been retired, and the air wing no longer existed. There would be no air support for the coup or an airborne quick reaction force.

CHAPTER 22

IT WAS NOW THE 27TH of November, three days before the planned coup. The SOG group and their loyalist allies were as trained up as they were going to get and both the Scantily Clad and the Shag McNasty were fueled up, loaded up and moored in the submarine pen ready to go.

At lunch, the team went over the plan a final time before everyone went down to the sub pen to check over their individual gear before going up to the shop to catch the last bit of shut-eye they were likely to get for the next few days. Cody and Taeng went into the office for some quality time before the operation kicked off.

Taeng was lying on her back between Cody's legs with her head resting on his chest relaxing when she had an epiphany. "You realize that if things don't go as planned, this might be the last time we see each other."

"This is true," observed Cody.

Taeng then rotated around on her short axis until she was looking up at Cody from her position on his chest and suggested that this being the case, it might be a good idea for him to go lock the door so that they could make the most out of their remaining time together.

This seemed like a very wise idea to Cody, so he got up, locked the door and they got down to business.

About an hour later the disheveled lovebirds casually walked out of the office and nonchalantly cruised by the line of cots acting as if they hadn't spent their time in the office studying each other's body geography and getting to know one another on an entirely new level. They would have gotten away with it, but as they walked past the 3Cs, Chiara called Taeng over and nonchalantly suggested that she should probably put her t-shirt on correctly and zip up her shorts all the way if she really was trying to make an effort of convincing everyone that her and Cody hadn't just spent the past hour in the pursuit of happiness. Without missing a beat, Taeng informed her that this was the latest island style as she kept walking away while blushing profusely. Once she was safely hidden behind some machinery and out of sight, she took her t-shirt off and turned it inside out as well as rotating it back to front to wear it the way it was originally intended to be worn. She also pulled her zipper up the final two and a half inches to avoid further snide comments and baseless assumptions.

Since the coup was supposed to kick-off at 2:00 in the morning on the 30th, Tony and the powers that be wanted both of the assault teams on the island early the previous morning, but not so early that they ran the risk of detection while staying under cover at the safe houses. Working backwards, since the distance from Pala Island to both the cement factory and the fish market was almost exactly 115 miles and assuming both boats would run at 30 knots, the transit time would be approximately 3 hours and 20 minutes. This meant that both vessels would need to be clearing the breakwater at 10:40 in the evening of 28th to get the teams ashore on Barbados by 2:00am on the 29th.

The Scantily Clad, with the group assigned to the radio station component of the operation, would tie up at the pier on the eastern side of the small harbor at the fish market formed by the two breakwaters and unload its cargo of equipment and personnel directly onto the doglegged pier which was usually occupied by vessels belonging to MC Buccaneer Party Cruises. MC Buccaneer had been convinced to park their boats elsewhere that evening.

The pier was only about 70 yards long and led directly to a large parking lot where transportation would be waiting to take the people and their equipment to a safe house located in the Whitepark area of Bridgetown.

The Shag would be dropping off its load of people and equipment far away to the north and west at the seaward end of the cement loading pier just off Fryers Well Point, where the bulk dry cement was loaded onto pneumatic and mechanical cement carrying vessels. No ships were scheduled to be docked at the pier and a loyal Bajan who worked at the facility would ensure that the gate at the shore end of the pier was unlocked at midnight that evening. If everything went according to plan, an old Tata 6-wheeled, double axle cargo truck with raised sides and a canvas covering would be waiting to transport the team and its gear to their safe house in the Parish Land suburb just to the northwest of the international airport.

At 10:00 in the evening of 28th, everyone turned up on the dock of the submarine pen, where the Scantily Clad was moored behind the Shag. Since the gear had already been loaded aboard the boats earlier, the teams split up according to their assigned vessels: Taeng, Tony, Carlos, Booker, Emmett, and five of the loyalists, including the woman, loaded up on the Scantily Clad with Tanawat at the helm to be dropped off at the fish market, while Autry, Dontrell, Garlan, Justus, Isaac and the remaining loyalists boarded the Shag.

According to the original plan, the 3Cs, having already completed their mission, would just hang around the island and relax until the overall mission was completed, but Tony had an 'if some was good, more was better' moment and decided to put Chiara on Tanawat's boat and Cheryl and Cathy on Cody's. The girls could handle the comms during the mission and jump in to support the direct-action component if required. All three had passed selection into the SAC/SOG program and would be an asset if things didn't go as planned.

Around 10:15, everyone shook hands or bumped fists and wished each other success before they boarded their respective vessels and the boats reversed back into the sub pen before heading out into the harbor and from there to the smooth water behind the breakwater and then out to sea.

The sea was running at about a 3 on the Beaufort scale, with winds at about 7-10 knots and wave heights between 2-3.5 feet, so the run up to Barbados at 30 knots for both boats was a walk in the park although a few of the passengers got a little seasick.

Cody pulled the Shag alongside the cement loading pier just before 2:00 in the morning to find an old Tata 712 LPT truck which had seen better days waiting for them. The team and all their kit were off the Shag and onto the truck in 5 minutes, which is when the Shag pulled away from the pier and the truck drove off to begin its journey to the south to the Parish Land safehouse in Bridgetown.

Miles to the south, and almost simultaneously, the Scantily Clad pulled up to the pier near the Bridgetown Fish Market and unloaded her cargo of arms and personnel as well. They were met in the parking lot by a 10-year-old Isuzu NPR box truck, which they managed to load up and get on its way to the Whitepark safehouse in just under 10 minutes.

Now the waiting began.

CHAPTER 23

THE CHINAMAN WHO HAD ORIGINALLY approached Wilfred Duguid, the Minister of Energy and Business, and the mastermind behind the coup in Barbados, was a senior agent in the Ministry of State Security named Xu Chunwang of the Second Bureau: Foreign Affairs.

As is usual for Chinese foreign intervention operations, it was imperative that no operatives, especially those associated with the Ministry of State Security, could be seen as being involved, much less instrumental, in an operation to subvert a foreign government. For this reason, in the days running up to the coup, Agent Xu and his cadre of Peoples Liberation Army officers who had trained the Special Operations Company of the Barbados Regiment on the Chinese weapons and tactics, as well as the group of MSS agents instrumental in securing the support of members of the Bajan government, had holed up in the Chinese Embassy on Gulf View Terrace along with the embassy staff.

Chunwang remained in communication with the elements at both St. Ann's Fort and the Paragon Army Base, but it was simply hands-off final tuning of the operation as both elements appeared to be ready, willing and able to execute the coup.

While at the safe house, Tony called Ian Gooding, the loyal Deputy Commissioner of Police, and had him start moving his people from all three divisions: the Northern Division, the Bridgetown Division and the Southern division into their assigned areas near the Voice of Barbados radio station and Government House. The Royal Barbados Police Service did not possess any heavy weapons, but they were armed with M16 and M4 automatic rifles, which would be more than adequate for the cleanup operations once the Chinese light armored vehicles were destroyed and the element of surprise was lost. Around midnight the police would begin infiltrating the areas surrounding the radio station and the neighborhoods bordering Government House and its grounds.

Tony did not foresee any of the opposition troops making it to Government House from the army base, but he still warned Ian to keep his people there on their toes just in case some of the disloyal soldiers from the base happened to squirt past the ambush at the army base and decide to carry on with their mission. The area around the radio station was another story, any of the coup members that survived the initial ambush would attempt to melt into the urban environment surrounding the radio station and would need to be rooted out.

Tony's next job was to get his people and their weapons into position around midnight, which is where Neville and his people again came into play. At 11:00 in the evening on the 29th, an AGS International moving van arrived outside the safe house on Gills Road in Whitepark. The van was quickly loaded with three Javelin Command Launch Units (CLU's) with four rounds apiece for each launcher, three 240B machine guns with 500 rounds apiece in five 100 round belts, four M4 carbines with eight loaded magazines for each, and 25 M67 fragmentation grenades. To operate all this weaponry, Taeng, Tony, Carlos, Booker, Emmett, and five of the loyalists, including the woman, climbed in as well.

At midnight, another van, from another moving company arrived at the safe house in the Parish Land suburb of Bridgetown. It was immediately loaded with the exact same weapons loadout, but it was Autry, Dontrell, Garlan, Justus, Isaac and the remaining loyalists who piled into the back of this truck.

The moving vans made their way to their respective drop-off points near the radio station and the army base, dropped off their cargos, then disappeared into Bridgetown proper.

The SOG crew at the army base set up their three Javelin missile systems on the high ground just outside the perimeter fence, inside a group of tamarind trees located off the perimeter road about 200 yards from where the perimeter road and the main entrance road met at the front gate. Since the range for the lightweight CPU (Command Launch Unit) is 2.5 miles, they could cover the entire base from the tree line. The minimum effective range for the Javelin is roughly 150 meters or 164 yards. At 200 yards, the missiles would have time to arm before impact.

Garlan, Justus and Isaac were the designated Javelin shooters with a loyalist loader assigned to each of them. Javelin rounds, complete with the sealed Launch Tube Assembly are just over 47.5" in length and weigh in at around 35 pounds. To reload the CPU, the 'loader' simply unlatches the used Launch Tube Assembly from the CPU and latches another in its place. It is an easy system to reload, but it is even quicker when you have a 'loader'. In this case, the trained loyalists.

Each Javelin team was paired with a 240B gunner, in this case Autry, Dontrell and a loyalist. The idea being that once a vehicle was hit by a Javelin, the gunners would target anyone who happened to make it out of the vehicle alive. The remaining loyalists would be armed with M4 carbines and grenades to provide rear security for the missiles and guns. The extra M4's and any spare grenades would be spread out through the missile teams as they exited the area after policing up all of their equipment, especially the empty Launch Tube Assemblies, essentially any equipment which might indicate an American presence if were to be left behind.

The SOG team at the radio station had a much more complex environment in which to set up their ambush. From the intersection of Fairchild Street and the H7, the Chinese armor and transport would need to travel about 160 yards in a straight line on Fairchild Street before angling off to the left as it passed in front of the radio station. Carlos, Booker and Emmett were the designated

Javelin shooters in this crew, again with three of the loyalists acting as loaders.

The problem, as mentioned earlier, is that the Javelins needed to travel 150 meters or 164 yards to arm, which means that the shooters had to be around 200 yards away to give the missiles time to acquire their targets and for their operators to pull the trigger. The only suitable location to place the Javelins was on the south side of Fairchild Street as it angled off to the left, but there wasn't much cover on that side of the street. With no other option available, Tony placed himself and his missile teams on the roof of the radio station itself. Although he hated to concentrate his forces, he simply had no choice if he was going to target the Chinese light armor and troop carriers as they turned off the H7 and drove towards the radio station on Fairchild Street.

The 240 gunners would be hidden behind the corner of buildings where Jossamy Lane and Nelson Street intersected Fairchild Street with the last one being set up at the ASAP Taxi stand directly across the street from the 240 where Nelson Street intersected Fairchild.

Taeng would be inside the studio, inside the radio station, waiting to broadcast the news regarding the failed coup.

The stage was set.

CHAPTER 24

THE COURTYARD AT THE PARAGON Army Base began to come alive at around 1:00 in the morning on Independence Day. The courtyard was actually a large parking lot bordered by the administration building and office spaces toward the east, and various maintenance and support buildings to the south and west. It was open to the north where it connected to the road leading to the entry gate of the base.

At precisely 1:30am, the five CSK-131 armored reconnaissance vehicles: four armed with 12.7mm heavy machine guns and 35mm automatic grenade launchers, and one with the four pack of TL-4 fire-and-forget anti-tank missiles, fired up their diesel engines and the crews ran through the digital diagnostics for their weapons systems.

At the same time the light armored vehicles were warming up, the officers were marshalling their troops aboard the six Dongfeng EQ2082 six-wheel drive troop carriers, ten fully armed and traitorous troops of the Special Operations Company of the Barbados Regiment to each carrier.

Once everyone was present and accounted for, the armored reconnaissance vehicles led the troop carriers out of the courtyard and onto the road fronting the courtyard to the north, which led to the main road out of the base complex to the west. Driving north towards the airport, they intersected the road leading to the front gate and began what they thought would be, the half hour drive to Government House. They were in for an unpleasant surprise.

The convoy had made it approximately halfway to the front gate and were roughly 300 yards from where Garlan, Justus and Isaac were hidden in the tree line, when the first salvo of three Javelin missiles, in Top Attack Mode, the default mode, rose to their programmed height of 160 meters, or roughly 525 feet, before they slammed down into the top of the three armored reconnaissance vehicles at the head of the convoy.

The FGM-148 Javelin missile system utilizes a tandem HEAT, high-explosive anti-tank, warhead, designed to defeat AKA, Any Known Armor. When the Javelins hit the lightly armored CSK-131 armored reconnaissance vehicles, they simply punched through the roof of each vehicle before explosively rearranging their components in a roughly circular presentation centered on a ball of fire and a pillar of sooty smoke. The 'shock and awe' of seeing their game changing Chinese reconnaissance vehicles suddenly disintegrate in a ball of fire for no apparent reason caused the remainder of the convoy to stop dead in their tracks, which gave the SOG 240B gunners six soft-skinned Dongfeng EQ2082 six-wheel drive troop carriers as stationary targets, which they raked mercilessly, setting all of them on fire and killing most of the personnel within them.

While the troop carriers were being riddled, the Javelins were reloaded and the remaining two reconnaissance vehicles, now caught between their explosively modified brethren to their front and the shot-up troop carriers to their rear, became easy targets for the second salvo of missiles. The last two remaining recon vehicles also exploded in fine fashion and were burning nicely. The remaining six Javelin rounds were fired at the troop carriers simply to ensure their destruction, to add to the 'shock & awe 'effect, and to get rid of them so that the team didn't have to carry them while they exfiltrated the area.

Any of the troops of the Special Operations Company of the Barbados Regiment that managed to survive the ambush simply stumbled like zombies back in the direction of the courtyard that they had left from earlier. They'd had enough of this coup silliness for one night.

While the Chinese vehicles were still burning bright, the SOG crew packed up their weapons and the used launch tubes for the Javelins before making their way about 300 yards due west to the Lion's Palace Bar & Grill, the joint that Cheryl and Cathy had originally began their recon mission at, where the same moving van that had dropped them off prior to the ambush waited across the street from the bar to take them back to their safe house in Parish Land. They would wait to hear how the other team had fared and how they were supposed to get off the island.

CHAPTER 25

THE OTHER TEAM AT THE radio station didn't fare as well simply due to the more complex urban environment battlespace. As mentioned earlier, Tony's choices to position his team were severely 'terrain limited', unlike the open fields that the other team had to work with.

Just after 1:30am, the five CSK-131 armored reconnaissance vehicles and six Dongfeng EQ2082 six-wheel drive troop carriers, along with their complement of the misguided members of the Special Operations Company of the Barbados Regiment tasked with taking control of the radio station, pulled out of St. Ann's Fort onto the H7 and began their journey north.

Everything was going fine, and they were in good spirits and ready to rock and roll as they turned right onto Fairchild Street, which was empty at this time of the morning, for the run-up to the Voice of Barbados building. The entire convoy of 11 vehicles bunched up as they made the turn from the H7 onto Fairchild Street. Once again, the heavily armed recon vehicles led the troop carriers. The problem for Tony and his crews was that the vehicle in front effectively shielded the vehicle immediately behind it as they drove towards the radio station. In an attempt to cause confusion and break up the formation, Tony told his Javelin crews to get ready and for Emmett to take out the lead CSK-131.

Once Emmett pulled the trigger and his missile soared up before slamming down on the target, things happened fast. The lead recon vehicle disappeared in a violent explosion. The second CSK-131 drove right through the explosion and Carlos took it out seconds later. The third recon vehicle attempted to drive around the remains of the two burning vehicles and became the third victim as Booker's missile slammed into it.

While the missiles were finding their marks, just as had happened at the army base, the troop carriers locked up their brakes and came to a halt trying to figure out what was going on ahead of them. This gave the 240B machine gun positioned at the corner with Jossamy Lane essentially point-blank targets to rake, which it did.

The problem was that the remaining two 240B guns positioned across Fairchild Street, where Nelson Street intersected it, didn't have an angle on the troop carriers and the remaining two heavily armed recon vehicles were now sliding past their burning teammates to the right, or the south side of the street.

Emmett was the first to reload his Javelin on the roof of the radio station and set his CLU to Direct Attack Mode, where the missile would fly directly to the target as opposed to looping up above it, and nailed the second of the remaining recon vehicles as it cleared the flaming wreckage. By this time the last remaining recon unit was approaching the target and began lighting up the entrance of the Voice of Barbados building with its 12.7mm heavy machine gun and 35mm automatic grenade launcher. Due to the angle from the roof of the radio station to the street below, and due to the fact that the missiles would not be able to arm at this distance, there was not a damn thing Tony and his crew could do about it.

The missileers still had eight missiles left, so they quicky targeted the shot-up troop carriers and turned them into scrap. While they were busy with that, Tony grabbed the three Bajan loaders from the missile crews, made sure that they were tooled up with M4 carbines and grenades, and ran back to the hatch they had climbed through to get to the roof of the station and dropped back into the Voice of Barbados building to deal with the recon vehicle and its crew who had survived the ambush and were now somewhere in the building after ramming the front doors off their hinges.

While the ambush teams had been setting up, Taeng and the only female loyalist in the crew, a fit, young, Bajan girl in her mid-20's named Lindsay, had made their way to the broadcasting booth on the second floor toward the rear of the building. After Taeng let the Voice of Barbados management know what was about to happen, several of whom knew and trusted her from her Caribbean News Agency days and vouched for her, she started getting set up to make her broadcast concerning the coup. She had just started her broadcast when the first Javelins found their targets outside.

Taeng's broadcast was straight and to the point. The Chinese had corrupted several members of the Parliament, both in the Senate and the House of Assembly, in an attempt to get Barbados to sign onto the Belt and Road Initiative, which was just a nice term for debt-trap diplomacy resulting in neocolonialism and economic imperialism. Due to resistance in Parliament to the Chinese initiative, the Chinese, with the help of some disaffected members of the Special Operations Company of the Barbados Regiment, had just launched armed attacks against both Government House and the Voice of Barbados radio station. A military coup was in progress.

She then advised that all loyal Bajans should shelter in place while the coup was being repulsed by the Royal Barbados Police Service. She then listed, by title and by name, the members of Parliament who had taken the Chinese coin: specifically, the Deputy Prime Minister who is also the Minister of Foreign Affairs and Foreign Trade, the Minister of Lands and Maintenance, the Minister of Environment and National Beautification which oversees the Green and Blue Economy and the Minister of Economic Affairs and Investment.

She then identified, by name and rank, the man who had corrupted members of the Special Operations Company to take up arms against the government, Warrant Officer First Class Gabriel Collins, ensuring he'd be stacking some hard time in His Majesty's Prison Dodds in the near future if he was apprehended.

Before signing off, Taeng said that the populace should stay tuned for hourly updates from the VoB.

CHAPTER 26

A CSK-131 ARMORED RECONNAISSANCE VEHICLE is usually manned by a crew of six: the driver, the vehicle commander, the remote heavy weapons operator and three infantrymen. The 'one that got away', the vehicle not destroyed by the Javelins, had fired multiple rounds from its 35mm automatic grenade launcher at the front door of the radio station before it rammed through them and ended up wedged in the elevator lobby behind and off to the side of the reception desk.

All six of the rogue Special Operations Company operators managed to climb out of their damaged vehicle and launched themselves through the emergency doors at the end of the small elevator lobby which led to the stairs at exactly the same time that Tony and his crew were coming down the ladder from the roof.

Tony had both heard and felt the recon vehicle smash into the building and had halted his group at the landing of third floor. When they heard the stairwell door open on the ground floor, they just simply tossed four of their M67 fragmentation grenades over the handrail and waited for the result. Just before the explosions, Tony heard a pair of combat boots pounding up the stairs, one of the Special Ops Company boys had made it to the second floor and into the broadcasting area just as his buddies were shredded by shrapnel down in the stairwell.

While Taeng was busy with her broadcast, Lindsay had been guarding the door into the studio with her M4 carbine. She just had just started to bring her gun to bear on the studio door when the surviving recon vehicle member slammed through the door and into her, knocking the weapon out of her hands and driving her to the floor. In her defense, Lindsay was only about 5'7" tall and weighed 110 pounds soaking wet. Her opponent was over 6' tall and weighed over 200 pounds.

The intruder had been instructed not to damage the broadcasting equipment as the coup leaders wanted it for exactly the same reason that Taeng did, to broadcast information concerning the coup, but these instructions did not prohibit damaging those in the broadcasting studio. As the man brought his weapon to bear on Taeng, Lindsay launched herself off the floor and straight into the man.

What the rest of the team hadn't known about Lindsay was that she was a UFC MMA straw-weight contender with a 16-3-1 record. Her last fight had been four months earlier in Miami when she had defeated the 7th ranked fighter in her division by TKO in the second round. Since then, she'd been training while teaching third grade at The Saint Michael School in Bridgetown. When Ian Gooding had approached her and asked if she wanted to take part in breaking up a coup, she had jumped at the chance.

Within seconds, Lindsay had disarmed the man, punched him in the throat, kicked him hard in the nuts and then, to everyone in the studio's amazement, she climbed right over the top of the guy like a monkey, reversed herself and ended up on his back with him in a rear naked choke. In seconds, he'd passed out. Taeng and Lindsay decided that this would be good time to make their exit. Just as they got to the battered door of the studio, Tony and his boys showed up. After Taeng had described what had happened, Tony gave an appraising look at Lindsay before he zip tied the man's wrists and elbows behind him as well as his ankles. He was well and truly trussed up as Tony, his missileers, Lindsay and Taeng made it back out onto the roof to pick up the 10 used disposable Launch Tube Assemblies and the two unused rounds as well as anything else that would indicate outside assistance before they all made it back down to the ruined front door of the radio station on Fairchild Street where an old American deuce and a half army truck, which had already collected the gun teams, appeared to take them back to the safe house in Whitepark while the Royal Barbados Police Service mopped up the surviving coup members.

It would take the police and the military weeks to finish rounding up all the conspirators and to calm things down on the island, but that was a job for the Bajans and they didn't need or want any more outside help. It was time for the SOG teams and their accomplices to slide into the shadows and make their withdrawal.

CHAPTER 27

AFTER CODY AND TANAWAT HAD dropped off their respective teams, they'd decided to meet up at the Driftwood, just west of the Blue Lagoon on St. Vincent to try and relax until they were called back to pick up their people.

The idea was that the loyal Bajans who participated in the kinetic operation to derail the coup, including Taeng, would simply disappear back into the fabric of Barbados, while the 12 SOG people would be transported back to Cody's Island for a debrief and eventual repatriation back to the States.

At around 4:00 in the evening on Independence Day, the day of the failed coup, Cody got the call to come fetch the crews. He and Tanawat were supposed to meet them at the Victorian Pier at the Radisson Aquatica Resort on Carlisle Bay. Since the weather was good, it was only about a two-and-a-half-hour run, so the Shag and the Scantily Clad slipped their moorings at the Driftwood and made their way back to Barbados.

Pulling up to the pier at the Radisson resort, the crews had started making their way back to whichever boat that they had arrived on, when Cody received another a call on the marine radio from Ian Gooding telling him that his policemen who had been watching the Chinese Embassy on Golf View Terrace had reported that a couple of Ford Transit vans had shown up and that approximately 15 people, including Ms. Qu Ching, the Economic and

Commercial Counsellor of the Chinese Embassy, and possibly the Ministry of State Security agent named Xu Chunwang plus a few other Chinese without portfolio, that is the other Ministry of State Security operators, had climbed in and were now making their way along the coast. If Ian had to guess, he'd say that they were heading toward the little pier by the Saint Lawrence Anglican Church to make their getaway. Apparently, a blacked-out Viking 65 sportfishing yacht had just tied up there for no apparent reason.

Both Tanawat and Cody were familiar with the blacked-out yacht from their run up to Barrouallie on St. Vincent, when Taeng met up with Lacy, A'lynn and her other conspirators. Ian asked if either Cody or Tanawat were in a position to intercept them.

Looking at his GPS, Cody saw that it was only about three and a half miles from where he was at the Radisson to the Anglican church pier. If he left now, depending on how much of a head start the Viking had and where the Chinese planned to go, he could make it, but he'd need to leave immediately.

As quickly as possible, Cody had most of the operators assigned to his boat and their personal equipment transferred to Tanawat's boat. He kept Tony, Booker and Emmett onboard as well as two Javelin Command Launch Units and the two remaining Javelin rounds. He also kept one of the 240B machine guns with 500 belted rounds. Cody asked Tanawat to take everyone back to his island and relax. He and the rest of the crew should be back later in the evening if all went well. With that, he reversed away from the pier and came up on plane to see if he could catch the Viking.

CHAPTER 28

A VIKING 65 SPORTFISHING YACHT has a listed top speed of 42 knots, but this is while running empty and not crammed with 15 Chinese MSS personnel, whatever they had taken from the embassy, plus the captain. Assuming each Chinese national weighed only 120 pounds, Cody figured this was an additional 2,000 pounds or so to haul around. Cody was guessing that even with the optional 2,000 horsepower engine package, the boat would be hard pressed to hit 40 knots.

On the other hand, the Shag, with the two Napier-Deltic turbocharged diesels cranking out about 6,200 horses, and with the guns and torpedoes removed, could get up to 50 knots fairly easily. Doing the math in his head, Cody figured that once he located the Viking, he could close on it at about 10 knots or 11.5 miles every hour, the first thing he had to do was find it.

Cody had installed a Raymarine Cyclone Radar on top of the wheelhouse back when he'd refurbished the old gunboat. This was a 55-watt open array with CHIRP Pulse Compression running a 4' antenna array, which let him see out to about 72 nautical miles. The problem in the Caribbean was that there were literally hundreds of boats, of all sizes, at any given time, running between the islands.

Patience is supposed to be a virtue, so when Cody pulled the Shag up to the now empty pier by the Anglican church, he decided to just watch the targets on his radar and see where everyone was going. Assuming that the Viking had a 15-minute head start at 40 knots, or 46 miles per hour, it would be out about 12 miles, but in what direction?

The word would have already gone out to all the islands in the Grenadines concerning a Chinese sponsored coup attempt on Barbados, so the rational choice for the Chinese would have been to head roughly south by southwest and hope that their socialist brothers and sisters in Venezuela would take them in after botching the coup.

The radar showed several ships and boats heading roughly in that direction, but none were making a beeline for Venezuela at around 40 knots, which is what Cody and Tony would have expected them to do. Oddly enough, one target on the radar had just rounded the southernmost tip of Barbados and was now running at 40 knots due east, out into the open ocean.

After discussing the options and with no other fast-moving targets on the radar, Tony and Cody surmised that the Viking was taking the Chinese out into the shipping lanes to rendezvous with a Chinese flagged vessel. Cody backed the Shag away from the pier and throttled up to give chase, rounding the bottom of Barbados at 40 knots, the radar told Cody that he was now 15 miles behind the Viking. Doing the math again, he figured that they should come up on the Viking in about an hour and 20 minutes if the Chinese stayed on their present course at their present speed, which would put them about 75 miles out to sea, in the middle of nowhere and nowhere close to an established shipping lane.

With no idea of what weapons were aboard the Viking, while Cody drove the boat, Tony took the 240B gun out on the front deck of the Nasty boat where he loaded a 100-round belt in it and secured it to an old recessed tie-down ring that must have had a purpose when the M2 .50 caliber heavy machine gun was originally mounted there.

While Tony was busy doing this, Booker and Emmett attached the two remaining Javelin Launch Tube Assemblies to the reusable Command Launch Units. Better to have them ready and not need them, than to need them and not have them ready. It was now just a matter of catching the Viking, which according to the radar, was still heading out into an empty ocean.

An hour into the chase, the Shag was closing on the Viking and was now only about 3.5 miles behind it. The moon was in its waning crescent phase, but the skies were clear and before long they could make out the phosphorescent wake kicked up by the props of the Viking and simply followed the photoluminescence to its source. The curious thing is that there were no ships of any type within 50 miles of the yacht according to the radar, which gave both Cody and Tony some concern, but they were coming into small arms range of the yacht now and had other things to worry about. Tony went out on the foredeck, readied the 240B for action and got down in the prone position to see what sort of welcome they would receive.

The Viking also had radar and had known for a while that they were being chased. Two of the MSS operators onboard had the presence of mind to bring along their QBZ-95 bullpup assault rifles, so Ms. Qu Ching, being the ranking Chinese person onboard, instructed them to 'prepare to repel boarders', or whatever the equivalent phrase was in Mandarin.

Only Ms. Qu knew who and what they were supposed to rendezvous with and although they were close to the GPS coordinates she'd been given, they needed a few more minutes. But as Americans are fond of saying, close is only good when playing horseshoes or tossing hand grenades. Ms. Qu told the MSS operators to open fire on their pursuers once they were within range.

When the range between the boats narrowed to about 500 yards, the MSS operators both began firing at the Shag. This was a mistake on a variety of levels: First, the QBZ-95 is a light weapon shooting a 5.8x42mm intermediate cartridge, which is fine for perforating human beings, but not worth crap when trying to take out an 80' long, 80-ton aluminum hulled torpedo boat. Second, it pissed off Tony, who was manning a belt-fed medium machine gun firing the much more powerful 7.62x51mm round. As soon as the two MSS clowns started firing their weapons, Tony unleashed a hail of his heavier rounds straight through them. These rounds carried on into the salon under the bridge and flying bridge, through the sleeping area under the foredeck and out the fiberglass bow, killing another 5 Chinese nationals in the process. Tony fired the remainder of the belt through the transom and into the engine compartment, bringing the boat to a halt.

It was at this point that Tony, Emmett and Booker heard Cody exclaim, "That can't be good," and turned to look at whatever he was looking at, which was about a mile ahead of where they had pulled alongside the Viking.

The sight which had caused Cody alarm was a black shape rising out of the water. It took Tony a minute to recognize it as a Chinese Type-039C Song Class Submarine. This was the reason that there were no other vessels in the area, the Chinese who had organized the coup were being picked up by one of their submarines. They'd scuttle the Viking and simply disappear.

Cody was contemplating the fact that he'd possibly taken his final voyage aboard his beloved Shag McNasty when he heard Tony shout at Emmett and Booker to grab their Javelins and to get up front on the bow and fire them at the submarine. As Tony came up on the bridge to watch the show, Cody asked him if he was mad.

"Look, Cody. A modern submarine has no deck guns and is optimized to fire missiles and torpedoes at capital ships, not ancient patrol boats. We can't sink her, but we can ring her bell. Think about it, how many of your Special Boat Team boys can say they successfully attacked a Chinese sub and lived to tell about it?"

"It's the 'lived to tell about it' part that has me worried," replied Cody.

At about this point in time both Emmett and Booker let fly with their Javelins. One missile dove into the conning tower while the other impacted just forward of it. Although the strikes were impressive, they didn't really seem to have any effect on the submarine except to cause it to quickly dive back under the surface.

Cody didn't want to hang around, in his mind a Chinese submarine that just got swatted by two anti-tank missiles would likely want to send a torpedo up his butt. Turning to Tony, he asked, "What do you want to do about the Viking and the survivors?"

"What survivors?" responded Tony as he, Booker and Emmett pulled their SIG P226's out of the holsters they had strapped to their thighs and stepped over onto the Viking.

A few minutes later they stepped back on board with a somewhat disoriented Ms. Qu Ching. She was bleeding from a head wound where one of Tony's original 240B machine gun rounds had ricocheted off the coffee machine in the lounge before it bounced off the side of her head. Although she was bleeding like a stuck pig, all head wounds do, it wasn't serious, but it had knocked her for a loop. They'd cable tied her wrists behind her on the Viking, and once she was on the Shag, they cable tied her ankles as well before they unceremoniously dumped her on the deck behind the wheelhouse like a sack of potatoes.

"What about Xu Chunwang, the MSS guru?" queried Cody.

"He's not onboard. Probably making his way off the island another way," replied Tony.

"What about the Viking? Are we going to tow it back?" queried Cody.

"Nope," said Tony. "These fruit bats wanted to play hardball, so we will as well. There were seven including the captain still alive over there and I decided to leave them that way, I must be getting soft in my old age. Anyway, the captain knows where the life rafts and survival kits are located, so they'll have a chance. I did take the liberty of smashing his radios and broke the antennas off all the EPIRB's I could find. They may or may not make it, I don't really care.

"But just to make things interesting, since we know there is a submarine around here that is interested in them, I need to go back over there for a minute."

Before going back on the Viking, Tony asked Emmett and Booker for their M67 fragmentation grenades. He then hopped back over to the other boat, climbed down into the engine room, pulled the pins on both grenades and tossed them in before running back up on deck and jumping across to the Shag.

The resulting explosion in the engine room blew out the transom below the waterline and the boat began to sink by the stern. At about the same time, the submarine began to surface again about half a mile away, which was just the cue that Cody needed to throttle up and get the heck out of Dodge. He began zigzagging as he pulled away from the now foundering Viking and the submarine approaching it.

"What the heck are you doing?" Tony asked Cody as he zigzagged.

"I'm making myself a harder target for torpedoes! Everybody knows you zigzag so they can't get a bead on you."

Tony just shook his head. "Moron, that worked back in World War 2, but even the Chinese are using homing torpedoes these days."

"Oh, hadn't thought of that. Torpedoes weren't really a big issue while I was running rivers back in the day," said Cody as he took a more direct path home.

On the way back, Emmett, Booker, Tony and Cody lounged around on the bridge and tried to figure out why the sub had resurfaced. The captain had to know that they had stopped the Viking, and he had to assume that the Shag was in radio contact with the authorities, so his only logical option would have been to cut and run.

Tony thought about it before asking everyone where they thought the second missile had impacted forward of the sail, or conning tower. Everyone was adamant that it had hit several yards in front of the sail.

"From what I could see through the binoculars, that was a Chinese Type-039C Song Class submarine which was the first diesel-electric boat to be made in China. Thirteen were built between 1999 and 2006. This was one of the early ones since the conning tower did not have the step design where the conning tower 'steps' higher toward the stern.

"If I remember correctly, the Type-C has two escape hatches: one about midway between the conning tower and the stern and take a guess where the other one is located?"

Cody grinned at Booker and Emmett before he made his guess, "Just a few yards in front of the conning tower?"

"Correct," said Tony. "If I had to make a guess, I'd say that the Javelin that hit in front of the conning tower miraculously made a direct hit on the escape hatch, and due to the nature of the Javelin warhead being a tandem high-explosive anti-tank round, where the first charge is meant to defeat the reactive armor on tanks and the second one does the actual damage, I'm betting that the first of the tandem charges blew through the cover of the escape hatch and when the second one detonated inside the escape trunk, keep in mind that a Javelin can penetrate 48" of rolled homogenous armor equivalent, it likely damaged the integrity of the lower hatch located in the forward torpedo room.

"These escape hatches penetrate the pressure hull so that the sailors can escape in an emergency and are the only two penetrations we could have possibly hit with the Javelin in Top Attack Mode.

"We might not have killed it, but I'd be willing to bet they can't submerge now without flooding the forward torpedo room. A good night's work all the way around and likely the only successful attack on a submarine by a PT boat since the Second World War."

"What is the top speed of a surfaced Chinese Type-039 Song Class submarine?" Cody asked Tony.

"No worries, she's only rated at 15 knots surfaced, so you should be easily able to outrun her in this crate."

"What about torpedoes or cruise missiles?"

"Well, I'm guessing that their forward torpedo room flooded through the escape hatch when they submerged after being hit, and who knows what damage the Javelin strike to the conning tower did. I think they have enough on their plate to keep them busy at the moment. Also, they'll need to rescue any survivors from the Viking, so I think we'll be okay if you'll stop asking questions and kick this thing in the ass."

CHAPTER 29

THE SHAG PULLED UP AGAINST the dock in the sub pen just after the sun had cleared the horizon that morning and tied up behind the Scantily Clad, which had been tied up in the Shag's dedicated position just behind the fuel barge. Once Booker and Emmett had secured the bow and stern lines around the old bollards on the dock, Cody shut everything down on the boat while Tony grabbed the now useless Command Launch Units and carried them onto the dock before going back onboard to collect the 240B gun. Cody collected Ms. Qu Ching from where they had dumped her on the deck behind the bridge like a bag of trash prior to attacking the submarine, cut the zip ties off her wrists and ankles and marched her off his boat.

Tony, Booker and Emmett had placed all their equipment on the old hand cart and rolled it around the front of the sub pen to the utility elevator, while Cody frog-marched Ms. Qu to the elevator. Once they were all inside with the equipment, they took it up to the shop floor. When the door opened, they were confronted by a wall of sound and the nine SOG operatives, the 3C's, and Tanawat partying and feeling no pain as they had obviously raided Cody's beer supply up at the house and had moved his compact hi-fi system complete with his Technic SL-1500C turntable and vinyl collection from his office out into the shop and set them up on one of the workbenches. At the moment AC/DC's 'You Shook Me All Night Long' was playing at an earsplitting decibel level as Tanawat approached them with a six-pack of Carib. After locking Ms. Qu in a utility closet in the office for safekeeping, the new arrivals, in the spirit of teambuilding, joined in.

Around noon everyone decided that it would be a good idea to get some sleep after their recent adventures and the follow-up festivities. Later that afternoon, everyone gathered up at the house where Cody and Tanawat prepared shrimp tacos by the dozens to feed the crew. Cody had driven Qu Ching up to the house and cut her loose in Taeng's room so that she could use the bathroom, clean up and get some circulation going. He also brought her a plate of tacos and a beer before he wedged the door shut from the outside to keep her from causing any trouble.

After the late lunch, the SOG crew sat in the living room drinking even more beer and listened to Tanawat's lies while Cody and Tony went to the comms hut in the back to get in touch with Mike in Puerto Rico to see what the fallout from Tony's after-action report would be. He had used the comms in the shop office to send the report before he'd joined the party in the shop. Sinking the Viking, kidnapping Ms. Qu, and attacking a Chinese submarine with anti-tank rockets had not been in the original plan and would likely rattle some cages.

Mike wanted to know a few more specifics concerning who had been left alive on the sportfishing yacht and the condition of the submarine when they left the scene. He also was concerned about Ms. Qu's state of health. After Tony answered as best he could, he really didn't know the identities of the living or the dead on the yacht and he really didn't get a good look at the sub in the dark after it resurfaced, Mike went ballistic.

"What in the heck were you guys thinking?"

"Hey, dickhead." Tony was getting annoyed. "We were tasked by Ian, who by the way is still the Deputy Commissioner of Police, to go after the Chinese who'd left the scene of the crime on that Viking."

"True, but you were not told to shoot up the boat and sink them. To the best of my knowledge, you were never authorized to attack a Chinese submarine!"

"You weren't there, and we didn't have time to call you up to ask how you wanted to play it. The Chinese opened fire first, I might add. Regarding the submarine, we didn't know if they had the ability to go on the offensive against us, and besides, it was a golden opportunity to see what a Javelin could do to a sub. Tell me you wouldn't have taken the shot yourself?"

Mike thought about this for a second. "Okay, I have admonished you for your decidedly imprudent decisions as per the powers that be in Langley, and you are correct, given the opportunity to fire a Javelin at a Chinese sub, I'd have done it.

"But this has opened a can of worms. A bunch of Chinese nationals have been killed, the mastermind of the coup, Xu Chunwang, was not among those on the boat and is likely in the wind, you have kidnapped the Economic and Commercial Counsellor of the Chinese Embassy to Barbados, you have committed an act of war against a Chinese warship in international waters and damaged it to the point where it now has to travel on the surface to Augustin Armario Naval Base at Puerto Cabello in Venezuela for repairs.

"These Type-039 Song Class submarines have high resolution cameras built into their periscope masts that are night vision capable, so there is a very good chance that the Chinese now know exactly what boat sunk the Viking and attacked their submarine. There is also a better than even chance that since there was a planned coup on Barbados, that they had a satellite overhead tasked to watch the show. When things didn't go as planned and they found out some cowboys smacked their sub with anti-tank missiles, they in all likelihood re-tasked the satellite and tracked you back to Pala."

Cody looked over at Tony and commented, "That is not good."

Mike heard the comment and continued, "No, not good at all. Since Pala Island is technically an island owned by a private individual, who also just happens to own the old Nasty boat that kidnapped their Economic and Commercial Counsellor to Barbados, regardless of the fact that she was instrumental in planning the failed coup, it is within the realm of possibility that they are very pissed off and will be planning an attack on the island as we speak, if for no other reason than to save face. Never underestimate the Chinese concept of saving face."

"Okay, so what's the plan?" asked Tony.

"Well, there is a CH-53K King Stallion helicopter from the USS Tripoli that will be heading your way shortly. The Tripoli just happened to have transited the Panama Canal a few days ago and was on her way to fly the flag in Puerto Rico. We asked her if she could send a chopper to Pala to pick up some of our wayward children.

"I would suggest that you destroy all the comms or sensitive equipment on the island before you and the rest of the SOG crew get on the chopper. Don't forget Ms. Qu, we'd like to have a word with her. The Chinese will be there sooner rather than later."

"What about me?" asked Cody.

"Well, you and Taeng will have to die. If you don't, the Chinese will be after you until they can confirm that you are. To be a convincing death, we'll need your boat. I'd suggest you climb into your old Jap seaplane and get yourself up here as soon as possible and we'll discuss it then. Give me a call from the air when you get close to Catano Park Pier, where you and Taeng parked before, and my guys will collect you there."

"What about Taeng? She was the voice on the radio, the Chinese are bound to be interested in her as well," asked Cody.

"The Puerto Rican Air National Guard kindly lent us the use of a Blackhawk chopper. It will fly to Barbados and collect Taeng, she'll be here when you arrive. Just get your butt here and we'll figure this out.

CHAPTER 30

IT DIDN'T TAKE LONG FOR Cody to point out the sensitive communication equipment and for Tony and his crew to rig it with the thermite demolition charges which had thoughtfully been supplied during the installation of said equipment, both in the communications hut and down in the office in the shop area above the sub pen. They also wrapped det cord around the base of the comms mast behind the house. After bringing the mast down, they unbolted all the cameras and antennas from it and placed them in the middle of the comms hut so that they would be destroyed with all of the other communications equipment in the hut.

After rigging the comms hut and it's associated equipment to blow, the SOG crew gathered up anything and everything that could point to their presence on the island, including their cots and their weapons and stacked them in the field in front of the house and prepped them with C4 and thermite charges to destroy the evidence while they waited for the big chopper to arrive.

Needless to say, Cody was not very happy about having to leave his island, his house and his work behind, but Mike had a valid point in that the Chinese wouldn't forgive and forget what had happened on Barbados, and that Taeng and himself had to get themselves 'off the X' as soon as possible. Hopefully, the powers that be in Langley and Fort Meade would make things right at some point in the future. Cody would need a new island and a new boat.

The chopper finally arrived and after all the incriminating evidence that wasn't about to be destroyed had been loaded onboard, everyone shook hands and had a group hug before the SOG team got onboard and the big CH-53K King Stallion helicopter lifted off and began its journey back to the Tripoli.

Cody waved as it disappeared to the northeast and then made his way down to the sub pen to fuel up the old Aichi E13A floatplane before he slipped the plane from its moorings, did his preflight checklist then fired it up and headed up to Puerto Rico for whatever the future might bring. As he lifted off from the 'runway' behind the breakwater, the thermite and C4 charges detonated in the house, the comms hut and in the shop, leaving them burning nicely as Cody banked the old Jake to the north.

As Cody came in to land just offshore of the Terminal de Lanchas de Cataño, where he and Taeng had parked the plane on their previous visit, he noticed what appeared to be the same black Jet Ranger as before, again parked at the shore end of the T-pier with the rotors turning. Once the old Jake was tied up at the top of the T-pier, Cody shouldered his seabag and made his way toward the little chopper. As the Jet Ranger took off, Cody once again noticed a Jeep full of Puerto Rican soldiers had pulled onto the pier to watch over his old warbird.

When the helicopter had touched down at the listening station, Cody climbed out while the rotors were still turning and made his way over to where Mike, Taeng and Tanawat were waiting for him just off the helipad. Taeng had actually worn a proper dress for the occasion; a white on black polka dot sleeveless halter neck knee length summer dress, which Cody had never seen before. He actually couldn't remember ever seeing her in a dress.

Being the smart-ass, Cody addressed Mike first, "I see that you still have your dangly bits, so I guess none of Taeng's associates got bent, spindled or mutilated during the recent fandango over in Barbados."

"It was close, apparently Lacy cut herself shaving. I am still having a problem picturing a mental image of this as from the photos I've seen of Lacy, she has no facial hair. This being the case she must have been shaving her legs or perhaps even a bit further north, but I'd be willing to investigate the matter in detail at some point in the future," replied Mike.

"I'll let Lacy know that you're concerned," piped Taeng. "Can we get off this helipad before that chopper blows my dress up?"

Mike and Cody held back a moment hoping for the best, but the chopper started winding down, so Mike ushered them off the pad and into the same low building in which they had had their original meeting before the Barbados thing kicked off. As Cody and Mike walked behind Taeng and Tanawat, a friendly gust of wind blew across the mountain top and finally lifted Taeng's dress to a respectable viewing level. Both Cody and Mike agreed that there is something about a woman that takes the time to color coordinate her lingerie with her dress, and that the thong undergarment, in a black on white polka dot motif, was a nice touch.

Cody had to get another visitor's badge before the group made their way back into the familiar conference room, where Mr. Doe and Mr. Smith were waiting for them. Neither one of them looked very happy, which was a little odd since the coup had been handily routed.

After everyone had taken their seats, Mr. Doe got started.

"First off, I'd like to say that both the NSA and the CIA appreciate your help with sorting out the recent coup in Barbados. If not for your heads up, we'd likely have missed the opportunity to stop the coup, and the Chinese would have gained yet another foothold in the Caribbean.

"That said, the decision to shoot up the yacht and then to hit the sub with anti-tank missiles was very ill advised." Mr. Doe looked pointedly at Tony as he said this.

"We now may have to deal with an international incident. Not only has a Chinese diplomat been essentially kidnapped, but a Chinese warship has been fired upon in international waters. The only saving grace is that the Chinese have lost a significant amount of face and do not wish to publicize the fact that they sponsored a failed coup, they have a missing diplomat and that they have a damaged submarine."

Tony had enough of this second guessing. He was pensive for a moment before he rose to his feet and placed his hands on the table while leaning forward and alternately looking between Mr. Doe and Mr. Smith.

"Okay, fair enough, but I would like to remind you that when all of this took place, we were acting for Ian Gooding, the Deputy Commissioner of Police, and that time was of the essence. Furthermore, nobody, including you two, issued any further guidance concerning the situation. What did you want us to do? Let Ms. Qu and the MSS crew board the sub and escape? Once you knew they were heading out into the open ocean you knew that they would either be picked up by a Chinese flagged vessel, and as you well knew from satellite surveillance, there were none in the area, so it had to be a submarine coming to collect them.

"We were fired on first and then returned fire, the only weapon we had available to return fire with was perhaps overkill, but it is all we had. We did manage to stop the yacht, but the sub surfaced suddenly. We didn't have a lot of options open to us at the time, so thinking out of the box, we fired the Javelins that we had onboard at the sub. We boarded the yacht, kidnapped Ms. Qu for interrogation, who we thought may have been one of the masterminds behind the coup, and then fled the scene after disabling the yacht and forcing the sub to resurface and check for survivors, hopefully buying us some time. At no point during this whole incident did either Langley or Fort Meade suggest a different course of action. Hindsight is 20/20, which is why they don't make glasses for assholes."

Neither Mr. Doe nor Mr. Smith seemed fazed in the least by Tony's outburst and simply asked him to sit back down.

"That is true, Tony, but before you get your panties in a knot, no offense, Ms. Skeete, nobody in this meeting room has said anything other than that your course of action was ill advised, and it was, but as you so colorfully pointed out, this is looking in hindsight," explained Mr. Smith.

Continuing, Mr. Smith detailed the present situation. "As of now, Ms. Qu is being strenuously interrogated on the USS Tripoli. We'll wring her dry, but at some point, we'll need to figure out what to do with her. At this point she'll have realized that she is onboard a US vessel and that she has been kidnapped by a foreign power. This is not a good look for the US and again, the only saving grace is that we know that the Chinese actively attempted to overthrow the government of a sovereign nation, which is an equally bad look for the Chinese. We'll probably just lodge her in Guantanamo Bay until we need to trade her for someone of equal value. This is simply how the game is played."

At this point, Mr. Doe took over. "We can handle the diplomatic fallout from the sinking of the yacht, the kidnapping of their Economic and Commercial Counsellor to Barbados and the attack on the sub, but the loss of face, especially to a non-state actor living alone on an island, will not go unpunished.

"Recent communications which we have intercepted between the sub, the Song Class submarine presently in port at Augustin Armario Naval Base at Puerto Cabello, Venezuela, and Beijing, suggests that after the submarine is repaired, it will set sail for Pala Island with a full complement of PLA Special Forces to affect some sort of payback. We'll prepare a surprise for them, but this means that Mr. Morgan can never return to his island and that Mr. and Ms. Skeete should probably take an extended vacation outside the Lesser Antilles Islands to be on the safe side."

Taeng and Tanawat erupted in disapproval, they did not like the idea of being instrumental in preventing a coup of their nation and then being told they had to leave. Cody, on the other hand, was concerned about the loss of his research shop, his island and his beloved Nasty boat.

Mr. Doe held up his hands for quiet before continuing. "To make matters even more complicated, Taeng and Cody have to die, there is no other way around it. If you do not cease to exist, in a believable manner, the Chinese will never stop hunting you. This is why we needed Cody's boat. Once that is accomplished, and you'll need to leave that to us, Taeng, Cody, and Mr. and Mrs. Skeete will be relocated to another location which is being prepared for them as we speak.

"Mr. Morgan's work on hypersonic propulsion is too valuable for DARPA to abandon it, so the new location will not only have accommodations, but your new shop will be comparable to the one on Pala. I assume you have your research stored either on a hard drive or in the cloud?"

"Both, actually." Of more concern to Cody was his beloved Shag McNasty. "How about my boat, will it be replaced? There aren't that many seaworthy Nasty boats still around," asked a concerned Cody.

"We are considering replacing it with a later model German S-boat hull that was sitting in the basement of the Smithsonian Museum. We'll remove the three Daimler Benz marine diesel engines, which only produced around 2,000 brake horsepower apiece and install the two twin supercharged Napier-Deltic diesel engines, which we will take out of your Nasty boat before we kill you in it and have them installed in the new S-boat. We'll also install a state-of-the-art electronics and radar suite as well as the latest, greatest automation and engine management system. The 6,200 horsepower of the Napier-Deltic engines should give the old S-boat some serious grunt. What do you think?" asked Mr. Doe.

Cody just grinned. "I'll need a place to work on her when we get wherever it is we are going."

Now Mr. Doe grinned. "A suitable boathouse for both your plane and your new boat has been factored into your new location."

Tanawat became concerned. "Are me and my wife also at risk?"

"We can't say for sure. You really only shuffled people around on your boat and you were not involved in the submarine or yacht incident. That said, we'd rather not take the chance and would like to move you and Mrs. Skeete to the new location as well.

"The Chinese will be looking for a single man and a single woman, we plan to set things up at the new location as a man and a wife, with the wife's parents nearby."

Taeng and Tanawat just looked at Cody and grinned at this news. Cody was beginning to think that this plan might actually have some merit.

"How about my boat, is it at risk as well?" asked Tanawat.

"Again, we can't be sure, but better safe than sorry. We'll take your boat too."

"Are you going to replace it also?"

"You won't be getting a reconditioned S-boat or anything as classic, but what would you say to a rebuilt 1996 Breaux Brothers 135' Fast Supply Vessel?"

"What motors are in it?"

"Four Cummins KTA193M3's rated at 2,800 horsepower, I believe. 22 knots top speed."

Tanawat had to think about this for a minute. "Can you trade out the Cummins for Cat 3512C HD's? This will get me about 6,300 horses and a top speed of around 40 knots. Just to compete with the hippie, you understand."

"I'll see what I can do, Mr. Skeete, but no promises," replied a chuckling Mr. Doe.

CHAPTER 31

THERE WAS A LOT TO be done in the next few weeks: the Chinese had to assault Pala Island to save face, Cody and Taeng had to die, and the 'newlyweds' and Taeng's parents needed to have a place to stay out of the public eye until their new digs were ready.

Two weeks after the meeting at the listening station on top of the mountain above Santa Barbara in Puerto Rico, the Chinese Type-039 Song Class submarine which had been licking its wounds while refitting at the Augustin Armario Naval Base at Puerto Cabello, Venezuela, released her mooring lines and headed out into the Caribbean before once again she slipped beneath the waves on a heading that would soon bring her to Pala Island.

While the Chinese were busy contemplating revenge, Mr. Doe and Mr. Smith sent the 3Cs: Chiara, Cathy and Cheryl back to Barbados to do a little breaking and entering at the office of Taeng's dentist off the Spring Garden Highway in Bridgetown. While in the office they exchanged Taeng's X-ray file with those of another young lady.

The young lady whose files were substituted for those of Taeng would not be needing them anymore, she was just another one of the unnamed and unclaimed victims of sex trafficking who had inebriated herself then simply walked into the ocean off the beach at Plage de l'Anse Tabarin on

Guadeloupe a few days earlier and drowned herself. She bore a passing similarity to Taeng, and her pimp had paid for some dental work and whitening before he had put her to work in the hotels, which would be readily apparent on her X-rays.

Mr. Doe and Mr. Smith had also been checking the morgues on all the islands in the Caribbean, not only for a corpse that could be mistaken for Taeng, but also for a male corpse with a passing similarity to Cody. They didn't need to worry about dental identification on the male corpse since only the CIA retained his dental records by this point in time.

They got lucky, if you will, with a young Russian tourist on Saint Kitts who had overdosed on heroin at the Saint Kitts Marriott Resort on Frigate Bay. Judging by the tattoos on the body, he was somehow associated with the Russian Mafia. Obviously not very high up in the organization since nobody had bothered to claim the body until Mike did.

After both bodies had been packed in ice and flown to Puerto Rico, they were put on the same C-130 that had originally delivered Tony and the SOG crew to Pala Island, where they were joined by Tony, Autry, Justus and Isaac from the original SOG crew and the necessary equipment to complete their new mission. The C-130 then retraced its path to Cody's island where Tony and the boys once again jumped out, after they had tossed out the now embalmed and frozen bodies of the Russian Mafioso and the girl from Guadeloupe, followed by their equipment bundles. Once on the ground, they got to work as time was of the essence, and the clock was ticking.

The Chinese knew that they were walking into a 'scorched earth' scenario, they had watched the house and the shop on Pala Island burn via satellite. Nonetheless, they wanted to investigate to determine what had been on the island, and what it had been used for. Their signals intelligence people had been aware of significant encrypted traffic coming from the island months before the debacle in Barbados and they wanted to see if anything useful was suitable for salvage and reverse engineering or of any value to the tech geeks back home. If they happened to find a certain Cody Morgan on the island, this would just be icing on the cake. From their surveillance, they knew that the torpedo boat had not left the island, so there was a chance that the owner might still be there even though the house and shop had been destroyed. They obviously didn't know about the old Japanese reconnaissance plane and their satellites couldn't see into the sub pens.

The sub came to periscope depth at midnight, about a quarter of a mile off the breakwater leading into the harbor. The mast containing the infrared and thermal vision optics was raised and the leader of the PLA Special Forces platoon took his time surveying everything he could see. There was not a 'hot spot' anywhere, but from the sub's position they could not see directly behind the breakwater or into the small harbor and sub pen behind it.

Once the periscope mast was retracted, the Chinese commando informed the submarine captain that they would stay in position and take another look once the sun came up. If nothing of concern was visible in daylight, the sub would maneuver closer to the breakwater before surfacing to let the commandos unload their inflatable boats and make their way ashore.

While the Chinese submarine was outside the breakwater with no view as to what was going on directly behind the breakwater or in the small harbor just beyond it, Tony and his crew were busy rigging the Shag for her final voyage. It had been decided that removing the original Napier-Deltic engines, so that they could be installed in Cody's new S-boat, was impractical and would give the game away if the Chinese dove on her later and found modern diesels installed, so they had remained in the boat.

They did, however, install a device that would allow them to operate the boat by remote control. On the deck behind the helm were two body bags, complete with an embalmed body apiece packed with ice. The bodies were no longer frozen stiff and were quite pliable. Finally, inside the bridge itself was a 55-gallon drum of 100-octane gasoline which had originally been intended to go into the old Jake seaplane but was now being re-purposed as an incendiary device complete with a remote-controlled detonator.

Tony, Autry, Justus and Isaac were well aware of the submarine's presence as it had been tracked continuously by satellite and by a P-8 Poseidon anti-submarine aircraft out of Leeward Point Field at Guantanamo

Bay in Cuba since it had slipped its moorings in Venezuela. A couple of remote-controlled, high-resolution day/night/thermal cameras hidden in the rocks on the ocean side of the breakwater allowed them to view the area where they knew the submarine to be in real time.

This being the case, they knew exactly when the sub raised its periscope again around 10:00 the following morning and they got to work on their ruse. First, they took the bodies of the Russian drug addict and the poor girl who had been trafficked and then took her own life and prepared them for their Viking-style funeral. The Russian was dressed in an old t-shirt and an old pair of khaki board shorts to resemble Cody before a wig of long blonde hair, tied into a ponytail, was glued to his head. He was then propped against the helm and tied in place with cord that was designed to dissolve in seawater in the event he was blown overboard before the thermite could do its job. The young lady was dressed to resemble Taeng in a bikini under cut-offs and an old red Tecate beer t-shirt. She was then strapped, with the same dissolvable cord, to the hatch on the starboard side of the bridge that led below decks.

With everything in place, Tony piloted the old Nasty boat to the end of the 'runway' behind the breakwater, the end toward the desalination plant where the waterway behind the breakwater made a 90° turn toward the harbor and left it idling while everyone got off and made their way into the desalination plant where they could watch the show.

Sure enough, about 11:30 that morning, the Chinese sub surfaced and a hatch at the bottom of the sail or conning tower opened, and three black rubber rafts were dragged out of the sail and inflated on the deck aft of the sail. An electric outboard motor was then attached to each transom before the boats were lowered into the water and six Chinese commandos climbed into each and began heading toward the breakwater.

Tony had the remote control for the Shag in his hands while he watched, via the day/night/thermal cameras hidden in the rocks, the Chinese beach their rafts and begin climbing up the rocky breakwater. Just before they reached the top, Tony throttled up the old Napier-Deltic engines and aimed the boat directly down the center of the 'runway' at full speed, as if Cody and Taeng were making their escape.

The Chinese, thinking that this is exactly what was happening, unslung their rifles, all 18 of them, and emptied them into the boat as it passed them on top of the breakwater. Some of the QBZ-95 rifles had been equipped with the QLG-10 35mm under-barrel grenade launchers and these were employed as well. At least two grenades found their mark on the Shag.

Justus had been given the radio controller for the detonator which had been placed on the drum of aviation fuel on the bridge. When he saw the grenades detonate on the deck behind the bridge, he triggered the detonator. The 'detonator', a misnomer if there ever was one, had been sized so that it would not only ignite the aviation fuel and the thermite strapped to the barrel, but it would also obliterate the bridge, which it did. The Shag erupted in a huge fireball with bits and pieces of the old boat raining down on the breakwater, the surrounding waters, and the Chinese commandos.

While the Chinese scrambled toward the burning hull to check it out, Tony and the boys packed up their kit and exited the desalination plant from the door on the far side opposite the breakwater, to remain out of sight of the Chinese, and made their way to the eastern side of the island where an SDV, SEAL Delivery Vehicle, collected them. The SDV then travelled about 10 nautical miles due south of the island, to put the island between them and the Chinese sub, where an American submarine took them aboard and whisked them away.

After investigating the burnt-out hull of the Nasty boat and finding no identifiable human remains whatsoever, the commandos took the rest of the day to search the burnt out remains of the house and shop, as well as the submarine pens and the desalination plant. Nothing of interest was found.

Cody and Taeng had, as far as the Chinese were concerned, now ceased to exist.

CHAPTER 32

AFTER THE MEETING ON PUERTO Rico, the powers that be had decided that they needed to keep Cody and the three Skeetes out of the public eye until Tony and his crew could execute a plan to convince the Chinese that Cody and Taeng were no longer on this mortal coil. With the idea of keeping them 'close, but not too close to home', Cody, Taeng, Tanawat and Miriam were put up in the Ritz-Carlton San Juan, between Isla Verde and the Pine Grove beaches. They had been given adjoining suites on the fifth floor overlooking the pool and facing out to sea. The view was spectacular, but the adjoining rooms, with her parents in the next room, was cramping Taeng's style.

Miriam, being an old-school conservative mother, did not want her daughter living in sin in the adjacent room, while her daughter, not so old-school or conservative, suggested that she needed to stay next door to give credibility to the ruse, since they had checked in as husband and wife.

Miriam, even after Tanawat suggested that it was time for their daughter to get married and provide grandchildren for their old age, didn't budge. Her daughter would be sleeping in their suite for the duration of their stay at the Ritz.

This caused much 'weeping and gnashing of teeth' for Cody and Taeng. Ever since the episode in the office on Pala Island prior to the operation to stop the coup, when Chiara had correctly pointed out that Taeng's shirt was on inside out and back to front, they had been waiting on the right set of circumstances for a repeat performance, but they just hadn't really had the time or opportunity to do so and now with Miriam in the mix, it just didn't seem like the stay at the Ritz was going to provide the proper environment for getting to know one another better on a non-platonic, carnal level.

This being the case, they did spend a lot of time together shopping in town, lounging on the beach, learning to surf at the Pine Grove surfing beach, and at the hotel pool in the evening. At the beach, surfing or at the pool, Taeng was constantly teasing Cody in her tasteful yet revealing swimwear. The shopping was performed simply to provide a variety of said swimwear. Her favorite shops seemed to be Everything But Water at the Plaza Las Americas, Victoria's Secret in the Mall of San Juan, Costazul in San Francisco, and the Playero Surf Shop in Parque. Cody would go along to provide commentary and rank the various swimwear that was modeled at each shop. It was driving him nuts and was not doing anything beneficial for his blood pressure, but he decided that it was very entertaining as long as he didn't blow a gasket.

Eventually Cody and the Skeetes were relocated to a small island located within the British Virgin Islands. It was called Ginger Island, and it was about two miles due east of Cooper Island. The US Government had bought the uninhabited 258-acre island from the Texas oil billionaire William Harrison six years previously with the idea of building a satellite tracking and communications facility on it to be operated by the National Reconnaissance Office.

The island is in the shape of a three-tined fork lying on its side with the short handle of the fork pointing west and the three tines pointing east towards the open ocean. The middle tine is short and extends into the shallow bay created by the two outer tines. Both of the outer tines terminated in hills rising to an elevation of 305' on the northern prong and 351' on the southern prong. The NRO facility had been built on the higher elevation of the southern tine. A dock suitable for resupply vessels and an industrial sized desalination plant had been built in South Bay, which was located at the neck of the fork, on the south side of the handle where the root of the tines formed. A road had been built from South Bay to the NRO facility, but other than that, the rest of the island had been left as it was.

The CIA realized that they now owed Cody for the loss of his island, which he could never inhabit again, they were also aware that DARPA would want him to continue his work on hypersonic propulsion systems, and finally, Mike was aware of the budding romance between Cody and Taeng and knew that they'd need some separation from Tanawat and Miriam in the upcoming scenario. In Cody's mind, his old house on Pala Island was perfect. Taking this all into account, the government had leveled the top of the hill at the end of the northern prong of the 'fork' and built an exact replica of the old house there with the front of the house overlooking the steep rocky cliffs but welcoming the morning sun. Just down the hill to the west, a smaller guesthouse in the same style was built facing south for Taeng's parents.

A nice, crushed oyster shell road was built from South Bay to the houses on the northern prong of the island, which was handy for the new Kawasaki 450X dirt bike and the new Gator utility vehicle and 2-wheeled trailer that replaced those which had been left back on Pala.

Down at South Bay, a separate pier extending out into South Bay had been built for Cody's newly refurbished S-boat and Tanawat's new 135' Fast Supply Vessel, complete with the new Cummins engines he'd asked for. Sadly, the Napier-Deltic turbocharged diesels in the Shag had been sacrificed in the effort to disappear Cody and Taeng, but the government had replaced the three Daimler Benz marine diesel engines with three Caterpillar 3512C 4-stroke diesel mills, each cranking out somewhere around 2,450 horsepower. Cody was looking forward to running them in.

Along the north side of the new pier, close to shore, was a 300' concrete enclosed boathouse that could easily house both Tanawat's and Cody's boats with all the tools, equipment and bridge cranes necessary to maintain and operate both. On the other side of the pier, just across from the boathouse, was another concrete structure similar to the old sub pen, but much smaller. The lower section contained moorings and a service area for the old Aichi floatplane, while the upper level contained all the equipment, machine tools and so forth as well as office and engineering spaces for Cody to perform his actual job of propulsion/materials engineer.

All in all, the new location was pretty nice. The fact that they had neighbors at the NRO facility to interact with was a bonus. Pala Island had been a lonely existence for Cody prior to Taeng washing up. True, he could fly to the other islands for some fun, but eventually he had to return to enforced solitude. Even with two people on the island, if you weren't busy stopping a coup or flirting with the other inhabitant, the island tended to become monotonous and boring.

The NRO attachment consisted of a rotating squad of US Marines as well as the actual NRO technicians and operators, both men and women. Hormonally fueled cookouts and volleyball tournaments on the small beach between the original resupply pier and Cody's pier, became regular events.

Six months after the failed coup, and after the CIA had wrung her dry of information at Guantanamo Bay, the CIA traded Qu Ching for an agent who had gotten nabbed in Hong Kong, and from what the NSA could deduce from intercepted signals traffic, the Chinese were no longer looking for Cody or the Skeetes. They had lost some face, but they had other games to play. At the end of the day, they much preferred people to think that it was the CIA and their SAC/SOG crews that had thwarted the coup, not some Bajan bimbo and her long-haired hippie associate.

This being the case, Cody or Tanawat would often travel incognito and take their new boats on runs back to Barbados so that Taeng and Miriam could visit old friends, or to pick up friends of Miriam and Taeng and bring them back to Ginger Island for parties that were held on the island.

At one of the hormonally fueled get togethers, the Gunnery Sergeant in charge of the squad of Marines on one of the rotations had run into Lacy, and had understandably, considering her cheeky personality and outstanding physical attributes, begun to develop feelings for her. Gunny Ramón Garcia was just a few years older than Lacy. His parents were legitimate Cuban asylum seekers, who were thrilled that their son had become a US Marine.

Ramón had originally made the grade and served with the Marine Raider Regiment, but during a series of classified operations in Syria against President Bashar al-Assad and his Iranian and Russian allies, Ramón received shrapnel wounds to his back and was no longer able to effectively play ball with the Raiders anymore and had been relegated to the security force on Ginger Island. The young Gunny Sergeant was infuriated at being taken off the tip of the spear, but once he ran into Lacy, and became infatuated by the Bajan beauty, he began to enjoy his posting much more. When he learned the story concerning her name, as it supposedly related to her choice of undergarments, he decided to investigate further and the rest as they say, is history. Lacy couldn't help but be attracted to the slim, fit Cuban-American Marine, and the scars he'd earned in Syria turned her on. He wasn't a bad volleyball player either.

At the end, it wasn't the Chinese that caused the problem; it was Warrant Officer Class 1 Gabriel Collins, the ex-Regimental Sergeant Major of the now disbanded Special Operations Company of the Barbados Regiment and a few of his cohorts that were the problem.

In an effort to heal the wounds opened by the attempted coup, President Griffith made the questionable decision to pardon Collins and the three other ex-Special Operations Company soldiers that had been tossed into jail once they were rounded up after the failed coup.

The Bajans were not very happy with or forgiving of anyone who had been involved in the coup, and Collins and his three comrades had been ostracized on Barbados and had been forced to relocate to Antigua under assumed names. Gabriel Collins was now known appropriately as Kenrick Roach. He and his three friends had found work at the Crabbs Power Plant and the adjoining Northern Marine Services Boat Yard as dogsbodies and they lived together in a small, rented house in the Parham area.

One Saturday afternoon, while Kenrick and his buddies were sitting at Cloggy's at the Catamaran Marina on Falmouth Bay drinking beer, they noticed a wicked looking, storm gray, patrol boat looking vessel pulling into a berth at the marina. They had no idea that they were looking at an old

German S-boat. Once the boat had been moored, four people disembarked and walked up the dock and right past Cloggy's drinking establishment. One of the women was obviously pure Caribbean, one of the men was a big, rough Hispanic looking guy while the other looked like a surfer with long blonde hair and a rangy build. It was the last woman that caught Kenrick's eye.

After the attempted coup, Taeng had become a national hero and icon after people realized that it was her who had broadcast the original message out of the Voice of Barbados studio. Although she was never interviewed on TV or radio, old photos of her in school and as a journalist surfaced and were shown on TV and in print. Kenrick knew for a fact that the incredibly sexy girl walking down the dock in a halter bikini top and cut-offs was one of the people responsible for ruining his life.

Once the group had reached the end of the dock and hailed a taxi, Kenrick told his friends to stay where they were while he walked down to the old patrol boat to take some pictures of it with his phone. Getting back to Cloggy's, he sent the photos off to an old friend in the Bahamas that knew how to access and search for boats on vesselfinder.com, Lloyd's Register and other sites, and asked him if he could identify the storm gray boat and perhaps the owner as well.

When his three friends decided to go back to their house in Parham, Kenrick hung around the marina in the hopes of getting some decent photos of the four people on the boat. He thought that there was a chance that they would be either leaving for points elsewhere this evening or perhaps they were roughing it by living on the boat in between ports. Whatever their plans, he wanted good photos to pass on to others who may be interested.

Around 6:00 in the evening, Kenrick had decided that he'd had enough beer, rum and sun for the day and made his way to the end of the dock and then up to Matthews Road to see if he could flag a taxi. Just as he passed the Catamaran Hotel, he saw his four targets getting out of a taxi loaded down with shopping, obviously for the girls judging by the brand names shown on the bags.

Kenrick quickly turned around and walked into the hotel lobby. Kenrick had shaved his head and thinned down after his stay in His Majesty's Prison Dodds, and after six months of working as a laborer at the power plant he doubted his own mother would have recognized him. The targets were busy checking in, so Kenrick sat on a sofa across the lobby facing the check-in desk and surreptitiously took a series of photos with his Samsung smart phone. Checking that the resolution was acceptable, he stood up and strolled out the front door. He finally flagged down a taxi on Matthews Road and had it deliver him to the house he shared in Parham. He had some work to do now.

Kenrick's career in the military, as well as his life in general, had come crashing down after the failed coup. Besides being publicly humiliated and shamed, his wife had left him while he was in prison and taken herself and their two daughters to live with her mother on Dominica. Once he was pardoned and released from prison, with nothing better to do with his time and with his anger boiling over at what had happened to him, he began investigating who and what had contributed to the failure of the coup. Besides the politicians who had actively been against any Chinese intervention on the island, the only 'face of the resistance' he could identify had been Taeng Skeete.

The following morning, while Cody, Taeng, Lacy and Ramón had a late breakfast at the Captain's Quarter Cuban style restaurant in the hotel, much to Ramón's delight, Kenrick was sending his photos of the people and the strange gray boat to his few remaining contacts in the old Chinese Embassy, now downgraded to consulate status, who would even speak to him.

Later that day, Kenrick received a call back from his now consulate, not embassy, contacts on Barbados, and it was not what he wanted to hear. The Chinese could confirm, due to their constant data mining of US military personnel, that the Hispanic male was a US Marine by the name of Ramón Garcia who was presently stationed on Ginger Island in the British Virgin Islands as head of the security detail at the not-so-secret NRO facility there, which could explain his presence on Antiqua. The ropy muscled, long haired hippie type and the stunning mixed-race woman seemed to be the recently deceased Cody Morgan and Taeng Skeete, which came as a surprise to the Chinese, but again, they were not interested in them any longer. Once Ms. Qu Ching had been traded and repatriated to China, she had positively identified Cody as one of the crew who had shanghaied her, no pun intended. The hot and healthy pure Bajan woman was thought to be Lacy Cumberbatch, an associate of Taeng's from their time with the Caribbean News Agency, and again of no further interest to the Chinese.

Before hanging up, the person on the consulate side of the call reiterated to Kenrick that the Chinese no longer considered the people that Kenrick had photographed to be of interest and were no longer interested in any retribution being paid to anyone involved with the counter-coup. They had failed fair and square, and nothing was to be gained by a vendetta.

Kenrick didn't agree.

CHAPTER 33

KENRICK'S BUDDY IN THE BAHAMAS who was looking into the various shipping registers and boat finder websites, had determined that the boat in question was an original World War 2 Schnelleboot or S-boat, which the British had dubbed an E-boat for 'enemy boat'. From the pictures he'd received, he could say for certain that it was an S-38 Class Schnelleboot, likely launched in between 1943 and 1944. This had come as a surprise as the only known surviving S-boat was the S-130 which was presently being restored in Cornwall, England.

Delving further into the records, the Bahamanian buddy found where the Smithsonian Museum had fairly recently sold a late model S-boat hull to a shell company in Bermuda, who had sold it to a shell company in Panama, and so on and so forth until the actual ownership of the hull could no longer be ascertained, which is all Kenrick needed to know. He was sure that the questionable providence of the boat and the resurrection of Cody and Taeng pointed to something shady, but more to the point, it gave him a target for his pent-up frustration and anger.

Over the next few months, Kenrick kept his eyes and ears open for any reports of the unique gray boat. The boat never seemed to appear in any harbor or marina north of Puerto Rico or south of Montserrat. Although this narrowed down the area where the boat was likely home ported, it was still a vast area. Kenrick needed to figure out where Cody, Taeng and the boat were hiding out.

The name painted on the stern, Cheap Trick, didn't help since the name was apparently unregistered, nor did the home port of Nassau painted underneath it. Some way of tracking the boat needed to be found.

After shopping around on the internet for a decent tracking device, he decided that he required a LandSeaAir 54 GPS tracker. This only cost about $30, plus a $20 per month service plan. The tracker attached magnetically and would update its location every three minutes to the app downloaded on Kenrick's phone. The only problem was that he needed to have the opportunity to attach it, which occurred as if by magic a couple of days after the GPS tracker arrived.

Kenrick and one of his cohorts were slaving away at the Crabbs Power Plant, when lo and behold the mystery gray boat cruised into Parham Harbor and pulled alongside the dock at the North Sound Marina, which just happened to be next door to the Crabbs Power Plant.

Kenrick's other two associates were working as menial labor at the marina that day and had dropped Kenrick and the other man at the power plant prior to taking their only vehicle over to the marina. Kenrick quickly called one of them and told him to go out to the old Toyota HiLux and get the tracking device out of the glove box. Kenrick would meet him in the marina's onshore boat storage yard which fronted on the harbor in 15 minutes. After Kenrick had collected the GPS tracker from his associate, he simply strolled along the dock until he came to the old S-boat.

There seemed to be some issue with the new cooling lines in the engine room. When the CIA had made the decision to leave the two Napier-Deltic turbocharged diesels in the Shag, when Cody and Taeng were killed, they made the decision to buy three additional Cat 3512C HD's, identical to the two engines in Tanawat's new boat, for Cody's S-boat. This not only got them a healthy volume discount from Caterpillar, it also simplified the issue of spares and maintenance items. With one of the 3512C's for each of the boat's shafts, this gave the Cheap Trick a total of roughly 7,350 brake horsepower. The old Schnelleboot could really scoot now, but they were still having some problems with the modified cooling system. While everyone's attention was focused on what was going on in the engine room, Kenrick slapped the magnetic tracking device underneath the portside torpedo tube door hinge where it was unlikely to be noticed, and then just made his way back to his job at the power plant.

That evening, Kenrick accessed the LandSeaAir 54 app on his phone and discovered that the boat was now moored in Jolly Harbor on the other side of Antigua, which was not helpful. He needed to track the boat to the out-of-the-way anchorage where it was hiding out.

The following day was a Saturday, so Kenrick drove the ratty old HiLux pickup over to Jolly Harbor and just followed the tracking app on his phone until he found the old German S-boat moored against one of the piers in front of the Jolly Harbor Marina Office. Apparently, Cody and whoever was with him had spent the night at one of the hotels between Jolly Harbor and Jolly Beach. This suited Kenrick perfectly, he'd just hang out at the Sea Dream Restaurant and Bar, which was conveniently located at the end of the harbor near the Jolly Harbor Marina Office, and see who boarded the boat and then watch where it went on the tracking device when it left.

Just after noon, a hippie-looking blonde guy in faded jeans and a white t-shirt came walking down to the docks from the direction of the Tropical Breeze Villas, with a very attractive mixed-race girl alongside him. The tart was dressed in jeans and a t-shirt as well, but Kenrick was of the opinion that she looked a heck of a lot better in them than the guy did. As they got closer to the bar where he was drinking, Kenrick positively identified them as Taeng Skeete and Cody Morgan.

Cody went onboard and did his pre-start checks, he'd upgraded all of the engine management systems and steerage controls so the boat could be easily crewed by two people if necessary, while Taeng waited on the dock to get ready to slip the mooring lines off the cleats on the pier when Cody gave the word. Eventually the boat slipped its moorings and idled out into Jolly Harbor. Kenrick had another beer while watching his smart phone app and followed the Cheap Trick out to the entrance of the harbor and then out to sea on a northwest heading.

That evening, while Kenrick's three amigos were engrossed in a meaningless local football match on TV, Kenrick watched the GPS icon on his phone as it made its way further northwest on his screen until it finally stopped at a small island between Virgin Gorda and Cooper Island. Getting out his old ASUS laptop he called up Google Earth and found that the island was named Ginger Island, and that it was supposedly solely inhabited by the personnel required to man the NRO facility there. But then Kenrick remembered that the Chinese had mentioned that the Hispanic male he'd seen from Cloggy's was a US Marine by the name of Ramón Garcia, who was presently stationed on Ginger Island. This was getting interesting.

CHAPTER 34

KENRICK CLAIMED THAT HE HAD contracted Covid again and took the next week off work. During this time, he flew to Tortola, the largest of the British Virgin Islands, and rented a cheap room in Road Town close to Port Purchell. Drinking in the various dive bars, and buying drinks for others, he soon discovered that the government facility on Ginger Island was resupplied every two weeks. The supply vessel, an old oilfield workboat, left from the CSY docks near the ferry terminal. He further discovered that half of the island was now privately owned and that they managed their own supplies. By this time, Kenrick had a pretty good idea as to who owned the other half of the island.

After relocating his drinking hole to Rotten Ronny's, the ambiance matched the name, just on the other side of Blackburn Highway from the CSY docks, Kenrick ingratiated himself with the locals and got a fairly accurate picture of the layout in South Bay, the two different jetties, and which pier the workboat tied up to and so forth. As a bonus, one of Rotten Ronny's regulars, who just happened to be a deckhand on the workboat, mentioned that every Saturday that they had tied up there, there seemed to be a party going on at the little beach between the jetties and that there was some prime female flesh on display. Kenrick was certain that he knew the identity of one of the women who was displaying that flesh.

Flying back to Antigua, and after a remarkable recovery from Covid, Kenrick went back to work at the power plant. In the evenings, he'd huddle up with his associates to come up with a workable plan to hit the island. The problem was, they needed a suitable boat to execute the plan that Kenrick had in mind.

Some people call it luck, and others might consider it serendipity, but whatever you chose to call it, it happened that week at the North Sound Marina. A wealthy Dutchman pulled his 2020 Conch 47 against the pier at the marina at almost the exact same point where the old S-boat had tied up. She was named the Wicked Wench, likely in reference to the fictional ship popularized in the Pirates of the Caribbean movies as the ship that was burned and sunk by Davy Jones before Jack Sparrow resurrected her as the Pearl. Anyhow, after tying the center consoled boat against the dock with fore and aft lines, the Dutchman walked over to the office, where it just so happened that one of Kenricks' buddies was busy filling out some paperwork. It seemed that the Dutchman's boat had a problem with two of the engines, the Conch 47 ran four Mercury Verado 400's for a total of 1,600 horsepower and a top speed of 34 knots. He had to be back in the Netherlands for the next two weeks and he wanted to leave the boat with the marina to sort out the issue. He'd pick it up when he returned to Antigua.

That evening, back at the rented shack in Parham, the buddy who had overheard the Dutchman made Kenrick aware of the situation. He was told to keep an eye on the boat to see what the problem was with the engines. As it turned out, the problem was relatively simple to fix, the two middle engines attached to the transom had clogged fuel filters. The marina did not have any of the required fuel filters in stock but had found four filters at a marina in Grenada and they would be coming in within a week. The Wicked Wench should be seaworthy again shortly thereafter.

The fuel filters were replaced on a Friday, and the boat was given a test run around the harbor and a clean bill of health late that afternoon. That evening, Kenrick and his boys loaded all their kit and two large coolers of provisions into the old HiLux and drove to the power plant. Shouldering their duffle bags while they carried the coolers between them, they sauntered along the dock shared by both the power plant and marina until they came to the Wicked Wench. Throwing their bags and the coolers onboard, they checked that the vessel had a full load of fuel before they hotwired the ignition and stole the boat.

The problem with the Conch 47, and the fact that it ran four Mercury Verado 400 outboard motors, was that its fuel economy left something to be desired. Even with a full load of fuel, the range was only about 400 miles. For what Kenrick had in mind, they'd need to refuel at some point during their upcoming escapade.

Thinking ahead, Kenrick had made a deal with a smuggler, ironically one of Tanawat's old friends and partner in crime, to rendezvous with him just off the North Curve of Ile Tintamarre, which is about 2.5 miles off the northeast tip of Saint-Martin. With the Wicked Wench anchored in the shallow bay fronting the Curve, the smuggler would pull his old 45' aluminum pilot boat alongside the stolen vessel. A hose would then be run from the five 55-gallon drums of gasoline on the pilot boat to the Wicked Wench and a hand pump would be used to top off her tanks. Kenrick had calculated that it would take roughly 225 gallons of gas to make it from where they had stolen the boat to Ile Tintamarre. If they topped off the tanks there, it would give them another 400 miles to play with and by his calculations the run to Ginger Island and then to their final destination was only about 145 miles. Fuel shouldn't be an issue for the rest of their undertaking once they had topped up their tanks. Kenrick couldn't afford to pay the smuggler in cash but had told him where he could find the Wicked Wench a week or so from when they met to refuel the boat and he could do whatever he liked with it afterwards. Smugglers are not a trusting lot, but they'd take a risk on trading 275 gallons of gas for a boat worth at least $250,000 on the black market.

Timing was important. They needed to come up to Ginger Island around mid-afternoon, while the beach party was well underway. The trip from Antigua to Ile Tintamarre would take about two and a half hours. The fuel transfer from the smuggler would take another an hour and a half. The run from Ile Tintamarre to Ginger Island would take three hours or so.

Since they stole the boat and got underway at roughly 10 o'clock Friday evening, this put them at Ile Tintamarre at 1:00 Saturday morning. The transfer of fuel was completed by 2:30 that morning. Working backwards from a desired arrival time at the pier at Ginger Island at 2:00 in the afternoon, they would need to leave Ile Tintamarre around 11:00am on Saturday. This left them with nine and a half hours to kill at Ile Tintamarre.

After a hearty breakfast of mangú and quesito from their coolers, washed down by coffee that they had found in the galley, they laid their duffle bags out on the deck and began going through their gear.

Each of the men had the Glock 17 9mm service pistol which had been issued to them during their days with the Special Operations Company back on Barbados before the failed coup, and which they had hidden prior to being incarcerated. Kenrick also had a Heckler and Koch MP5 A3 which the Chinese had gifted him for use during the coup, which he had also hidden before going on the run and getting caught and jailed. Other than the firearms and ammunition, each man had a combat knife, in this case an OKC-3S bayonet usually issued to US Marines, these were to be for intimidation purposes if required. Other than this, the duffle bags just contained a change of clothes, snacks and personal items.

After cleaning and lubricating their weapons, they reassembled them, and then just relaxed or took a swim to burn daylight until they left for Ginger Island.

CHAPTER 35

MEANWHILE, ON GINGER ISLAND, TANAWAT, Ramón and Cody were getting up and getting ready for a day of fishing off Anegada Island about 16 miles north of Virgin Gorda Island in the BVI, or British Virgin Islands. Cody didn't really care much about the fishing, but he was always up for any excuse to get his old S-boat out to sea and up on plane.

Lacy and Taeng were not quite ready to get up. They were sleeping in what would have been referred to as Taeng's room back at the old house on Pala. Usually, Taeng would be nestled up against Cody, but she and Cody had made the run down to Barbados on Friday to collect Lacy. The evening before, once they thought that Lacy had gone to bed in 'Taeng's room', Cody and Taeng decided spice things up and play a little strip poker in what used to be referred to as Cody's room, but was now their room. Things were just getting interesting when Lacy burst into the room without knocking to have a talk with Taeng, which sort of took the ardor out of the game. Since Cody had to get up early to go fishing with the boys, Taeng and Lacy had relocated to Lacy's room and decided to stay up late drinking wine while rehashing coup stories and discussing the men in their lives in vivid detail. Eventually they both fell asleep.

Early the following morning, as Cody drove down past Tanawat and Miriam's guesthouse on the Gator, he stopped to pick up Tanawat and his rucksack before driving down to the new boathouse where Ramón met them on the pier. Ramón was working a five week hitch this time as his back-to-back was down with the flu, this being the case he had chosen to give himself a day off to go fishing.

After Cody unlocked the double doors about midway down the boathouse, the three men carried their rucksacks inside and then onboard the Cheap Trick. The fishing gear, food and beverages had been loaded the day before. Tanawat went down into the engine room to check that everything was good to go while Cody went up on the open bridge above the wheelhouse to run through his 'pre-flight' checks. Ramón had gone back on the dock waiting to cast off the lines.

When all was ready, Cody fired up the three Caterpillar HD engines and let them warm up before he gave the signal to Ramón to cast off. Once Ramón had jumped back onboard, Cody backed the old S-boat out of the boathouse and into South Bay before spinning her around and giving her some gas, or diesel in this case, and making his way around the handle of the sideways 'fork' before heading north to their fishing spot off Anegada Island.

Little did Cody know that an interested third party had been keeping track of him via radar. This interested party was well aware of Cody's habit of taking his boat out fishing most Saturday mornings and was actually counting on it. Kenrick watched the blip on the SIMRAD radar that came with the stolen boat as it cleared the western end of Ginger Island and headed north.

Those that intended to party that afternoon finally woke up, some at the NRO facility and some on the other side of the island. After a light breakfast, they all dressed somewhat immodestly, as you do when you attend a beach party in the Caribbean, and began to make their way down to the beach to set things up and get things going.

Since Cody had taken the Gator earlier, Taeng had to jump on the Kawasaki dirt bike and run down to fetch it so that her and Lacy could load it up with food and beverages, towels, and beach chairs. The girls, it was to be a girls' day on the beach, at the NRO shop had an Air Force supplied Gator of their own and they loaded it up with the same plus the volleyball net and ball. After double and triple checking on their respective load-outs, the girls met at the beach to begin their day. The guys that had to man the NRO facility were extremely upset since they knew what they were missing after attending previous beach events with the island's female inhabitants and their friends, but they did have a government supplied pair of Zeiss Victory SF 10x42 binoculars which would allow them to closely follow the action at the beach a mere half mile from the facility.

The two girls from the NRO side were named Kelly and Monica. They were both in their mid-20's, both from Minnesota, both had long-blonde hair, and both were as pale as marshmallows. This wasn't really surprising as they were both of Scandinavian descent. This made for an interesting contrast to Taeng and Lacy, whose skin tone was down toward the other end of the melanin content spectrum. The two blondes were best friends, and both had played volleyball for the University of Minnesota Golden Gophers, and they had both kept fit after following each other into the NRO as Overhead Intelligence Analysts. Their co-workers sincerely appreciated their attention to fitness.

Neither Kelly nor Monica was romantically attached at the moment, which originally tended to make their male counterparts on Ginger Island think that they would be easy targets for their affections. Although Kelly and Monica were not above some good-natured flirting with the guys, they were professionals and kept their professional lives separate from their personal lives. Everyone at the facility recognized that the flirtation was all in fun and it just made the time at the remote location pass a bit quicker.

It was perhaps fortunate that the guys manning the NRO facility were not able to attend this weekend's beach party. The girls were stunning, all four were so hot they'd make a jalapeño pepper sweat bullets. The ladies were dressed, or perhaps more accurately undressed, to the point that would have caused much 'weeping and gnashing of teeth' of those of the male persuasion who were able to read the menu but not place an order.

Kelly was attired in a strappy side sunburst stripe low-rise bottom with a matching triangle halter top, while Monica made do with a strappy triangle bikini top in a blue and white tropical motif and a black Miami tie side bottom. They had both obviously gone shopping together at the Venus store back in Virginia at some point in the past.

Lacy, of the Nubian princess appearance, who had the largest bust, probably in the 34D range, had opted for a tie sided hiked bikini bottom in the Western Sky motif with a matching underwire top to keep her assets firmly in place.

Taeng, not to be outdone, was sporting a knotted halter bandeau top with a Brazilian styled bottom in the Seven Seas pattern by Lulifama that accented her mixed heritage perfectly while showcasing the rest of the package to a mouthwatering degree.

Dressed, so to speak, as they were, they could have turned back the tide by simply walking down the beach.

After they had set up the volleyball net and laid out the rope boundaries and organized seating arrangements to suit, they each had a couple of beers while they gossiped and got caught up before they paired off into teams. Apparently, it was to be those with a higher melanin content against those who were melanin challenged. The game was on.

The melanin challenged team won the first game 15-12, which wasn't surprising as they had both been volleyball stars in college. Then Taeng teamed up with Kelly against Lacy and Monica. Lacy and Monica barely won the game at 17-15. At this point it was time for lunch, so they pulled sandwiches and chips out of the coolers beside the beach chairs and had lunch while the voyeurs at the NRO shop took turns taking a good look at the flesh on display via the Zeiss binoculars. The girls assumed that this was the case and made every effort to stretch or strike poses guaranteed to excite the boys. Even though the viewing was through high powered optics as opposed to physically being present, there was still much 'weeping and gnashing of teeth' in the NRO facility that morning.

After lunch, Monica paired with Taeng and Lacy teamed up with Kelly. Taeng and Monica came out on top with a 15-13 performance. The girls then once again paired up based on melanin content and once again the girls from Minnesota beat the Barbadians like a drum, 15-10.

It was now about 2:00 in the afternoon and the girls had had enough volleyball and were just lounging in their beach chairs drinking beer and talking about whatever sexy women talk about while hanging out on the beach, when a boat rounded the western tip of the island, which would be the same end of the fork handle that the Cheap Trick had rounded earlier that day, and slowly made its way to the private side pier. There appeared to be two local guys on board, and one jumped onto the pier to tie up the boat before he jumped back on and both men leaned over the transom and appeared to be studying the outboard engines.

All four of the girls threw on either t-shirts or cover-ups and then began walking down the pier to where the boat was tied up about 25 yards from the end on the north side. As they approached, one guy, the larger of the two, stepped off the boat and waited for them to approach. As they did, Lacy taking charge as she usually did, told the man politely that this was a private island, but asked if he needed any help with his boat.

The man on the dock explained that they were having trouble with two of his engines and motioned for the Lacy and Taeng to go aboard to take a look so that they could see the problem for themselves and perhaps help them out. While the girls' attention was focused on the engines, the man on the dock whistled. When the girls turned around to see what he was whistling at, they saw that the man on the jetty was now standing behind Kelly and Monica while casually pointing it in their direction.

The man still on the boat at the transom, where they had been examining the four outboard engines, now pulled a matching pistol out from under his shirt while two other men came out of the accommodation area, each with a pistol to match the other two.

At this point, Taeng whispered to Lacy that she recognized the last man out of the hatch leading to the accommodations. Lacy nodded and said, "It's that asshole Gabriel Collins."

CHAPTER 36

"WELL, IF IT ISN'T TAENG Skeete and Lacy Cumbersnatch," commented 'that asshole' Gabriel, using a vulgar play on words regarding Lacy's actual surname of Cumberbatch.

"It's nice to see you again after you managed to derail my little operation back home and sent me to jail. I will try to repay the favor today. Get them under cover before someone decides to check on them," Gabriel instructed the other men as he went up to the bridge to fire up the Mercurys.

The guy on the dock hustled Kelly and Monica onto the boat while taking the liberty to fondle them as he did so. Kelly managed to kick him hard in the nutsack and dropped him, but one of the others cracked her on the side of the head with his pistol and dropped her out cold beside him. As Kenrick, now back as Gabriel, made a sweeping turn to port away from the pier and headed back into the open ocean, the girls were subjected to more fondling as their hands were zip tied behind their backs and they were placed on the bench seat just below and behind the bridge, facing aft.

As the Wicked Wench cleared the western end of the island and headed west, one of the guys in the NRO shop picked up the binoculars hoping to get a view of some prime female flesh, when he noticed that the girls were no longer on the beach and that a strange boat was just exiting South Bay to the north. He immediately contacted Ramón's second in command of the security detail, a black corporal whose given name just happened to be Derek Black and told him what he'd seen.

Corporal Black left two Marines at the shop and crammed himself and the remaining four Marines, now armed with M4 carbines, onto the remaining Gator and hauled ass down to the beach. What he found was disconcerting; all of the girls' kit was still lying on the beach as if they had simply disappeared. There was no sign of a struggle, and nothing looked as if they had decided to go somewhere else on the island. Realistically there was nowhere else on the island to go to enjoy yourself. Since Kelly and Monica were classified senior Overhead Intelligence Analysts with the National Reconnaissance Office, the abduction instantly became a national security issue. Corporal Black got on his radio and told one of the Marines left back at the shop to get on the encrypted net and raise the alarm with NRO headquarters back in Chantilly, Virginia and to await instructions.

Leaving everything as they had found it, Corporal Black and the rest of the Marines went back to the shop. While they were waiting for orders concerning the abduction, Corporal Black thought that it would be a good idea to contact Ramón and let him know what had happened. Getting on the VHF radio, Corporal Black ensured that it was on channel 16 before keying the mike and calling repeatedly, "Cheap Trick, Cheap Trick, this is Ginger 1, over." After the third attempt, Cody came back, "Ginger 1, this is the Cheap Trick, go to channel 68."

Corporal Black couldn't broadcast what had happened on an open channel, so he'd have to be clever about it. Once on channel 68 and re-establishing contact with Cody, Derek transmitted, "Are you familiar with the police 10 codes?" Cody told him to hold on while he asked Ramón and Tanawat, who were fishing off the stern where the old depth charge racks use to be, if they knew the police 10 codes. As soon as he asked such an odd question, they knew something serious was going on and they both came up to the bridge. Ramón took the mike and identified himself and told Derek to go ahead.

"10-24, 10-31, 10-57, 10-78. 18 US Code Section 1201 all the girls."

Ramón asked him to repeat what he'd just transmitted then hung up the mike and told Cody to head back to Ginger Island and not to spare the horses. When the boat was up on plane doing close to 45 knots, Cody asked Ramón what was going on.

Addressing both Cody and Tanawat, he said it didn't look good.

"10-24 is an emergency at the station. 10-31 means there is a crime in progress. 10-57 indicates a missing person, 10-78 means he needs assistance. 18 US Code Section 1201 relates to kidnapping. It looks to me like all the girls on the island have been kidnapped, Derek needs help, and we need to get back there as soon as possible."

Cody nudged the Cheap Trick up to 50 knots.

When they pulled into the boathouse, they found Derek Black waiting for them. He briefed them on the situation to that point and indicated that NRO headquarters had told him to hang tight and they'd be back to him shortly.

Shortly turned out to be an hour later, by which time everyone was up at the NRO facility waiting for the call. The security chief for the entire NRO worldwide didn't waste time, he asked Derek if he knew whether or not Kelly and Monica had worn their Apple watches, which sounded like an odd question to Cody and Tanawat. Thinking back to what he'd seen through the binoculars and not really wanting to admit to his voyeuristic urges, he simply replied that he believed that the girls had been wearing them when they left for the beach as per protocol, and that they wore them religiously.

"Good," replied the security chief in Virginia. "We are re-tasking a satellite as we speak, I'll get back to you within the hour."

After the chief had disconnected the call, Cody asked Ramón what the big deal was about the Apple watches.

"I'd totally forgotten about the watches. All NRO employees working outside of the US are given a watch: some are given Apples, some a Timex, some a fake Rolex, others a Casio G-Shock. It all depends on who they are, their age and what they could reasonably be expected to wear. Nowadays a lot of people don't bother with watches and simply rely on their phones to tell time, but the first thing somebody takes from you these days is your phone. These watches are all fitted out with a GPS transmitter that the NRO can track from space. Once that satellite is in place, we'll know where the girls are at so long as the watches remain with them."

57 minutes later, the call came in on the secure laptop.

Again, the security chief did not mince words. "The watches are located on an island almost directly due east of you called Prickly Pear Cay, whether the girls are still attached to them, we have no way of knowing. We have an Air Commando team at Hurlburt Field in Florida, but it'll take at least 24 hours and more like 36 to get them organized, equipped and on their way. If you guys have a better idea, let's hear it, time is obviously of the essence."

"Hold one," replied Ramón as he muted the mike on the laptop and turned towards Cody, who was looking very thoughtful.

Signaling Ramón to unmute the mike, Cody addressed the chief. "It's about 90 miles from here to Prickly Pear Cay, I can make that in about two hours. I'll need some weapons for Ramón, Tanawat and myself, preferably three suppressed pistols in 9mm or .45 ACP with three full magazines of hollow point rounds for each. We'll need one M110 Squad Designated Marksman Rifle complete with the Sig Sauer 1-6x24mm optics and three full 20-round magazines of the M118LR 175 grain sniping round and I'll need one 870 Remington combat shotgun with a regular synthetic stock and ghost ring sights along with a box of 3" double-ought buckshot and a box of 3" Brenneke Special Forces Maximum Penetration slugs.

"The problem is that we have not heard from the kidnappers and have no idea as to what they want, but while we are waiting, I want to get closer to where the girls are. I'm going to fuel up my boat now and get on the water. Can you get those weapons together and air drop them to us about 20 miles to the west of Prickly Pear Cay? I want to be over the horizon from the island when the drop is made."

"You seem to know your weapons, Mr. Morgan. Why is that?"

"A few years spent as a misguided member of the Navy Special Boat Teams," answered Cody.

"That would explain it. I'll start putting together your shopping list while you get on the water. Take a sat phone with you and I'll be in touch."

CHAPTER 37

BACK IN THE BOATHOUSE, RAMÓN and Cody had taken all the fishing gear off the boat and piled it on the pier while Tanawat rummaged through the coolers that had been left on the beach and consolidated all the food and drinks he could find into a single large cooler and brought it onboard.

While Tanawat was busy scavenging for supplies, Cody had pulled the Cheap Trick alongside the fuel barge at the far end of the boathouse and begun topping off the fuel tanks. Once the tanks were full and Ramón and Tanawat were aboard, Cody climbed up onto the bridge, backed the boat out of the boathouse, turned her around, and began the mission to find and rescue the girls.

While passing between Old Jerusalem Island and Virgin Gorda, Cody was discussing the situation with Tanawat and Ramón and suggested that you had to give the kidnappers some credit. If you were going to risk lifelong incarceration or possible death for kidnapping women, then these would be the caliber of women you would want to risk it for, you couldn't really consider any of the girls as anything other than top shelf. They were all prime examples of feminine pulchritude, and each and every one of them could launch more ships than Helen of Troy ever thought about doing. That said, he still intended to kill each and every one of the bastards when they found them.

Roughly an hour after leaving Ginger Island they were about 40 miles out to sea and running at 40 knots, when the sat phone rang. Ramón picked up, it was the NRO security chief letting them know that an Air Force C-21, the military version of the Learjet 35, had recently landed at Luis Muñoz Marin International Airport in San Juan with the kit they had requested. The weapons and ammo were being loaded onto a Coast Guard Search and Rescue UH-60 Blackhawk chopper as they spoke. Since the Blackhawk cruised at 140 knots and had 145 nautical miles to travel to the drop off point 20 miles to the northwest of Prickly Pear Cay, the flight time was going to be about 62 minutes. Since the Cheap Trick only had another 26.5 miles to go to reach the drop off point, and he didn't want to get there early and just cruise in circles waiting for the chopper, Cody backed the throttles off to a sluggish 23 knots to arrive at the same point in the ocean at roughly the same time the Blackhawk did.

The Cheap Trick was running with all lights on to make themselves more visible to the chopper and Cody had apparently run the calculations correctly in his head since the chopper flew right over the top of them and hovered just above the water about 100 yards ahead of the boat. The starboard door slid open and a bright orange box about the size of a refrigerator box slid out of the door and bobbed around in the rotor wash before the helicopter gained altitude and continued on its way to the Clayton J. Lloyd International Airport on Anguilla.

Cody coasted alongside the orange box and Tanawat and Ramón muscled the box onto the deck amidships after snagging the thoughtfully supplied ropes with a gaff hook. The box was big, but most of it was floatation material so it wasn't overly heavy. Ramón and Tanawat unpacked the weapons and ammunition while Cody aimed the boat toward Prickly Pear Cay.

Since it was only 9:00 in the evening when the chopper made the weapons drop, and the fact that they had still not heard from the kidnappers, Cody made the command decision to pull into Road Bay, Anguilla and drop anchor there to wait for the call that he knew was coming. After eating some of the sandwiches and drinking some of the Gatorade that Tanawat had scrounged from the girls' beach supplies, the guys just hung out on the bridge while waiting for the call.

It was a convoluted method of communication when the call finally came in around midnight. Knowing that they would be monitoring VHF channel 16, the International Hailing and Distress Frequency, one of the kidnappers hailed the Cheap Trick and told them to go to channel 9. Once comms was regained on channel 9, the kidnapper told them to go to channel 72, the intership non-commercial channel.

At this point Cody gave the person on the other end of the radio the 15-digit satellite phone number for the Iridium unit he was using. Once the kidnapper had successfully dialed the sat phone, Cody hung up the mike for the VHF radio and continued the conversation.

"Who am I talking to?"

"You don't really need to know who I am. What you need to know is that we will trade these four women, unsullied and unharmed, for 10 million US dollars and not a penny less. What do you say?"

"I'm interested, but before we go any further, I'll need proof of life from all four women."

"A reasonable request for 10 million dollars, hold on a second."

A few moments later, Lacy was put on the phone and told Cody that so far, they were fine. Kelly and Monica come on next and indicated the same. Taeng was last and she also indicated that all four of them were fine, with an emphasis on the word 'them'.

"Satisfied, Mr. Morgan?"

"For the moment. You realize that getting 10 million dollars together is going to take some time, don't you?"

"Of course, I am not an unreasonable man. From what the skanky Oriental half breed here has told me, you are a wealthy man and familiar with international banking transactions. I'll give you 24 hours to get your funds together. I'll call you back on this number at that time and give you an account in the Turks and Caicos that you can wire the money to. Once the transaction is complete, I'll tell you where you can collect these slags."

"That's not going to happen. You don't honestly expect me to hand over the money before I actually have the women, do you? If you have an internet connection I'll wire you the first half in 24 hours, then the other half when we meet face to face and the women are safely aboard my boat. You can check that the first wire has cleared before I actually lay eyes on the girls and wire you the second half, which you can also check at that time as long as you have internet. At that point we'll go our separate ways."

"A reasonable precaution. I'll be in touch in 24 hours," said the kidnapper just before he disconnected the call.

Ramón looked at Cody funny and asked him if he was really going to pay the asshole.

"No, of course not, but I want him to think that I am, pin him in place, and keep the girls healthy. We'll be going in tomorrow morning at 2:00, you'd better get some shut-eye if you can."

Tanawat said it would be nice if they knew how many people they'd be going up against. Cody said there were four and then related his short conversation with his daughter. There was no need for her to let him know that there were four of 'them', they already knew how many girls had been kidnapped. Also, there was no need to tell him that they were all fine as the others had already confirmed that. By emphasizing the word 'them', she was letting him know how many kidnappers were involved.

"Obviously I have raised a very smart girl, wouldn't you say, Mr. Morgan?"

"I can't answer that, Mr. Skeete. I'm still working on her physical attributes and haven't worked my way up, in a manner of speaking, to her mental qualities."

"Understandable," was all that Tanawat would say.

CHAPTER 38

PRICKLY PEAR CAY ACTUALLY CONSISTS of two cays: west and east. The western cay is smaller with rocky shores and no place to land a boat. The eastern cay, which is what most people are referring to when they mention Prickly Pear Cay, is about 720 yards east to west, and 560 yards north to south, about 50 acres altogether. A large salt pond nestles in the shallow peninsula that comprises roughly half of the north shore.

Both cays are mostly shrubland, with thickets of trees mixed in. This is due to the thin soil on top of limestone bedrock. The dominant vegetation is prickly pear, pope's head cactus and sea grape interspersed with mauby bark, balsam bush, cockspur, milky thorn, loblolly and nicker trees.

Prickly Pear Cay's only claim to fame had been the Misguided Mermaid Bar and Grill, an establishment that tended to cater to backpackers and the more financially challenged of the tourist spectrum, but with the beautiful white sand beach along the north shore, it managed to stay in business from around 2010 until 2020 when it finally could not compete with the other low budget venues in the Caribbean. Towards the end it had become a destination of choice for those who simply wanted to party on a budget and a place for island smugglers to stop off whether to re-supply or refuel either on their way to, or on their way from, other islands in the easter Caribbean.

The original bar and various outbuildings had been of cinder block construction and still remained standing, although some of the corrugated metal roofing had blown off many of the buildings. None of the glass in any of the windows had survived the neglect.

Just after 2:00 in the morning, the Cheap Trick raised her anchor and made her way out of Road Bay to make the six and a half mile run to Prickly Pear Cay. Originally the old S-boat displaced 115 tons with a draft of 9'6", but when it had recently been refurbished all of its armament: 1 x 40mm Flak cannon, 1 x 20mm cannon, the stern depth charge racks and 4 x 21" torpedoes had been removed, although the torpedo tubes had been retained as storage bins. This reduced its displacement while decreasing its draft by about two feet, with a corresponding increase in performance.

Even with the reduced draft, the old S-boat could not approach any of the beaches on Prickly Pear Cay due to the rocky shoreline along the western and southern shores of the island, and the coral reefs guarding most of the northern and eastern approaches, except for a channel which had been blasted into the reefs directly in front of the old Misguided Mermaid which allowed for vessels with less than 10' of draft to pass through the reefs offshore and come into the lagoon fronting the old bar and grill. Tanawat, due to his years spent smuggling in the region, was well aware of all of this.

With this information, a rough plan had been put together while the guys had been anchored off Anguilla.

CHAPTER 39

CONSIDERING THAT RAMÓN AND CODY were the only ones in the rescue team with any combat experience, that Ramón was actually responsible for Kelly and Monica's security due to his position as head of the NRO security team, and that Tanawat was the only one besides Cody who could handle the old S-boat, it was decided that Cody and Ramón would go ashore to find and actually rescue the girls.

While barely maintaining steerageway, Tanawat brought the Cheap Trick as close to shore as possible near the rocky point located at the southeastern corner of the island. This allowed Cody and Ramón to launch the little 4-man inflatable boat which was usually kept strapped down on the engine room hatch aft of the wheelhouse and paddle it to the very end of the sandy beach which looped around the northern and eastern shores of the cay.

While Tanawat backed the old S-boat into open water, Ramón and Cody paddled ashore and drug the inflatable about 25 yards over the beach and into the loblolly and nicker trees growing there to hide it. Once this was done, they both grabbed one of the suppressed CZ P-09 pistols out of the waterproof bag in the inflatable along with two extra magazines. Cody also grabbed the 870 Remington combat shotgun and loaded it with double-ought buckshot and crammed a few extra rounds of buckshot and a few of the 3" Brenneke Special Forces Maximum Penetration rounds into his cargo shorts for good measure before they started slowly making their way through the trees and underbrush towards the old bar in the dark.

It was slow going and they got off track a few times, but once they hit the edge of the saltwater pond they knew exactly where they were at and turned further west and continued on. Eventually they could hear waves rolling onto a beach and got down on their bellies to crawl the remaining few yards to the edge of underbrush above the beach. They found that they had ended up about 60 yards down the beach from the old Misguided Mermaid to their left.

Although the stolen Conch 47 was anchored out in the lagoon, not a soul could be seen either in or on the boat, or around the old bar and outbuildings, although there was woodsmoke rising through a hole in the roof of the bar.

They waited until first light before inching their way back into the foliage on their stomachs and then making their way around to the back of the bar. The bar had been built in a little clearing at the opposite end of the beach that wrapped halfway around the island from where they had been put ashore. Remaining in the tree line about 15 yards behind the bar, Cody took out a compact pair of Leica 8x20 binoculars from the case hanging around his neck and took a good look at the bar and all the buildings in the clearing before handing them to Ramón so that he could do the same.

They then pulled back about ten yards into the trees and underbrush to discuss what they had seen.

"What did you see?" Cody asked Ramón.

"All the doors of the bar have been ripped off, probably for firewood, which means you can see all the way through the structure. All the windows are gone. I didn't see anyone in the kitchen but did see a guy out on the veranda facing the lagoon having a smoke. What did you see?"

"Same. We need to know where they're holding the girls. I need you to stay here and cover my back while I go do a little recon. If I'm not back in 30 minutes you'd better come and rescue us all," replied Cody.

"Why do you get to run the recon? I'm the Recon Marine."

"Because I outrank you, Gunny."

"You were in the service? What, must have been the Coast Guard? What was your rank?"

"Technically I was in the Navy Special Boat Teams, which is sort of like the varsity Coast Guard team, as a Master Chief Petty Officer. I probably do not need to remind you that a Gunnery Sergeant is an E-7 while an esteemed Master Chief is an E-9. That being the case, I am giving you a lawful order to come save my ass in 30 minutes if I'm not back by then."

"I always knew that the Special Boat Teams hired the mentally challenged. Get going."

Cody left the shotgun with Ramón, then low crawled up to the back wall of the old pub. Pulling the CZ P-09 out of his waistband at the back, he reached into the cargo pocket on his right and pulled out the YHM R9 suppressor and threaded it onto the pistol. Getting up on his knees, he took a quick peek into the old kitchen from each of the three broken out windows along the back wall. No sign of the kidnappers or the girls.

The exterior wall to the right of the kitchen had no windows, so he duckwalked along the back wall to the lefthand exterior wall and hit paydirt immediately. Without even having to peek, he heard women's voices. When he did peek in the window, he found himself looking into a garbage strewn room, which would have been in the far right-hand corner of the building if you were walking in the front door. It must have been the office back in the day.

The next window along, toward the front of the building would have been behind the bar that had run along that side of the building. A quick pop-and-peek revealed four black guys sitting in ancient beach chairs at a table made from an old cable reel. There were beer bottles on the table along with a bottle of Jamaican rum. There were also four Glock 17 pistols on the table and a Heckler Koch MP5 submachine gun leaning against the cable reel. These guys may have been sloppy, but they were well armed.

Going back the way he came, Cody got back to Ramón and told him what he'd seen. They needed to get the bad guys out in the open and away from the girls to do this right and to keep the girls out of the line of fire.

After a half hour of brainstorming the problem, they'd come up with a plan.

After synchronizing their watches, Cody took the shotgun from Ramón and asked him, "Are you sure you know how to hotwire a boat?"

"Man, I'm a Marine of Cuban descent! If it has wheels, I can hotwire it!"

"I was afraid of that. I'd like to point out that there are no wheels on a Conch 47. It is a boat, if you hadn't noticed," Cody pointed out.

"I was speaking figuratively, Squid."

Ramón had just started moving back the way they had come when Cody hissed at him and held out his Swiss Army knife.

"Makes stripping the wires a whole lot easier, Jarhead."

"I, being a Marine, would have just gnawed the insulation off the wires with my teeth."

"Yeah, but you'd have probably chipped or cracked those annoyingly white teeth, ensuring that Lacy would likely have never run her tongue across them in the future."

"Good point. Give me the knife," said Ramón taking the Swiss Army knife and shoving it in his pocket before going back in the undergrowth to set their plan in place.

After an hour and a half, Cody low crawled to the back wall of the derelict bar and grill and just waited. At exactly two hours since he'd watched Ramón disappear back into the woods, he heard all four of the Mercury outboards on the Wicked Wench come to life.

Ramón had made his way back through the underbrush until he was at a spot on the shallow peninsula that was out of the line of sight from the pub. Easing across the beach and into the water, he swam out into the lagoon, using the combat side stroke taken from the SEALs and taught to Recon Marines which gave him mobility as well as stealth. When the Wicked Wench was between him and the Misguided Mermaid, he swam directly towards the boat keeping it between him and the pub until he could crawl up and over the center two Mercury outboards and up and onto the bridge.

It turned out that Ramón did not need the Swiss Army knife or to fret about Lacy refraining from running her tongue across his teeth in the future; the keys had been left in the ignition. Showtime!

As soon as the outboards fired up, Cody got to his feet and slowly walked through the kitchen at the back of the old pub and then into the old bar proper. The kidnappers had grabbed their pistols and jumped to their feet when Ramón fired up the Wicked Wench with their attention focused on the boat out in the lagoon.

One of the men, obviously the boss, grabbed the MP5 and started running out of the front of the building closely followed by his three henchmen. Cody strolled out after them.

It was only about 50 yards from the front of the pub to the lagoon, and soon the leader was at the water's edge yelling at Ramón with his buddies spread out behind him.

"What the hell you doing, mon?" the boss asked Ramón.

"What's it look like, asshole. I'm stealing your boat." Marines like to rub situations like this in your face.

"You see this here?" asked Gabriel, also known as Kenrick, raising the MP5 subgun. "You get off my boat and maybe I don't shoot you."

It was at this point that Cody shot the three henchmen center of mass in the back from about 10 yards away with the 870 Remington loaded with buckshot. This buckshot made a gory mess out of the midsections of the hired help as it exited out the front of them, but it did get Gabriel's attention. The shotgun was now trained on Gabriel, who had looked over his shoulder to see what all the commotion was about.

"Drop the piece, or not, I really don't care," suggested Cody.

After seeing what a 12-gauge shotgun loaded with buckshot would do to a man at close range, Gabriel wisely dropped the sub gun and his Glock as well after taking it out of his waistband.

"Now face away from me, get on your knees, interlock your fingers behind your head and cross your ankles."

Once Gabriel complied, Cody yelled to Ramón to shut down the engines and call Tanawat on channel 72 and tell him to come on in. When Ramón had done what he'd been asked to do, he jumped overboard and swam to shore.

"Look what I found on the boat." Ramón had found the bag of zip ties that the kidnappers had used on the women.

"I'd say that is poetic justice," commented Cody. "Go take care of the girls, but don't bring them out here until I get this mess cleaned up. I'll holler at you."

So, Ramón went up to the pub and cut the girls free. They were starving and dehydrated, but they found the coolers that the kidnappers had brought with them and chowed down on jerked chicken sandwiches while downing copious amounts of bottled water.

While the girls were being fed and watered, Tanawat expertly threaded the reef and brought the old S-boat into the lagoon and helped Cody load the bodies of the hired help and Gabriel onto the Conch. Using the Conch to ferry the bodies out to deeper water where the Cheap Trick was anchored, the dead were cross-decked to the Cheap Trick and then placed under a tarp on the engine room hatch where the little inflatable boat usually resided. Gabriel was eventually brought onboard as well before being securely roped and tied to a D-ring set into the aft deck where the depth charge racks would have been originally located.

After sluicing the blood out of the Conch 47 where the torn-up bodies had lain, Cody and Tanawat took it back to shore and after raising the props, gently ran it aground.

Ramón had already been suitably thanked by a semi-naked Lacy, but not to be outdone, an equally barely dressed Taeng jumped into Cody's arms, wrapped her legs and arms around him and they began to tongue wrestle. Tanawat thought this was a vulgar display of affection, but he'd seen worse.

Kelly and Monica didn't have anyone to wrestle tongues with, but they were just happy that the ordeal was over.

The problem was that all four girls had been kept out in the open all night with hardly any clothes on, and they had been a feast for the mosquitos. The girls looked like they had chicken pox, but even in this condition they were still an eyeful.

Everyone was now ready to get back to the normalcy of Ginger Island, so Cody had everyone load up on the Wicked Wench except Ramón and himself, which aroused Taeng's curiosity. Cody assured her that he just had to get rid of the bodies and he and Ramón would be back on Ginger Island later that evening.

With that, Cody and Ramón pushed the Conch back into deeper water. Tanawat lowered the four outboards back into their running position before he turned her around, threaded his way back out through the reef and headed home with the girls.

CHAPTER 40

SHARKS ARE A MUCH-MALIGNED species. Not all sharks present a threat to humans, and many are docile creatures. There are ten shark species common to the Caribbean, these are the great hammerhead shark, tiger shark, nurse shark, blacktip shark, whale shark, Caribbean reef shark, bull shark, lemon shark, oceanic whitetip shark, and the silky shark.

Of these ten species, only three have been known to attack humans: the tiger shark, the nurse shark, and the bull shark. The nurse shark has been identified in nine attacks on humans, but none were fatal. Bull sharks, although aggressive, only live in shallow coastal waters and just wouldn't do for what Cody had in mind.

The tiger shark is the second largest predatory shark in the world. They are known to be highly aggressive like the great white and bull sharks. Perhaps due to their aggressive nature, these sharks have been known to attack humans. Tiger sharks can grow up to 14 feet long and have streamlined, torpedo shaped bodies. They have serrated teeth designed to kill and ingest bony fish, sea turtles, dolphins and seals. These sharks would work just fine for what Cody had in mind.

While Tanawat and Cody had been shuttling Gabriel and his recently deceased buddies from the beach to the Cheap Trick, Cody had quizzed Tanawat about tiger sharks and where they could be found locally. Tanawat said that he and his fishing and smuggling buddies were aware of a little-known breeding ground for tiger sharks about half mile off the east coast of Sombrero Island.

Sombrero Island is a little 94-acre rock that sits 34 miles northwest of Anguilla. It has been uninhabited since 1890, when its phosphate reserves had been exhausted. It was an ugly, barren place with little to no vegetation. A perfect location for what Cody was planning.

Once the Wicked Wench and crew were safely out to sea, Cody and Ramón followed suit in the Cheap Trick and took a heading of 323°, which would take them directly to Sombrero Island. At 20 knots, the trip took them about 25 minutes, which gave Gabriel time to ask what Cody had planned for him and to beg for his life. Cody and Ramón remained silent on the bridge, but Ramón was a little curious as to what Cody had in mind as well.

Cody pulled his boat to an idle about half a mile offshore with the old derelict lighthouse on Sombrero Island directly off his port beam. Turning to Ramón, Cody informed him that as a serving member of the United States Marine Corp he might want to go below now so that he could maintain plausible deniability and honestly say that he had no idea as to what was about to happen and would not be a witness to what Cody was about to do.

"Nope, in for a penny, in for a pound. I'll see the mission through to its conclusion."

"Suit yourself, come give me a hand."

They went back down on deck to the engine room hatch amidships and pulled the tarp off the bodies and drug them over to the starboard gunwale. With Ramón taking the feet and Cody taking the hands, they tossed all three of them overboard. While Cody went back to the bridge to get the shotgun, Ramón went astern and untied a very nervous Gabriel from the D-ring and brought him back amidships where he had a good view of his three ex-buddies bobbing in the waves about 10 yards from the side of the boat.

Cody joined them, and while Gabriel watched in silence, Cody jacked the remaining buckshot loads out of the 870 and reloaded it with five of the 3"

Brenneke Special Forces Maximum Penetration slugs which he still had in his cargo shorts pocket.

After giving Gabriel an evil smile, Cody turned to face outboard while bringing the shotgun to his shoulder and calmly blew the heads off each one of the cadavers. Placing the shotgun on the engine room hatch, Cody came back to the rail to watch for what he knew was about to happen.

"Are you familiar with chumming?" Cody asked Gabriel, who didn't seem capable of answering at the moment.

"No? Well chumming is the blue water fishing practice of throwing meat-based bait, usually ground up fish and guts, into the water to lure various marine animals to a designated area. The scent of blood in the water tends to attract predatory fish. Since we are presently in a tiger shark breeding area, I would expect to see some action shortly."

Sure enough, before too long, several triangular shaped dorsal fins broke the surface. Tiger sharks will often circle their prey slowly, then when they get close, they will suddenly sprint to reach the intended victim before it can escape. When attacking, tiger sharks tend to try and eat their prey whole, although larger prey will be devoured in several large bites.

At this point Cody had Ramón cut the zip ties off Gabriel and had forced him to don a life jacket. Gabriel was almost catatonic with fear by this time. Suddenly one of the sharks, a nice 12-footer, lunged toward the body furthest from the boat and literally bit it in two, carrying the upper half with it back into the deep while leaving the hips and a pair of legs remaining on the surface. Gabriel moaned as he watched the resulting feeding frenzy that didn't leave a trace of his associates.

Now that Cody was sure that he had the shark's attention, he pulled the boat ahead about a quarter of a mile before he pulled the throttles back to idle and went back on deck to where Ramón was watching over a petrified Gabriel as he sat on the engine room hatch cover. On the way back he grabbed a coil of 1/2" rope off the wheelhouse bulkhead.

Both Ramón and Gabriel watched curiously as Cody made a loop out of the rope he'd brought down from the wheelhouse. Cody then had Ramon stand Gabriel up so that he could drop the loop over his head and arms before pulling it up under his armpits and adjusting the overhand loop knot so that the loop itself was not constricting and the knot was directly in front of Gabriel. Cody then took the other end of the rope and tied it securely to the D-ring that Gabriel had originally been tied to before he stood up and inspected his handiwork.

Motioning for Ramon to bring Gabriel to the stern of the boat, Cody looked Gabriel in the eye and simply said, "Your turn," before he shoved him over the stern.

Ramon followed Cody back to the bridge and asked what he was up to. "We're going trolling," replied Cody. Gabriel looked at Cody for a second before grinning and telling him he was a wicked man.

Cody throttled up and made a slow circle before heading back to the area where he'd just fed the sharks. Gabriel was trying to scream the whole way back to the feeding area, but since he'd grabbed the knot in front of him with both hands, he was being towed face down and he'd get a mouthful of water every time he opened it.

It didn't take long for the sharks to find Gabriel. One must have taken a nip out of him from below as Gabriel gave a shriek of sheer agony as he was jerked underwater before the life jacket brought him back to the surface. Gabriel was still very much alive when another fin rose behind him and an enormous shark hit him from behind and took what remained of Gabriel in its jaws and swam with it for a good 20 yards on the surface before diving into the depths with its meal, breaking the line.

"You are one twisted individual," observed an awed Ramón.

"Could be. Go pull in that rope before it gets wrapped in the props. We left our inflatable back on Prickly Pear Cay, we'd better go get it before we head home," replied Cody.

After going back to the island and picking up the little 4-man boat, Cody got the Cheap Trick up on plane before he rammed the throttles forward and made a beeline for home. They actually arrived at Ginger Island less than half an hour after Tanawat and the girls.

CHAPTER 41

ONCE EVERYONE WAS HOME SAFE and sound, Kelly and Monica were taken up to the NRO facility to get an extensive medical check-up. Afterwards, they were allowed to take long, hot showers before putting on proper clothes prior to attending the encrypted video conference call where they were debriefed by the security chief at NRO headquarters back in Virginia. Kelly and Monica were given the option of two weeks of R&R in Virginia or finishing out their hitch. The girls chose to stay. Once that was resolved, the exhausted girls went back to their quarters and slept like the dead. They'd had a long couple of days.

Ramón stayed down at the boathouse with Cody to tie up both boats and secure the weapons while Tanawat took his daughter and Lacy back to Cody's house in the Gator before he also went home. He was a little older than the rest of the crew and the past few days had tired him out. He needed a nap.

Since both Gators had been taken already, Cody and Ramón hopped onto the Kawasaki dirt bike and Cody drove Ramón back up to the NRO facility. Before dropping him off, he suggested that they should plan to finish the party that the girls had begun on the beach prior to their recent adventure. Around noon the next day sounded good.

When Cody finally got back to his house, he found Taeng dead to the world in his bed, and he assumed Lacy was in a similar state in Taeng's old room. He quietly undressed and showered before putting on some old gym shorts and climbing into bed beside her.

Everyone woke up late the following day, around 10:00 in the morning, and shortly thereafter the word began to circulate regarding the celebratory party to be held on the beach. Cody left their portion of the party requirements to Taeng and Lacy while he jumped back on the Kawasaki and stopped by Tanawat and Miriam's guesthouse to collect the old man. They rode back to the boathouse so that they could do the preventative maintenance on the Cheap Trick and to clean up both the Trick and the Wench after the miles and the blood they'd put on them over the past few days.

Afterwards, while Cody went into the shop above the seaplane hangar on the other side of the pier to touch base with Ramón, who was preparing an after-action report for the NRO powers-that-be, Tanawat was running his eye over the Wicked Wench thinking that it would make a nice addition to his stable of boats. When Cody came back down to the dock and went inside the boathouse and saw this, he reminded the old coot that the boat was stolen property and they had to give it back, much to Tanawat's chagrin.

Walking outside the boathouse and then turning down the pier towards the beach, the two men could see that the party had already started. Everyone that was not required to be on duty at the NRO facility was there, including Kelly and Monica. Representing the private side of the island were Miriam, Taeng and Lacy. Miriam was scowling at the girls, apparently she did not approve of their beachwear. This was a little odd since all the girls on the beach appeared to be wearing one-piece swimsuits for a change. Most people would consider a one-piece swimsuit on a woman these days as a sign of modesty. As you got close enough to these girls to really appreciate the suits, this was definitely not the case.

The girls must have all gotten together at some point in the past and decided that they all needed the most revealing one-piece swimsuits available. The suits chosen appeared to be from the one-piece bikini Wicked Weasel collection, and today was the day to wear them since they were still covered with healing mosquito bites over whatever portions of their bodies which had not been covered while in captivity, which was the majority of their bodies. Granted, the one-piece bikinis did not cover much more real estate than the previous two-piece models which they had worn while being held captive, but you had to give them credit for at least making an attempt at propriety.

The party was in full swing after the required volleyball tournament, when Taeng asked Monica if she'd seen Lacy. With a sly smile, Monica said that the last time she'd seen Lacy, she'd been walking hand-in-hand with Ramón down the pier toward the boathouse. Apparently the newly acquired Conch 47 had a reasonably comfortable mattress in the cabin under the front deck. She assumed that is where Taeng could find her. Taeng was somewhat annoyed that she hadn't thought of this first.

After the sun set in the west, the party slowly came to an end. After everyone had pitched in to pack up all the gear and to clean up the beach, the NRO crew went back to their place, and the private citizens went to theirs. Except for Ramón and Lacy, who opted to spend the night camped out on the Wicked Wench.

EPILOGUE

WHILE PARTYING DURING THE DAY, both Cody and Taeng had managed to overserve themselves with rum drinks and beer. This being the case, not much friskiness was actually possible when they finally arrived home, and they essentially just passed out in Cody's bed.

The following morning Cody was up early and sitting on the couch having a coffee while perusing the local news on his phone when he heard Taeng come out of his room and go into her old room. Eventually a freshly washed, perky Taeng, sporting a mischievous grin came out of her room wearing the same cut-off jeans, with the same crimson bikini top, under the same Banks beer t-shirt, dry this time, that she had on when she initially washed up on Pala Island.

She plopped herself on the couch near Cody, sitting cross-legged while facing him, which was weirdly erotic from Cody's point of view. Cody laid his phone on the coffee table and asked her what was on her mind.

"I was just curious if we were going to finish what we started now that our guest is occupied elsewhere and we are finally home alone."

Cody was at a loss. "You are going to have to be a little more explicit, Ms. Skeete. We've both been a bit busy lately and I am not sure what you are referring to."

Taeng leaned forward and pushed him back down on the couch. "You are such a dolt sometimes; I'm not talking about the kidnapping you moron. I'm talking about picking up where we left off the night before the whole kidnapping thing got going," a frustrated Taeng explained.

A light finally went off in Cody's head and he decided to play the game as well. "You mean when you were losing so badly at strip poker, and I had you down to your bra and panties before Lacy burst in without knocking?"

"That would be correct, Mr. Morgan," answered Taeng. "Although I would like to point out that at that point you were only attired in your Fruit of the Looms and one flip flop."

"True. We didn't really get to finish the game, did we?"

"No, we didn't, and I've been thinking that you or I may have missed out on a treat, so to speak."

Cody took a good look at Taeng before saying, "I don't know, Taeng, I am a bit older than you, and at my age I need a meal not a snack."

"Really?" replied Taeng as she stood up and began walking back to Cody's room while slowly and seductively shedding her attire one piece at a time. First, the Banks beer t-shirt hit the floor as she moved toward the kitchen island. At the island she slowly unzipped her cut-offs and seductively wriggled them down to her ankles before stepping out of them, leaving her dressed in nothing but that little crimson bikini, which just accentuated the positive and really highlighted her 'Georgia peach' attribute.

Leaving the cut-offs where they fell, she continued toward Cody's room while reaching behind her to untie the bikini top and letting it drop to the floor as well.

Without turning around, she informed Cody over her shoulder, "When you get hungry enough, you know where to find me," as she made her way past the French doors which separated the living room from the little courtyard with the water feature and headed back towards Cody's room.

It didn't take long for Cody to realize that he was absolutely famished, and what was looking more and more like a five-course meal was waiting for him mere yards away wrapped in nothing more than a clingy, bikini bottom.

Later that day, Taeng slyly asked Cody if his appetite had been satisfied.

Without missing a beat, Cody looked at Taeng in surprise and said, "You call that a meal? I was just getting warmed up. I thought we were going for a five-course meal. Sadly, I seem to have been served only the hors d'oeuvres, appetizer and salad courses. I was looking forward to the main course and especially the dessert. Please tell me that you're not sated already, I had plans for you!"

"Really? Well, we can't let those plans go to waste, Mr. Morgan. Due to your advanced age, I was pacing myself earlier," admonished Taeng. Standing up in her bathrobe, she held out her hand to Cody and said, "Let's go see if I can put some meat on your bones."

AFTERWORD

IN XINJIANG PROVINCE, THERE IS a place called Quxi Village. It is located in a flat, dusty plain north of Xinjiang proper. It is remote and is the location of a special re-education camp for MSS agents who have failed to live up to expectations. This particular camp was home to an extensive solar farm.

It had been two months since the man previously known as Ministry of State Security agent Xu Chunwang had been invited to Quxi Village after he had managed to leave Barbados after the failed coup and had made his way to Havana from where he had been repatriated to Beijing.

Technically, Xu Chunwang was looking at a minimum five-year stretch at Quxi Village for his apparent incompetence as the agent-in-charge of the coup. In reality, he could be there for the rest of his life doing the same task over and over until he died.

He could just see the tops of the snow-covered peaks to the south and wondered if he would ever actually walk in mountains again; it was something that was out of his hands.

Walking out of his assigned hut, he got into his assigned CFMOTO Chinese made utility vehicle and began the short drive to the one square mile solar farm to the north, which contained the 700,000 solar panels that he was tasked with keeping clean. A mind-numbing chore what would be his only task, rain or shine for the foreseeable future. Failure while in service to the

Chinese Politburo was often fatal, so Xu Chunwang was actually grateful for the opportunity to clean solar panels for the next few years.

And here ends our tale of romance and chaos on the Lesser Antilles side of the Caribbean. The names of the players have not been changed in an effort to commend the upright and fairly virtuous, while humiliating the unjust and unprincipled.

www.ingramcontent.com/pod-product-compliance
Lightning Source LLC
Chambersburg PA
CBHW020800250626
47155CB00003B/1167